LESSONS FOR *Survivors*

CAMBRIDGE FELLOWS MYSTERIES

CHARLIE COCHRANE

RIPTIDE PUBLISHING

Riptide Publishing
PO Box 6652
Hillsborough, NJ 08844
www.riptidepublishing.com

Cover Art by Lou Harper, louharper.com/Design.html
Editor: Delphine Dryden
Layout: L.C. Chase, lcchase.com/design.htm

ISBN: 978-1-62649-158-8

Second edition
January, 2015

Also available in ebook:
ISBN: 978-1-62649-193-9

CAMBRIDGE FELLOWS MYSTERIES

CHARLIE COCHRANE

To my family, because a) they believe in me and b) they come up with solutions to my plot problems.

TABLE OF Contents

CAMBRIDGE, 1919

Chapter 1

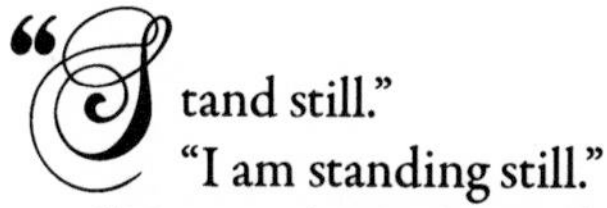

“Stand still.”

“I am standing still.”

“You aren’t. You’re jiggling about like a cat after a pigeon.” Jonty Stewart made a final adjustment to Orlando Coppersmith’s tie, then stood back to admire his efforts. “I think that’s passable.”

“You should wear your glasses, then you wouldn’t have to go back so far. You can’t use that old excuse about your arms getting shorter so you have to hold the paper farther away.” Orlando turned to the mirror, the better to appreciate the perfectly tied knot. “Faultless. Thank you.”

The hallway of Forsythia Cottage benefited from the full strength of the morning sun through the windows and fanlight, enough for even the vainest creatures to check every inch of their appearance in the mirror before they sauntered out onto Madingley Road. Still, what would the inhabitants of Cambridge say to see either Jonty or Orlando less than immaculate, especially on a day such as this?

“It’s as well you had me here to help, or else you’d have disgraced yourself and St. Bride’s with it.” Jonty smiled, picking at his friend’s jacket. If there *were* any specks on it, Orlando had to know they were far too small for Jonty to see without his glasses. “I’m so proud of you. Professor Coppersmith. It will have a lovely ring to it.”

Orlando nodded enthusiastically, sending a dark curl springing rebelliously up, a curl that needed to be immediately flattened, although even the Brilliantine he employed recognised it was fighting a losing battle.

His hair might have been distinctly salt and pepper, but he was still handsome, lean but not angular, nor running to fat like some of his contemporaries. He'd turned forty when the Great War still had a year to run, so there was a while yet before he hit the half century. Jonty was a year closer to that milestone and never allowed to forget it. "I won't believe it until I see the first letter addressed to me by that title."

"Conceit, thy name is Coppersmith." Jonty nudged his friend aside and attended to his own tie. Silver threads lay among his own ruddy-gold hair now, and the blue eyes were framed with fine lines. He knew he could still turn a few heads and young women told him he was handsome. If the young women concerned were his nieces . . . well, that didn't invalidate their opinions.

Orlando snorted. "Conceit? That's a case of the pot calling the kettle black." He slicked back his hair again, frowning.

"You seem unusually pensive, even for the new Forster Professor of Mathematics." Jonty stopped his grooming, turned, and drew his hand down Orlando's face, remapping familiar territory. Coppersmith and Stewart. Stewart and Coppersmith. They went together like Holmes and Watson, Hero and Leander, or strawberries and cream. Colleagues, friends, lovers, and amateur detectives, they were partners in every aspect of their lives, and neither of them entirely sure whether the detection or the intimacy was the most dangerous part.

"I was just thinking how sad it is that neither your parents nor my grandmother are here today." Orlando fiddled with his tiepin, at which Jonty slapped his hand away and straightened the offending object once more.

"Leave that alone. I'd only just got it right." Jonty stuffed a hat into Orlando's hands—not the one he was going to wear today, but one he could twist nervously to his heart's content, with no damage done. "Perhaps it's as well they're not here for your inaugural lecture. They might have had to put on a magnificent act to cover their boredom. Computable numbers? Hardly the stuff of gripping entertainment." Jonty smiled, trying to keep his lover's spirits up. He knew how deeply Orlando still felt the horrible series of losses he'd suffered during the years of the Great War.

So many people he'd been close to, now gone; it had left a gap in his life that Jonty knew even he couldn't entirely fill. Not that, as Orlando swore, he loved Jonty any the less—nor, as Orlando frequently said, was there any less of him to love. The reports of the college veterans' rugby matches still referred to him as a little ball of muscle, and Orlando said he was beautiful beyond the power of words or numbers—even imaginary ones—to describe. Both of which were nice, if perhaps biased, compliments.

"Thank you for your vote of confidence." Orlando ruffled his lover's hair, grinning smugly as Jonty scurried back to the mirror to begin priddying again.

"My pleasure. I'm looking forward to the lecture, of course. I've a list of keywords that I'll tick off as they come. If I get them all, I'll win five quid off Dr. Panesar."

"Does he have a list as well? Does everyone?" When they'd first met, Orlando would have been thrown into a panic at such a statement. Now he was older, wiser, and alive to Jonty's attempts to make game of him. "And do I get a cut of the proceeds? I'd write my lecture specifically to help out the highest bidder."

"That's the spirit. I'll start the bidding." Jonty leaned forward and kissed Orlando as tenderly as when they'd first been courting. "That's the deposit. You can guess what constitutes the rest of the payment." He was pleased when Orlando, visibly happier, returned the kiss; he couldn't let Orlando succumb to melancholy now. The man might start blubbing through his inauguration.

"Oh, Lord, look at my hair!" The romantic interlude earned Orlando a return to the mirror to repair the damage to his coiffure. "No more of those before the big event, thank you."

"We're not turning into a pair of sissies, are we? I don't ever remember spending as much time in front of a looking glass, not even when I was in my twenties." Jonty resisted the temptation to have another glance at his reflection.

"This is an occasion without precedent. We can take as long as we want. You said it was a matter of the college's honour—surely we can't have people thinking St. Bride's is inhabited by scarecrows!" Inhabited by old duffers, eccentrics, and a pair of amateur detectives who had the habit of getting their names into *The Times*, certainly. "Anyway, make the most of that kiss. There may be no more forthcoming before I give my lecture."

"That's hardly the spirit I expect, Orlando. If I were ever to gain a Chair in Tudor Literature or some such wonderful thing, I'd insist on regular romantic activity to fortify and inspire me. A man can't live by hair pomade and computation alone." Jonty made good the knot in his lover's tie for what seemed the umpteenth time. "How far have you got with your first draft, by the way?"

"First draft? At this rate, it'll never get written. Too many distractions. You being at the top of the list." Orlando screwed up his face. "Perhaps I should simply write it on the subject of 'Equations quantifying the known nuisance values of Jonathan Stewart.'"

"That would be impossible to quantify, I'm afraid. Didn't you tell me there are no numbers bigger than infinity?" Jonty pulled down his lover's brow to reachable level, but had second thoughts about kissing it, just in case hair and tie both got mussed up again. "If you're *that* distracted, we should deem it protocol to sleep in separate beds the next few nights. Then you could scribble away to your heart's content."

"It could be done. And the thought of resumption of bed sharing would be a positive incentive to get the wretched thing sorted out. I need something to give me the proverbial boot up the backside." Orlando deliberately moved away from the mirror. "Right, that's it. If I'm not fit for public view now, I never will be. Thank goodness it's just the official bit today and the lecture's all of a fortnight away."

"At least that'll give Lavinia the chance to buy a dress suitable for the occasion. She's dragging her heels about getting the right outfit. Worse than you. And she's almost as nervous as you are. Feels she's representing all the Stewarts and has to be on her best behaviour." Lavinia Broad, Jonty's sister and the matriarch of the family now that their formidable mother had died, was developing into the role with surprising dignity and good sense.

"She's bound to be better behaved than you, so everyone will be relieved." Orlando smiled, a twinkle in his eye to show that he didn't mean any—or at least much—of what he'd said.

"And you'll have Antonio there, to represent your illustrious relatives." Jonty took out his spectacles and gave them a special polish in honour of the occasion. Not that he intended to wear them. "He can sit next to Lavinia, looking proud and patriarchal."

"At this point, I'm glad my grandmother had to change her name. Professor Artigiano del Rame sounds a bit pretentious. And they'd never manage to paint all of that on the sign at the bottom of the staircase at Bride's. They had enough trouble with O'Shaughnessy." Orlando made one final adjustment to his jacket, ignored Jonty's whisper of *I was right when I said 'Vanity, thy name is Coppersmith,'* and turned to the door. "It shows you what a state I'm in that I don't object to turning up in the metal monster. If I was quite myself, I'd have insisted on a horse-drawn cab."

"The metal monster" was one of the kinder ways Orlando referred to whichever one in the procession of Jonty's cars was currently standing outside the house, allegedly polluting the vicinity. Only the fact that one of the earlier incarnations had helped save Jonty's life made the possession of an automobile tolerable, even if the current version was one that Orlando deemed deficient in the number of required wheels.

"You love it, really. Especially since we got the Morgan." Jonty grabbed their academic gowns, opened the front door, and ushered his lover through it. "Come on, let's get the bride to the altar."

"Not the analogy I'd have chosen, but it'll do. Lead on, Macduff."

"*Lay* on, Macduff, you mean. You're worse than the dunderheads at times." He closed the door behind them and took a deep breath of the autumn air. "It's going to be a glorious day, in more ways than one." As they reached the car, he dropped his voice to barely a whisper. "That moratorium on my bed doesn't have to start until tomorrow. Only don't think about that fact while you're being inaugurated or invested or installed or whatever it is they're about to do to you, as you won't look very good in the photographs with a lascivious grin all over your gob."

Investiture or not, Orlando couldn't resist calling into the porters' lodge en route to see if he had any post. It was customary for him when entering or even passing St. Bride's to see if anything of importance had appeared in his pigeonhole. Or failing that, just some desperate set of calculations from one of the dunderheads. No matter how Jonty tried to break him of the habit—"Once a day is enough for any man, and I do mean checking your post and not anything else, Mr. Filthy Mind."—the practice was ingrained.

"Dr. Coppersmith!" Summerbee, head of the porters' lodge in spirit if not in title, greeted him with a huge grin. "The lads were hoping you'd drop in today. We all wanted to wish you the very best."

"Thank you." Orlando couldn't help grinning in return. He'd always liked the denizens of the lodge, and today they felt like the absolute salt of the earth. There couldn't be a college in Cambridge with a more stalwart set of men in its employ, and they'd taken good care of him back in the darkest days when it had seemed like there was no light left in the world.

Tait, a relatively new porter who still seemed totally in awe of Orlando, whispered something to his colleague.

"Ah, thank you for reminding me. Dr. Coppersmith, would it be an imposition to ask a favour? The lads wondered if there'll be any photographs taken today for the newspapers and the like. And if so, maybe we could have a copy of one of them, to go up in the lodge?" Summerbee looked imploringly and as like an eager schoolboy as a fourteen-stone, middle-aged man could manage.

"If there are, you can." Orlando felt slightly overwhelmed by such a request; it always astonished him that anyone should take a genuine and affectionate interest in his affairs.

"Thank you, sir." Summerbee bent his head as Tait conveyed another whispered message. "Oh yes, that's right. And if it could feature Dr. Stewart as well, that would be very gratifying."

Gratifying? Orlando couldn't help wonder if the porters had twigged the exact nature of the domestic arrangements up at Forsythia Cottage. Well, if they had, they didn't seem to be showing any signs of disapproval. Not in public, anyway.

"I doubt we'll be able to keep the little blighter out of range of any cameras. Remember when His Majesty visited the college? Dr. Stewart seemed to get his nose into just about every photograph that was taken."

"He did that, sir. Mind you, he's what you might call photogenic." Summerbee grinned. "We could do a roaring trade with the ladies if we made postcards from those pictures of him dating back to when he was naught but a student here."

"I beg your pardon?" Orlando had once been taken to see *The Tempest* and had lost the plot around Act II, Scene 1. He felt the same way now.

"We keep photograph albums of college life—the students and the dons, the sports teams and the like. They go back years. When we have our Christmas party here, some of our missuses and sweethearts like to look through them." Summerbee tipped his head towards the inner sanctum where the picture albums were stored. "They always pick out Dr. Stewart, especially the one of him with the rest of the rugby fifteen."

"So long as it's not a picture of me milking a goat in the lodge, we should be thankful for small mercies." Jonty, distinctly red-faced as though he'd heard every word of the praise, entered the lodge bearing a handful of letters. "Mr. Summerbee, have you any idea how these ended up in my room and not in my pigeonhole?" He held up his bundle of post.

"Wasps." Tait at last seemed to find the courage to speak aloud, even if it was only in a monosyllable.

"Wasps?" Jonty and Orlando asked in unison.

"Yes. We've got a wasps' nest behind the wainscoting and we had the little blighters smoked out only yesterday. Trouble is, the smoke seeped through and was pouring out of a crack in the wood." Tait, gaining in confidence, illustrated his story with dramatic gestures representing pumping smoke and fleeing insects. "It was coming out into your pigeonhole and Dr. Panesar's, so we decided to rescue both sets of post in case either got damaged. We felt it was safest to put it in your rooms, rather than leave it in the lodge and risk it going astray . . ." Tait's burst of courage was clearly waning under Orlando's beady eye. "I'm sorry if we overstepped the mark."

"Not at all." Jonty smiled, dispersing all worries about people fiddling with his personal property. "Better safe than sorry."

Orlando shuddered at the thought of wasps, smoke, or worse still, porters interfering with his letters. "I think I'll just nip my post up to my study, if there's any risk of arthropod intervention." He smiled as if he'd made a wonderfully witty joke, and the porters indulged him with a chuckle. Naturally, it was human intervention that would have bothered Orlando more than the other two.

"It shouldn't happen again, sir." Summerbee was conciliatory. "We think we've got shot of all our unwanted visitors. A shame we can't employ the same techniques when we get waifs and strays from the college next door in here."

The college next door—how every true St. Bride's man loathed it. Often, although not always, with good cause. A den of plagiarists, scoundrels, cads, and cheats, or so every good Bride's man swore. The archenemy, camped at the gates. Jonty always said every dark cloud had a silver lining, and maybe he'd be proved right. All the great and the good of the mathematics department had been called to attend an urgent meeting on Thursday morning to discuss a case of possible plagiarism by one of their members, which was not an enticing prospect. But at least the suspect was someone from the college next door.

"Maybe you could get your man with the smoke to make a secret raid on Dr. Owens's lodge and see if he dislodges something worse than wasps." Orlando sniffed, clutching his post to his chest as if Owens, head of the much-reviled institution and thief-in-chief, was going to sneak around and purloin it. He'd stolen things from St. Bride's before and had even tried to get his hands on the notorious, precious, and totally befuddling Woodville Ward papers. Those papers had provided the key to solving a mysterious disappearance that had puzzled scholars for centuries. "Shall I put your letters somewhere safe, Dr. Stewart? Just in case you lose them halfway up King's Parade?"

Jonty sorted through the pile of correspondence, picked out two items to put in his inside pocket, then handed over the rest. "If you'd be so kind, Dr. Coppersmith. They'll make a terrible bulge in my jacket otherwise. Two whole papers to check through and both of them on *King Lear*, so that'll be a bundle of laughs. I'll hang about the Old Court while you do the necessary."

Orlando nodded and swept all the letters and papers to safety before any more wasps—or porters—could get at them. He was too consumed with thoughts and worries about the forthcoming ceremony to entertain any curiosity about the letters in Jonty's jacket.

As he came down the stairs from his room, he found Jonty lurking by the entrance, looking concerned.

"I was just a bit worried that you'd lock yourself in and refuse to take part."

"Don't tempt me. The thought's crossed my mind several times." Orlando hated fuss. Although there was more than that; he was distinctly miffed that he couldn't be Orlando Coppersmith, Sadleirian Professor of Pure Mathematics, as he'd always had a fondness for real analysis and Fourier series. But short of assassinating the present incumbent of the post—who looked like he had a good few years in him yet—there seemed to be little chance of him getting the job. So Forster Professor of Applied Mathematics he would be, and if anyone noticed that the title had been endowed by his almost-sister-in-law in honour of his almost-mother-in-law (courtesy of the handsome inheritance Lavinia had received), then they were too polite to mention it.

"You deserve this position. Completely and utterly. If anyone so much as hints otherwise, I'll belt them one. Anyway, you weren't even the first person to hold the post." With that, they began a slow, stately walk over the college lawns.

"True." Orlando had been in the trenches of France when the chair had first been created. The honour of being the original professor had gone to someone from the college next door, shoehorned into the post by that toad Owens, who had probably used blackmail to get his own slimy way in terms of the appointment. "Your Lavinia said Professor Mann was almost a gentleman, even if he came from such a disreputable place."

"Did she? Well, the old girl's always had good sense when it comes to getting the measure of someone, so I suppose we must give him the benefit of a rather large doubt." Jonty grinned, the great scar on his cheek—his souvenir, along with two medals, of the Great War—tipping up and giving him a piratical air. "She didn't arrange to nobble him, did she?"

Professor Mann had come to a sticky end, literally, falling into a vat of flour and egg when on a visit to a biscuit factory to observe particle and liquid flow through hoppers and tubes. He'd developed a phobia of machinery as a result and had retired to Devon a broken man. The professor elect wouldn't do anything as rash.

Orlando was pleased they'd not brought the motor car. Sauntering along King's Parade with Jonty at his side and not a cloud in the piercingly blue sky, he couldn't shake off the feeling that the shades of Helena Stewart and Grandmother Coppersmith were walking alongside him as well. He wasn't sure he believed in God or heaven, even though Jonty was enthusiastic about both, but the thought of the two formidable women who had so shaped his life for the better being in cahoots in some ethereal realm, bossing the angels and telling Gabriel off for going around without his vest on, made the day even brighter.

All he needed now were two things. The first was for the ordeal of the next few hours to be over swiftly and without incident. Please God, his dodgy Achilles tendon, which hadn't given him any gyp this last five years, wouldn't decide that today was the day it had its revenge for presumed maltreatment and gave out, sending him arse over tip in the face of the congregation. The second was for his guardian angels, if they did exist, to send him a nice juicy problem to solve. And if they couldn't manage a murder (which didn't seem like the sort of thing to be praying for), then some other mystery, maybe one that had evaded all solution for years on end and that he and Jonty alone could master.

"Are you thinking about violent crime of some sort?" The perky voice at his side cut into Orlando's daydream of knives, victims' backs, and convoluted inheritances.

"How did you know?" How did Jonty Stewart *always* seem to know what was going on in his brain? Did it read like ticker tape all over the Coppersmith fizzog?

"You've got *that* look in your eye. The one that only comes when it's been too long between cases." Jonty grinned, and Orlando had to admit he was right. Time was when he would have bitten anyone's hand off at the chance of a nice, complicated crime to investigate. Maybe those times were returning at last.

While there'd never been lean years, there had been the odd stretches of lean months when nobody had come forward with so much as a telegram gone astray that needed to be tracked down, let alone an unsolved murder for him and Jonty to get their brains about.

They didn't count the war years, when they hadn't felt any need to investigate anything; Room 40 work had kept their wits occupied long enough with cryptography and the like, and when they'd been at the front, they'd shut all curiosity off. If ever there'd been a time when Orlando hadn't wanted to think too deeply, that had been it.

"Is it too much for a man to want a little diversion when he's got such weighty matters as an important lecture on his mind?" Orlando tried to sound as if he believed passionately in every word he said. "It would help oil the wheels of contemplation. Working on one would aid the other, naturally."

"You talk such rot at times. I hope you don't stuff that lecture with such obvious lies." They stopped to let an idiot undergraduate from the college next door—instantly recognisable by the vile college colours he adorned himself with—hurtle past on a bike. "That reminds me of something Dr. Panesar was saying in the Senior Common Room about the circulatory system. A clot may be transported in many ways."

Orlando groaned, rolling his eyes. "And you have the nerve to accuse me of speaking rot."

"At least I don't deny doing it." They carried on walking, safe for a while from being impaled on anyone's handlebars. "You just won't admit that you miss the thrill of the chase. You're like a foxhound. You've smelled blood once and now you have to have your share of it. Regularly."

Orlando stopped, eyeing his friend closely. "And are you saying you don't?"

"Of course not. There's nothing I'd like more than a mystery. Been too long." Jonty's expression was rueful; their last case had been in the spring and solving it had been bittersweet. "It would prove to me that everything was back to normal. That the last five years hadn't spoiled the world forever."

They walked on in silence, each with his thoughts.

"Do you really think that the world's been spoiled?" Orlando hated to hear his friend so glum. This wasn't the Jonty Stewart he knew, loved, and sometimes had the overwhelming desire to murder. Especially when he changed cars and became besotted all over again with some metal monstrosity.

"It'll certainly never be the same. I feel we've all passed through the fire." Jonty slapped Orlando's shoulder. "Still, there's no point in grumbling. Some things are above and beyond the passage of time and the cruelty of the world affecting them. Maurice Panesar still tells appalling jokes." He lowered his voice to barely more than a whisper. "And we still love each other. Which is a miracle in itself when I consider what a miserable swine you are."

Orlando grinned, finding the insult a welcome sign that the old Jonty was back. "And you're still the cheekiest toad in Cambridge." If they'd been home at Forsythia Cottage, *sod* would have been substituted for *toad*, but that wasn't appropriate for King's Parade.

"Toad, am I? Then I might not feel inclined to give you the little treat I have here." Jonty patted his jacket through his gown.

"A reward for getting through this afternoon without strangling the vice-chancellor?" Orlando eyed the thick material, as if the layers might become as glass and yield the secrets of the inner pocket.

"Something like that. But you're not going to find out unless you stop frowning. Do try to smile at least once."

"Will whatever it is be worth it?"

"Oh yes. Trust your Uncle Jonty. It's even worth rousing a smile for Dr. Owens."

Chapter 2

"You survived, Professor Coppersmith." Jonty cuffed his friend's shoulder. All the solemnity and ceremony was done, Orlando had smiled at least three times and not snorted at anyone, and at last they could relax and enjoy some light refreshments. It might not have been champagne and lobster, but tea and finger sandwiches totally fitted the bill. The hall at St. Bride's had been especially spruced up for the occasion; even the tiniest indications of a lobbed sprout or a flicked black currant had been removed, and all traces of dunderheads with them. Jonty wondered whether they'd had the place fumigated, just in case.

"I did." Orlando broke into his fourth smile. "Not quite like going over the top, but it had its similarities."

"Comfier uniform, certainly. I suspect . . ."

Whatever Jonty suspected was interrupted as Dr. Panesar ran up to them. Or as close to running as an academic gown, the solemn occasion, and the press of people allowed for.

"Dr. Coppersmith." He clasped his hands to his mouth. "*Professor* Coppersmith." He shook Orlando's hand, pumping up and down enthusiastically. "I'm so pleased for you."

Orlando beamed. Maurice Panesar—fellow of St. Bride's, mechanical engineer and budding astrophysicist, inventor of prototypical time-travelling devices and one of the nicest men you could care to meet—was among the elite group of people Orlando labelled 'friend.' As he'd confessed to Jonty, he'd never once regretted it.

"Thank you, Dr. Panesar. I got your note. It was much appreciated."

"I wanted to wish you all the best. I knew I wouldn't get to talk to you beforehand." He turned to Jonty, who'd managed to sidle through the throng right at the start and hadn't budged since from his rightful place at Orlando's side. "He's done the college proud, hasn't he?"

Jonty slapped Panesar's shoulder, then gave him a big hug. It was probably inappropriately affectionate for the occasion, but clearly Jonty was beyond caring. "He's a credit to us all. It'll be your turn next, Dr. P., when they're filling the engineering professorship."

"The Chair of Mechanism and Applied Mechanics?" Panesar shook his head. "I'd like to think I had a chance, but I doubt my abilities are up to it."

"Nonsense!" Orlando cuffed Panesar's other shoulder. The poor man was buffeted about like a punching bag under the weight of affection. "You've more brains than all the dons down at Ascension College put together, although that's not saying a lot."

Panesar lowered his voice. There were a few Ascension men lurking about, and you could never tell if they were going to turn nasty. "Even Nurse Hatfield has more brains than the whole company of Ascension. Junior and senior members combined."

Jonty wanted to say that Nurse Hatfield, doyenne of the St. Bride's sickbay, had more bosom than all the figureheads in His Majesty's navy combined, but thought better of it. There was still a persistent rumour that Dr. Panesar sometimes was allowed to rest his head on that soft and expansive cushion, and so the subject had to be avoided if one wanted to escape a black eye. He sipped his tea and smiled to himself.

"I'll restrain my hopes, though. I suspect they wouldn't dare elect me. I'm too likely to blow up half the laboratories if they give me free run of the department." Panesar smiled, having hit on at least part of the truth. He was generally regarded—almost literally, the way his inventions had a habit of exploding—as a loose cannon. People who visited his laboratory were liable to hover at the door or don a steel-lined bowler hat if they had to enter the room. However, even if he hadn't been such a force for mayhem, he still might not win any promotion; whether Cambridge was entirely ready for someone of his humble background and Punjabi race to take an elevated position was a whole other issue.

"Will you come up to Forsythia Cottage for dinner?" Jonty wondered whether to invite Nurse Hatfield while he was about it, but thought better of that too. No one was supposed to *know*. "I wish we could invite you at some point over the next few weeks, but all parties and frolicking have been put on hold until Doctor . . . *Professor* Coppersmith has finished writing, and then delivering, his lecture. We've planned a celebration in three weeks."

"It might well be a funeral wake for my career if I can't get the thing written." Orlando studied the contents of his teacup, as if inspiration might lurk there.

Jonty and Panesar exchanged knowing looks and ploughed on, ignoring the doom-mongering. "We've our old friend Matthew Ainslie descending on us with his business partner. Mrs. Ward and her granddaughter will be doing the catering." Jonty's plans for the dinner party were escalating in proportion to Orlando's pessimism. Mrs. Ward might well grumble when informed, but she'd be secretly thrilled and her granddaughter would be delighted at the thought of a decent-sized company to try her developing culinary skills on. He gave Panesar another hug. "And I can promise you something a bit more exciting than the spread here."

"I'd be delighted to attend. Matthew Ainslie is a most entertaining man, and I'd like his opinion on a communications device I've been thinking about." Panesar's eyes lit up with enthusiasm as he spoke of his latest creation.

"A communications device? Dr. Sheridan would be interested to hear about that, as well." Jonty tried to look keen, but experience had taught him never to overestimate the capabilities of one of the good doctor's devices. Orlando should have been grateful that he only had automobiles to contend with. Those weren't likely to take out half of the university in one enormous blast. Still, maybe one day Panesar would make a breakthrough that would change the world.

"Dr. Sheridan will be there too? And his good lady wife at his side?"

"How could we invite him and not her?" Jonty pretended to be horrified. "It's always a delight to have Mrs. Sheridan gracing an event. Stops it being just a bucks' do and keeps us all in line."

"Dinner it is, then." Panesar made an elaborate bow and backed through the crowd, almost sending the dean of St. Thomas's College flying.

"Dear Dr. P. He doesn't even know what day the party is or what time he's supposed to be there." Orlando shook his head indulgently, more than pleased to see the dean nearly come a cropper. He'd never liked the man and suspected his views on Fermat were fundamentally unsound.

"Doesn't know what day the party is? I'm not sure he knows what day of the week it is today." Jonty eyed the assembly with indulgence. "And I suspect the same could be said of most of those present."

"I wouldn't have it any different." Orlando nodded. "Cambridge, in all her glory. Old-fashioned, out of touch with the times, a bit stuffy, but wonderful."

"Sounds just like you. No wonder you love the place so much." Jonty was pleased to be amongst such a crowd that Orlando couldn't whack him for the insult. "As for Dr. Panesar, we can leave a note in his pigeonhole, assuming the wasps don't eat it." Jonty lightly tapped his friend's arm. "Come on, we've a bit more meeting and greeting to do before you can honourably make your departure. As you said, not quite like going over the top but near enough." Now they could almost bear to joke about the war or to use phrases lightly in conversation that, even a few months ago, would have been too close, too painful.

"Though I never thought I'd ever say it, I suspect I preferred going over the top to facing this." Orlando looked around at the mass of people, all there in honour of him and his new position. He lowered his voice. "I couldn't have faced it if you hadn't been here."

"Oh hush," Jonty whispered, secretly delighted. For all his teasing, he liked the shy and reticent part of his lover's personality; thank God that hadn't disappeared during the months at the front. However much a hero Orlando had been out in France, he would never boast of what he'd done. Both of them kept their medals hidden away for secret appreciation. "And here's Dr. Sheridan."

The master of St. Bride's topped Orlando by a couple of inches; he was tall, thin, and handsome with a Puckish twinkle in his eye that sometimes flared and caught anyone who didn't know him well enough totally by surprise. Dr. Sheridan had astounded everyone by being given the post of master in the first place, not being a St. Bride's man, but he was proving to be more than able. Jonty envied nobody the job. The master had to be diplomat and arbiter when the situation required, rigorous academic and scholar if that was expected, and Sheridan had filled every role.

The fact that he was the loving husband to the sister of the previous master, and that their late-flowering love had filled the college with its joy, was a bonus.

"Gentlemen. This is a great occasion for St. Bride's and a greater occasion for you." Sheridan shook Orlando's hand for at least the third time that day, and then cuffed Jonty on the arm. "Mrs. Sheridan is furious, of course, not to have been allowed to come—although she understands the constraints placed upon us at such times. She looks forward very much to your inaugural lecture and hopes that she will understand at least part of it."

"I suspect she'll understand every word and pick me up on where I go wrong." Orlando smiled. "Please give her my very best wishes and thanks for her kind words."

"We could give her a blow-by-blow account of what's happened if she wishes. With all the speeches and actions." Jonty grinned. "If she can't wait until the dinner party, I'll drop into the lodge and give an impression of Dr. Coppersmith, when he was still a mere doctor and not yet professorified, trying to look dignified and not like a seven-year-old boy with a new kite."

Orlando was evidently trying not to look like a seven-year-old boy who wanted to murder his best friend. "I'm sure she'd prefer to hear a truthful description of the occasion from me, rather than your exaggerations."

"Gentlemen." Sheridan held up his hand like a referee intervening in a nasty set-to around a ruck at Old Deer Park. "You'll both be superfluous, as I'll be giving the full story the moment I walk through the lodge door. I won't be allowed to get my coat off until I've at least begun, anyway. You can repeat the tale over dinner, but your thunder will have been stolen."

The arrival in their midst of an emeritus professor of divinity from an obscure London college interrupted the laughter ensuing on the master's comments, and Jonty started to count down the minutes until they could make their escape with dignity.

Orlando's study at St. Bride's had never looked so welcoming. Despite aching legs from standing on their feet and being sociable for so long, he and Jonty threw caution to the wind and almost bounded up the stairs, then slumped into the armchairs, only stopping en route for two glasses and the decanter.

The sherry was very welcome. Orlando worried at times that taking to the bottle was becoming a bit too habitual for comfort, but Mrs. Stewart had always sworn that a small sherry—especially a sweet one at times of trial—practically counted as medicine. He felt as though he needed something therapeutic now, having been sustained after the ceremony by nothing stronger than milky tea and a few sandwiches. He and Jonty hadn't been able to make it as far as the porters' lodge, let alone all the way back to Forsythia Cottage, without nipping in to make use of what lurked in Orlando's study. Port felt too decadent for five o'clock in the afternoon, so sherry it had to be, and very welcome it was.

Jonty slumped into a chair with his drink and immediately loosened his collar and tie. "You were magnificent. Absolutely looked the part of the austere mathematical man." He took a swig of sherry and let out a huge sigh. "If only they all knew what you were really like. They'd have to be administered sal volatile at the very least."

"Oh, hush." Orlando wasn't displeased; he quite liked people supposing he was stern and logically minded. Really he was an old romantic—at least where Jonty was concerned—and a positive lion in bed. He didn't want people knowing that, though. He and Jonty might have a reputation throughout the university as two singular and rather eccentric men who had to share a house as no one else would put up with either of them, but what if someone put two and two together?

"And don't think I missed the 'like you' remark," he added, glancing at Jonty. "Am I really old-fashioned and a bit stuffy?"

"Don't forget the bit about being out of touch with the times. Yes, you have the capacity to be all of those, but you also said that Cambridge was wonderful." Jonty leaned forward and tapped Orlando's knee. "You're that as well."

"Hm," Orlando snorted, deliberately ignoring the compliment. "I'll have you know, I'm regarded as one of the most forward-thinking men in my department."

"Yes, well, given what I saw today of the great and good from your department, I wouldn't use that as any self-advertisement. I'm surprised half of them aren't on display with the iguanodon down at the museum. You'll be a breath of fresh air to them." Jonty leaned back again in his chair. "Been a bit of a strain for both of us today, hasn't it? I feel like the father of the bride or something."

"That makes me the bride, I suppose." Orlando grimaced. "Still, I hope that's the hard bit done. Even delivering that inaugural lecture can't be as daunting." He looked at Jonty for reassurance. "Can it?"

"I always think, with public speaking, that the best thing to do is imagine all your audience is naked. Takes away your nerves entirely, even if it gives you the collywobbles." Jonty knocked back the rest of his sherry; it had been a hard day. "Only maybe don't imagine Lavinia in her birthday suit, as Ralph will be round to thump you one. He has the capacity to read minds, I believe."

"I can't think of anything more ghastly than imagining the vice-chancellor and all the other great men of the university wandering round in nothing but their academic gowns and hoods." Orlando reached for the decanter and topped both of their glasses up. This was a 'take two doses of medicine' day. "We mustn't forget to take our post back home. What was so important about those two letters, anyway?"

"Which two letters? Oh." Jonty patted his jacket. "I'd forgotten about them. One's from Lavinia, although that's just family matters. Thought I'd take it with me so the old girl would be represented at your 'do,' figuratively if not literally. Seemed right."

"And the other one?"

"Oh, that's your reward for smiling so angelically today." Jonty took out his spectacles, slipped them on, and then caressed the envelope affectionately. "What you'd refer to as a professional enquiry. Someone wants to know if he can consult us. A case. Not one you pack your shirts in. Hey!" Jonty pulled away his fingers, which had come between Orlando's viselike grip and the letter. "Were you never told not to snatch?"

"And were you never told not to tease? You've had wind of a case all day and you hesitated to share it." Orlando held out his hand and tried to look appealing. "Please?"

Jonty passed the letter over. "See, all you had to do was ask nicely. We shouldn't run into taking it, though, just because it's come at what feels like the right time." In the run-up to the war, they'd been able to pick and choose what they took on, rather like Sherlock Holmes had done in the Conan Doyle stories that Jonty's father had so loved and Orlando completely detested. Even now, if anybody made the comparison between the two pairs of detectives, Orlando was at pains to point out that Jonty was far more intelligent than the Watson of the stories. Even if Jonty himself argued that Watson as narrator was probably downplaying his own skills while promoting his friend's.

The last few years, Orlando'd had the growing suspicion that Jonty was doing exactly the same thing.

"Would you care to give me the salient points while I peruse this?" Orlando held up the letter.

"No, that would take away all the fun. You read while I shut my eyes and think for two minutes."

"Think? You'll be having a crafty forty winks if I know . . . Ow!" Orlando rubbed his shin. It seemed to have a permanent bruise there at times, being one of Jonty's favourite kick-you-for-being-cheeky-or-not-paying-attention spots. He wished he'd had the foresight to move the armchairs farther apart, or to have worn shin guards. "Perhaps I should save reading this until you've had your nap. In deference to your slowing down with age."

"Slowing down, am I? By heavens, if you still kept a set of rooms here, rather than just this study, I'd have you over the bed and show you who's displaying no signs whatsoever of slowing down. Ow!"

"Taste of your own medicine." Orlando grinned at having managed to get a pretty sharp blow in. Jonty was usually on his guard and ready to shift his leg out of the way; perhaps this was further evidence of him showing his age. "Anyway, I've been thinking. Maybe we shouldn't take on anything before my lecture's done."

"What?" Jonty almost shot out of his armchair. "Where's all the enthusiasm from earlier on?"

"I just want to savour anything we get involved with solving." Orlando smoothed the letter in his hands. "Too often in the past, the investigation's all been a dreadful rush, and that's half the fun taken away."

"I suppose so. This one's got a pretty tight deadline attached, although the thought of that always seems to galvanise you. Still, if the timing's wrong, then maybe we'll just have to give this one a miss . . ." Jonty slowly took off his spectacles and put them away again. "I'll send the Reverend Bresnan a reply along the lines of us not having sufficient time at present." He reached out and took the letter.

"How long a deadline?" Orlando felt the words come out of his mouth, although he'd only intended to think them. For all his reticence, he *did* like solving a conundrum while the sands were running out of the hourglass, no matter how much he protested. It was like eating very spicy food—both a pleasure and a pain. And he wanted to prove they could still cut the investigational mustard.

"A month. So by your reckoning, we *definitely* haven't got time." Jonty made to throw the letter on the fire, although his grip on the piece of paper remained firm.

Little bugger, he knows I can't resist for long. He's playing me like a fish. Orlando stood his ground. "A month? It would be very easy to use up that much time without achieving very much. We'd have to be consulted pretty quickly, for a start, or the sands of time would already be trickling through our fingers." In that short a time, they might just fail too, which was untenable.

"Well, as a matter of fact—a splendidly convenient fact—that's not going to be a problem, as the writer is coming up to Cambridge on Thursday. But that wouldn't be any use, would it? We shouldn't tempt ourselves." Jonty made a show of putting the letter away, but it still didn't leave his hand.

"Where's he staying?" Orlando sighed, half-defeated.

"He'll be at the University Arms and we could leave a message there, assuming he starts out from home before I can telephone him." Jonty folded the letter up carefully.

"Starts out? Where's he coming from, the Pyrenees?"

"Almost. Deepest, darkest Gloucestershire, which is almost as remote and certainly as cold." Jonty looked particularly innocent, a sure sign he was winning the fight and knew it. "I *could* ring him as soon as we get home, if you want."

Orlando sat back, conquered. A lecture to write and give, new duties to assume in the department (another change Cambridge had seen that he didn't entirely approve of), newly arrived dunderheads to be licked into some sort of shape, this plagiarism case to be opened and (he hoped) swiftly shut. He didn't have the capacity for an investigation, especially one with time pressures. But to give up now, through fear of failure, would be an act of cowardice.

"We'll see him over lunch on Thursday, if that's convenient."

"Good man." Jonty returned the letter to his pocket, blissfully and blatantly triumphant. Orlando tried to console himself not only with the thought of a mystery to solve, but the prospect of trying to replicate that blissful look on his lover's face in bed that night.

Chapter 3

Jonty rang the Reverend Ian Bresnan, reporting to Orlando that an appointment over Thursday lunch had apparently proved to be, "Alas, already spoken for." He'd promised he'd be free later in the afternoon, so a mutually agreeable time was found when tea, biscuits, and investigation could be on offer in Jonty's study at St. Bride's.

Not Orlando's study this time, even though it had been the setting for many such discussions of mysteries. He'd become even more crabby about who was allowed in there than in his pre-Jonty days. It was, according to his lover, one of the developing (although still somewhat endearing) peculiarities of character, as much a hangover from the war as the diminution in his confidence and the huge scar across his chest. Jonty's study was messy, welcoming, and a place of refuge for the cares of the world. Orlando would have to explain at some point why the departmental meeting hadn't gone as well as anticipated, but for the moment, he'd put on a brave face.

Jonty had arranged for the college kitchens to send up tea for him and his guests. The refreshments arrived at almost the same time Thursday afternoon as Bresnan himself. The reverend was escorted in regal state through the college by Tait, who dropped him off at Jonty's study door like a proud father presenting his son with a view to admission. Ian Bresnan looked almost as nervous as any prospective student might have been.

The reverend was tall, slim, and extremely handsome for his age, which Orlando put at rising sixty. Despite the obvious nerves, there was something almost monastic about his appearance—pious, yet full of the milk of human kindness. The sort of rector any parish would truly welcome, if the man's outward appearance matched his character. Orlando wondered if he was married or widowed, and whether—if the former case was negative or the latter positive—the ladies of the parish made a beeline for him. Certainly, if he was the recipient of a stream of cakes and homemade jams, he either didn't indulge much in them or had a remarkable metabolism. As slim as a reed, he even made Orlando look tubby.

They quickly dealt with the formalities, shaking hands and offering their guest a seat and a cup of tea, both of which he accepted with alacrity. "Thank you for seeing me. I realise that you must be extremely busy, with Dr. Coppersmith's—sorry, Professor Coppersmith's—recent inauguration and his lecture to come. Such exciting times for the college."

"Exciting times for all of us. But we're not so busy that we couldn't find time for a St. Bride's man." Jonty took his seat at Bresnan's side, allowing Orlando to install himself in the prime information-gathering place opposite the clergyman. "Do you get back here often?"

"Not as much as I would like." Bresnan shook his head in evident sadness. "I try to take my parish duties as diligently as I can, although I suspect I could do better in that regard. Unfortunately, they don't allow me much time to travel all the way here."

"Not the easiest journey from Gloucestershire. I wish I'd had the foresight to put out a decanter of sherry as well. I'd forgotten what taxing work investigation is." Jonty smiled. "Is there a special occasion for your return?"

"Indeed. An old friend of mine has just been appointed the new rector of Archangel and I'm here to watch the installation tomorrow. It seems to be the season for ceremonies." Bresnan beamed enthusiastically.

"Ah yes." Orlando nodded approval. Archangel was another of the less fashionable colleges and one with which St. Bride's had never struck up a rivalry, both of them being brothers-in-arms against the bigger, more glamorous places. Even when St. Bride's had begun to gain in both popularity and status, in no little part due to having a pair of famous detectives in its midst, Archangel hadn't changed its opinion. As opposed to the college next door, which thought St. Bride's was getting jumped-up delusions of grandeur and complained to everyone about it. "Would that be Dr. Walcott? A very sound man. I'm sure he'll do a wonderful job."

"He always was the most able of my generation," Bresnan sighed. "So many men pass through Cambridge, some with shining potential that never quite fulfils itself. Still, it's wonderful to have reason to see the place again. I'm staying a few nights at the University Arms and taking the opportunity to renew old acquaintances and revisit old haunts. Especially St. Bride's." The sudden light in Bresnan's eyes gave him the innocent air of a callow undergraduate. "She's looking lovely, the old girl. Always does in the autumn."

Orlando waited to see if Jonty hastened the conversation on, in the way he always did when things were threatening to get maudlin. He did.

"You said in your letter that you had a matter of some importance you wished to seek our advice on?"

"My case, yes, I'm sorry. We seem to have deviated off the subject." The clergyman looked flustered.

"No need to apologise, as it wasn't even your fault. My colleague himself specialises in going off the subject. Should they make it an Olympic event, he'd be sure to win gold in Antwerp." Orlando sniffed meaningfully. If Jonty was going to so obviously avoid dwelling on autumn, just because Orlando got a bit sentimental about that time of year, then people needed to know *he* was the worst sort of wool gatherer. "Please enlighten us."

"I have—had—two uncles. Born within two minutes of each other and yet with birthdays a day apart. Is that enough of a conundrum to start with?" Bresnan's eyes began to twinkle; he was clearly fond of puzzles and riddles. This was just the sort of silly stuff that Orlando used to love, even if his appetite for trivial things seemed to have waned. He hoped that as the Forster Professor of Applied Mathematics, he would still find time for laughter, tickling, punting on the river, and other childish delights.

"It is. A nice easy delivery to get our eyes in." Jonty shared a happy glance with his friend. "Those two minutes straddled midnight, I assume?"

"You assume correctly. Simon first, then Peter. You'd be amazed at how many people—intelligent, sensible people—can't solve that one.

Maybe I should try another. Although they were born at the same time, of the same parents, they were not twins." Bresnan sat back in his chair, looking just like Dr. Panesar did when he'd propounded some miraculous theorem in the SCR and was waiting for anyone to dare argue against it.

"That's not possible." Orlando sat forwards, hands pressed together, intent on the riddle.

"Of course it is, if Mr. Bresnan says so." Jonty leaned on his elbow, his second-choice thinking position. The best place to work anything out was entwined in each other's arms, but that couldn't be used now. "It's a play on words somehow, I bet."

Bresnan nodded. "You could say so. And germane to this case, Professor Coppersmith, I promise you."

"Hold on." The tip of Jonty's tongue protruded from his mouth, as it always did when he had his best thinking cap on. "Not twins. Therefore . . . triplets or quadruplets or something. There was a third child who died, perhaps?"

"Absolutely. You show the true discernment of a St. Bride's man, Dr. Stewart."

Orlando snorted, cross at not having solved the problem first, although it was more a matter of linguistic pedantry than logic. He really needed to sharpen his wits again on these sorts of things. Couldn't have a mere scholar of the Bard getting one over on a Professor of Applied Mathematics, not when it came to solving puzzles.

Bresnan, if he'd heard the snort, politely ignored it. "There was a third child, Andrew, named after my grandfather. He did not survive the first day. He was very ill, and so was my grandmother. The children had to be taken and nursed by someone else for the first few weeks."

"Your grandmother survived, though?" Orlando thought fleetingly but fondly of his own beloved grandmother.

"She did, although she was never the woman she had been, understandably. She died when my mother was five. My uncles would have been barely a year old. I remember seeing pictures of her when I was a child, and thought she was very beautiful. Said to be clever, with it. My mother inherited her looks and my uncles her brains."

Orlando wondered where the grandfather had come in all this but kept his counsel to himself. Maybe he was reading too much into a few words, although Bresnan seemed to be a man who used words carefully, as his riddles had illustrated. He rose, rescuing the pot from under the cosy and offering another cup of tea all round. It seemed an apt moment to wet their whistles and whet their brains.

"The way you spoke at the start implies that your uncles are also dead." Jonty's eyes were alight, the thin lines around them like aureoles and the scar on his cheek almost disappearing into his smile. A greyhound in the slips, indeed.

"That is correct. Uncle Peter died the best part of a year ago and Uncle Simon followed him just two months past. And now we come to the nub of the case." Bresnan took a sip of his tea, as if fortifying himself. "Simon left me a substantial legacy in his will, part of which—the much smaller part—I am to receive in any case, while the larger part is dependent on me satisfying his executors on a particular point. If I haven't achieved this by the twentieth of October, his birthday, then the remnant of the legacy will be given to Great Ormond Street Hospital for Children. It is not an insubstantial amount, certainly to me."

"That seems very unfair." Orlando couldn't help bridling at what he perceived as innate meanness of spirit.

"I felt that at first, but I've considered the matter carefully since and I believe Uncle Simon felt so strongly about this . . . case . . . that it was the only way he could see of pursuing it. It's an issue of justice and the truth, so you might say it would be highly unfair if it were not to be resolved." Bresnan looked as if he meant every word. He didn't seem to be rationalising away the potential loss of the money and his aspirations with it. "Not, I hasten to add, that I begrudge the hospital a penny. If I do inherit, then I'll make sure I give them a handsome emolument. But I would like to travel, to see things I've only dreamed of, and this would make that possible."

"There's no need to apologise to us for wanting to collect your rightful bequest. We've experience of people being given conundrums to solve as part of a legacy." Orlando thought of his own puzzle, tracking down his real family, the search for his own real name. "Tell us what you're required to do."

"I have to establish the case for my aunt having murdered my uncle." The silence following the remark spoke louder than if it had raised a cacophony of disapproval.

"Heavens," Jonty said finally, breaking the silence with a single shot rather than a volley. He opened his notebook, which had lain alongside his teacup, almost forgotten in the puzzles and wordplay. This was no simple riddle suitable for the drawing room; this was murder most foul.

Orlando couldn't decide whether to be pleased at the nature of the case. He liked a nice, juicy, unlawful killing, or at least he always had before the war. He looked at Jonty, who'd turned unnaturally pale and was still bent over his notebook, as if all the death he'd seen at the front had taken away any pleasure in dealing with it now.

"Please can you give us the details?" Orlando spoke quietly, suddenly in the throes of inner debate about whether he wanted to proceed.

Bresnan nodded. "The particulars of the will were simple. The body of it said what I've already stated. A codicil outlined Simon's belief that Peter's wife, my Aunt Rosalind, had done away with him—Simon's words, not mine—although he had no proof, and little cause for suspicion other than his instinct. He must have long had his suspicions, to have written the main part before Peter died."

"How *did* he die?"

"Of natural causes, or so everyone said. He'd had the influenza, although he seemed to be fighting it off and making a grand recovery. Then one afternoon, they found him dead in his chair in the conservatory. They thought he was dozing, but he'd gone into his long sleep."

"You say 'they' found him. Who was that?" Orlando kept to the facts of the case, eager to skip over anything to do with influenza. They'd lost Jonty's parents to the disease and the thought of it still made him shudder.

"Aunt Rosalind and the housekeeper, Mrs. Hamilton. They wouldn't normally have disturbed him, but they'd had a plague of ladybirds in the house. The man had been in to treat them, and the ladies wanted to make sure he'd eradicated every one of the things from every corner." Bresnan sighed. "When they'd finished, they went to the conservatory and found my uncle."

"What made Simon suspicious about his brother's death? Would it be too presumptuous to suggest it was the usual cause, by which I mean a healthy legacy?" Jonty was busy keeping meticulous notes, and establishing motive had to be high on his list of priorities.

"Exactly that. Perhaps he was being unfair, judging that it couldn't have been a love match simply on the basis of disparity of age, but Rosalind was substantially younger than my uncle. Not even as old as I am."

"Now, or when they married?" Orlando, mind racing off, wondered whether there was a younger man lurking about in the case somewhere.

"Both. She can't be more than forty or thereabouts, now. When they were married, she'd have been thirty and he had just turned seventy." Bresnan sipped his tea again, even though it must have been turning cold.

May and December marriages—not so unusual, yet so often the cause for scandal or ribald remarks. Especially if there was money involved.

"That makes ten years of marriage." Jonty seemed pleased to have got his sums right. Even the dunderheads could have done that calculation, although some of Orlando's present crop might have struggled with anything more complex. "And she stood to inherit the entire estate?"

"She did, apart from some minor legacies to staff, past and present. Everything cleared probate surprisingly quickly."

"Your Uncle Simon didn't lodge some form of objection at the time?" Orlando wondered why everything had been left for nearly a year. Surely any potential evidence would be long gone?

"He didn't, for two reasons. There was a peculiar clause in Peter's will, as well. While Rosalind was to have a very comfortable allowance to live on, she wasn't to inherit the bulk of the estate outright until a year had elapsed from his death. That year finishes on the thirty-first of October."

"So all the dates seem to converge." Jonty steepled his hands before his chin, clearly relishing the way the little ends of the case were drawing together.

"Exactly." Bresnan laid out his hands, as if offering the mystery to both of them. "Perhaps this is meant to be. If she did kill him, then we're to establish that fact before she can claim her money. I wouldn't be surprised if Uncle Simon chose the date especially, the birthday being fortuitously placed."

"Where does the money go otherwise?" Orlando looked up from his own note making.

"To any living relatives of his father's line. Which I suppose means me. I was an only child and both my uncles died without issue."

"What about those other bequests in your uncle's will? Peter's, I mean."

"The sums involved were quite small, nothing that would constitute a sufficient reason to commit murder." Bresnan put his head to one side, considering. "No, not the price of a life."

"You'd be surprised what constitutes a reason to murder." Jonty shuddered, perhaps at the memory of some of their past cases; sometimes motive was as slender as a spider's thread. "And what seems a small amount to us might represent a fortune—or a lifeline—to some poor soul, especially if they were in desperate need. No hint of that?"

"Not that I'm aware. And Simon mentioned no suspicion of any other person, just my aunt."

Orlando tapped his fingers together. "You said there were two reasons for Simon not raising his suspicions immediately. What's the other?"

"Not a scrap of medical evidence. Simon saw the body himself and didn't notice anything untoward. When he began to wonder if there'd been foul play, he went back and spoke to the doctor."

"Who said . . .?"

"That he was certain Peter was just another victim of that dreadful flu. Apparently he'd been tending him for the past week and had no suspicions of anything else being to blame. You'll find Simon's notes about that interview in my papers."

"If the doctor had been suspicious, he'd not have signed the death certificate." Jonty nodded. "There was no inquest?"

Bresnan shook his head. "Not at the time. And Simon couldn't find enough solid evidence to justify applying for an exhumation, especially when he was trying to conduct his enquiries without raising Rosalind's suspicions. The undertaker said Peter looked like he'd just fallen asleep. That's in the notes too. I've verified as much of this as I can, and you can triple-check if required."

Orlando inclined his head gravely as though that would be the first job on his list, although they'd sub-contracted such seemingly mundane matters before. "Let us get the matter of the will absolutely clear. You have to clarify the case for Rosalind having murdered your uncle. Does that really mean you only stand to inherit the extra part of the money if Rosalind is proved guilty? Or will exonerating her count?"

"The former only." Bresnan gravely nodded. "Simon believed she would kill Peter and wanted to have that proven."

"Was Simon himself married?" Maybe there was some degree of jealousy present, either against Peter for having found himself a young wife or against the wife for having come between the twins. Maybe Rosalind had rejected Simon at some point in the past and he was taking his revenge from beyond the grave? Such rivalries and jealousies could run deep.

"No, he was a confirmed old bachelor, much like yourselves."

Orlando hoped their guest didn't know exactly *how* confirmed in bachelorhood he and Jonty were, although it might prove interesting to know whether Simon's inclinations ran along the same lines as theirs did. Who could tell, at this stage, what might prove relevant? But he wasn't sure he wanted to open that can of worms just yet. Better to go and do some groundwork, listen to local gossip.

"Actually, may I ask why you thought of getting in touch with us, rather than a solicitor or the police?" Jonty asked insouciantly. He and Orlando didn't mind taking on what the police hadn't or wouldn't, but they'd had a few run-ins with obstreperous inspectors along their detecting way and didn't want to fall foul of anyone again. Especially when there was always the threat of their relationship being viewed a bit too closely. "They're not threatening to strike again?"

"I sincerely hope not." Bresnan appeared horrified.

"So do I." Orlando hadn't been in England when anarchy had let loose the year before, but he didn't want it on his doorstep, thank you. Unless some kind soul wanted to come and steal that wretched motorcar. It would be quite in order for any policeman to refuse to deal with the matter.

"I'm not sure whether I'd call choosing you cowardice or discretion. I have no evidence against Rosalind, nothing to make accusations on. The death had been put down as natural causes, Uncle Peter was an old man, and there'd been no hint of scandal against my aunt." Bresnan smiled. "Oh yes, I kept my ears open. I did a little bit of investigating myself, in the way of visiting Aunt Rosalind and talking to some of the people in the village about my uncle. All hidden under the façade of a grieving nephew showing the right degree of interest, but I'm afraid I didn't turn anything up. My solicitor advised me to let the matter drop, as I didn't want a case of slander on my hands."

"But you wouldn't let it drop?" Orlando looked up again from scribbling his notes.

"No. And not just for the money. I felt I owed Uncle Simon the courtesy of taking him seriously. He was neither a stupid man nor a malicious one. If he believed there was something suspicious about his brother's death, then there must have been, even if it turns out not to be a case of murder." Bresnan sighed. "I'd almost given up when I came across some fortuitous Cambridge gossip. I met an old friend of mine in Cheltenham for luncheon. Not a St. Bride's man, I'm afraid. Someone from the college next door." Bresnan seemed suitably ashamed at consorting with the old enemy.

"Not everyone can be lucky enough to come here, I suppose." Jonty grinned. "Although I'd be highly embarrassed if I'd been *there*. I wouldn't admit the fact to anyone. Did you hear they made Owens head of the place last month?"

"Never! That plagiaristic scoundrel." Bresnan sat up, as though ready to dash over to the college next door and take up arms against such a scandalous decision.

"Gentlemen, we're digressing again." Orlando felt he had to bring some sense to the conversation.

"You're correct. I apologise once more." Bresnan bowed and continued. "As I spoke to my friend, I made reference to the need for a discreet and reliable investigator. I'm doubly afraid to say I pretended it was on behalf of one of my parishioners who had a personal matter to be dealt with. My friend made a bit of a joke about my going back to St. Bride's, as she had her own Holmes and Watson."

Orlando took a deep breath before replying; if he heard one more comparison to *those* two, he'd strangle the comparator, or whatever the appropriate noun was. "We're hardly that." He'd have liked to say that they were better, as Jonty wasn't as thick as Watson seemed to be and *he* was a lot nicer than Holmes.

"We don't take commissions for money, for a start." Jonty clearly recognised the signs of Holmes-loathing and leaped in. "Waive every single payment we've been offered."

Orlando couldn't remember being offered any payment, except a cake from Mrs. Ward when she'd mislaid her reticule, and it had turned up in the airing cupboard. He hastened to reassure Bresnan. "We do it for the public interest."

He hoped Jonty wouldn't chip in and say, "He's lying. It's for the love of the chase."

"I'm pleased to hear that, as I'm not sure I would be able to offer any fee at present."

Orlando was about to make some caustic remark along the lines of, *Do we seem like the sort of men who need to be* paid *to undertake our hobbies?* But he noticed a warning expression on Jonty's face and held his tongue.

"Then that works out admirably." Jonty's smile was patrician but not patronising. "And of course, I refuse to write up the cases, unlike Watson. That's mainly due to Professor Coppersmith's language being too dreadful to report."

Bresnan smiled benignly, evidently enjoying the banter. "Then I shall rephrase myself and say I was advised to contact Coppersmith and Stewart and seek their advice for my 'parishioner.'"

Orlando heard Jonty mutter "Stewart and Coppersmith" and hid his grin by pretending to scribble some notes. "We hope we won't let you down. We can't guarantee results, as I'm sure you'll appreciate."

"I *do* appreciate it, and I appreciate the fact that you'll do your best to help me." Bresnan put down his cup and saucer, looking suddenly old and tired. "I wish that there was something I could do in return for your time and efforts, irrespective of the outcome."

Before Orlando could say anything, Jonty cut in. "Say a prayer for Professor Coppersmith, here. He's a terrible old heathen and causes heaven more grief than any six righteous men put together."

"I will do just that," Bresnan replied, clearly not believing a word of what he'd been told. "And for you, too, should you be in need of one."

"I have one or two more questions," Orlando said, although he actually had a whole list of them. "Not least of which is why you left it so very late in coming to us. If Simon died two months ago, you'd have known of the clause in his will not long after. Why wait until you have only a month's grace?"

Bresnan appeared both flustered and slightly sheepish. "As I said, I was stupid enough to think I could solve the conundrum without aid, as I do my beloved word puzzles. It took me a while—and that threat of slander—to see the light. When you visit Downlea, where he lived, it might be as well not to mention any connection with me. When I was there, people simply saw me as a mourning relative, and would talk quite willingly and openly. Especially to a clergyman. And particularly when I bought them a pint in the pub. I'd hate to raise any suspicions that my actions were less than candid and that you've come to raise a scandal."

Which is exactly what they were meant to do. What would the Reverend Bresnan's congregation think if they knew what a wily old fox he was?

"And you're sure you turned out no malicious gossip while you were at Downlea?" Jonty was evidently struggling to hide a delighted grin. He was a fan of malevolent talk; the stuff could be highly informative if you could pick the truth out of it.

"Very little. Blind alleys and dead ends, I suspect."

"Would you care to enlighten us about some of these dead ends?" Jonty was a fan of those too. Sometimes it wasn't the alleys that were blind, just the people walking up them.

"No, I've decided not to. I would like you, if it's not an impertinence to expect it, to bring an entirely open mind to the case and not be influenced by what I've said or the conclusions I think I've reached." Bresnan shrugged. "Who knows if I've even interpreted anything aright?"

"But you *have* interpreted something?" Orlando, feeling like a hawk after a rabbit of a clue, swooped down.

"Perhaps. I'm sorry, I don't mean to be obscure, but I'd prefer you to just look at the facts for now." Bresnan picked up his briefcase, which had lain at his feet like a faithful hound. "There are some relevant papers here, with as many objective details of the case as I can muster. Dates, times, names, an approximate valuation of what my uncles inherited and what they stood to pass on."

"I'm glad to see you've such good sense and foresight. Is there a copy of the will among them?"

"Alas, not. I was unable to make one. There is a précis, however."

"Thank you. I don't suppose we'd be fortunate enough for you to have furnished us with any further details concerning your uncle's death?" Orlando cocked his head to one side, a gesture he knew he'd acquired from his lover, probably by some sort of osmotic process. It seemed to aid thought.

"I've jotted down a few extra notes about that day, as far as I can put them together. There appears to have been no one else in the house during the afternoon in question, and Aunt Rosalind and Mrs. Hamilton apparently stayed together all the time after my uncle went to sleep. Searching for insects, from the top of the house to the bottom. Perfect alibis." Bresnan turned his head sharply as Jonty snorted.

"You'll excuse my colleague, Mr. Bresnan. He has no truck with alibis and can't hide the fact on occasion. Important to note that the ladies said they weren't apart, though." Orlando furrowed his brow. "Those insects. When they were fumigating them, is there any chance your uncle might have inhaled the smoke or powder or whatever they used? Either accidentally or by somebody's deliberate intention?"

"That's the first thing I thought of." Bresnan smiled. "But apparently he kept in the same room all day, away from the workmen. They were most careful. And before you ask me how I know, I asked the chap involved, when I was in Downlea. They didn't see my uncle after they passed the time of day with him on first arriving."

"And if he'd been poisoned by something he inhaled, surely there'd have been some sign?" Jonty's voice was abnormally quiet. He and Orlando had witnessed too many men fall victim to modern warfare's nastier weapons. "Now, you spoke of more subjective things, things you interpreted, even if you think you got them wrong. I know it goes against your wishes, but would you please consider sharing *some* of those?"

Bresnan sighed. "I can see that I shan't be allowed to get away without giving you some sort of an answer. Very well. As I said, when I visited Downlea, I expected to come across all sorts of gossip and unkindness. Tempered, naturally, because people feel that they mustn't appear mean in the eyes of a priest, so they usually add some sort of moral basis to the tittle-tattle."

"Villages can be much harsher places than the city. Too close-knit, and everyone knowing everyone else's business. Like schools." Jonty shivered. "And where a young wife—a much younger wife—is concerned, one would expect spite in abundance, however it was dressed up."

"Indeed. And the remarkable thing is that's exactly what I *didn't* find. Hardly anyone seemed to have a bad word for Aunt Rosalind, even some of the people one would most expect it from. It's almost suspicious in itself, how universally liked she appears to be." Bresnan clearly had a perceptive and realistic view of the world as it truly was.

Orlando noted the "*Hardly* anyone," but let it pass. They'd find out soon enough where the few malicious tongues were wagging. "So we start with almost a blank canvas?"

"You do. And if you provide a picture within the month, I shall be forever in your debt." Bresnan at last fished into his case and produced a set of papers. "I give you all my hopes with these, gentlemen. Whatever you achieve with them is better than I could manage on my own."

"We'll try, won't we, Professor Coppersmith?" Jonty took the papers, laying them on his lap with care.

"We will that." Orlando summoned up a smile. Of course they'd succeed; they had to. "If we can't get to the bottom of things, then they can't be got to the bottom of." He covered up his bad grammar with a nod in Jonty's direction.

The man looked so happy, it seemed a crying shame to have to spoil the day with talk of Owens and chicanery. And something that felt awfully like blackmail.

Chapter 4

After escorting their guest to the porters' lodge, Jonty returned to find Orlando at *his* desk, already poring through the case papers. The autumnal light danced through the leaves of the plane tree, a huge branch of which had grown halfway across the window since Jonty had first acquired the room. He stopped to enjoy the dappling on his lover's hands and face, as well as the look of intense concentration. Orlando at work was a magnificent creature.

"Out with it." Jonty had leaned over the desk, applying his hot breath onto the side of Orlando's neck, one of numerous strategies he'd devised for getting the truth out of a certain mathematical person.

Orlando jumped a mile. "Out with what?"

"Don't try to play the innocent with me, Orlando Artigiano del Rame." The name had a rolling, dramatic feel to it; suitable for when the man was in disgrace or needed to be pinned down to the exact truth. "You've changed your tune about this case every five minutes. What on earth is going on now?"

"Well, I've been looking at things objectively. This village where Peter Priestland lived, Downlea, is barely twenty miles down the road from here, not far by either rail or the infernal combustion engine." Orlando gestured airily. "Not like going all the way to Gloucestershire, or even down to Romsey, where Simon lived. It'll make the time constraint much less intrusive."

"You couldn't have known all that when you changed your mind and decided we'd take the case." Jonty snatched up the papers. "That's all come from swotting up on these. Tell me the truth."

"It would be more interesting than writing my lecture." Orlando looked sufficiently shamefaced. "You have no idea how hard I'm finding it."

"Of course I do." Jonty would have thrown up his hands if it wouldn't have sent all the papers flying. "I have to live with you, don't forget, and all our years together have taught me a thing or two about your character. Give me *some* credit." He shook his head, amused by the way that such an intelligent man could still be so dim at times. "You want it to be perfect. Which it will be. And there's more, so out with it."

"I'm sorry?"

"You know damn well what's eating you. And I'm not saying it on your behalf."

"You must be the most annoying man in the whole of Christendom." Orlando turned in his chair, grabbed Jonty's face and brought it down for a huge smacking kiss.

"That was very nice, but don't think you'll make me forget you owe me an answer."

Orlando sighed. "I'm scared my lecture will be rubbish and I'm also scared that we've forgotten how to sleuth."

"I thought as much." Jonty perched his not insubstantial bottom on the desk, taking Orlando's hands in his. "Surely it's like riding a bike? We'll get started and after an initial wobble or two, we'll pedal along like billy-oh."

"Then come round a corner too fast and end up in a heap? With all the world standing round and laughing at us?" Orlando asked, closing his eyes and shuddering.

"We've not failed yet." *By luck if not by judgement.*

"No, that's true." Orlando didn't seem convinced. "Has my worrying been that obvious? And that annoying?"

"No more than the usual." Jonty ruffled his lover's hair. "You've yet to reach a level of grumpiness that's too much to live with. Be assured the thought of murder has been no more prominent in my mind than it is about thirty-one percent of the time."

"Only thirty-one percent? I must be getting better." Orlando still looked shaken, but the fight was back in him.

"Oh yes. Times past it's been as high as eighty-seven." Jonty picked up a pen, fiddling with it as if writing the aggravation of Orlando's ways and in fresh numbers listing all his annoyances. "And irrespective of reducing how much I want to resort to pickaxes and other weapons,

I like to see you with a case. You get a light in your eye when you're on the trail of a villain, a light that I only see there in two other sets of circumstances: when you've got your head over a tricky piece of differential calculus or when you're rogering me."

Orlando clearly couldn't stop himself glancing at the door at the mention of rogering. It was shut, and no noise could have penetrated it, but that bit of logic had obviously escaped him. Maybe he thought the dunderheads listened at his keyhole. "There'll be no rogering at all unless you stop being so wanton in public places like this." He dropped his voice to a whisper for the key word, and tried to look as if the threat was real.

"Says you. One day I'll call your bluff on that threat and then where will you be? You'd never stick to it." Of course he wouldn't. Orlando was a sight too fond of the double bed, and Jonty in it with him, for that to happen. "Now, you'd better get your head down over that lecture of yours and earn some playtime, because I'm going to take the bull by the horns. If there's a telephone number here, I'm going to ring our merry murderess and make an appointment to see her on Saturday morning. *This* Saturday. And if there's no number, I'll ask at the exchange. And if *that* doesn't work, I'll send a telegram."

"And what reasonable excuse will you give for the consultation? 'Please, Mrs. Priestland, I don't have much time, so can you tell me how you bumped off your husband?'" Orlando snorted, clearly put out that he hadn't thought about an interview with the prime suspect. Or, if he'd thought about it, hadn't acted quickly enough to put in dibs for doing it. "That's going to earn you a rousing welcome, isn't it?"

"Actually, I'm going to play the family name card. The more truth I can wangle into these things, the easier it is for my conscience . . ."

"And for your acting abilities," Orlando muttered.

"I heard that. That's one whack owed, to be collected later on." Jonty got out his spectacles and polished them vigorously, as if they were Orlando's backside getting the deserved thrashing. "I'm going to tell her that I'm paying my respects on behalf of the Stewart family. I'll explain that I'm behindhand in doing so because when the news came of Peter Priestland's death, I was abroad." He stopped, a chilling memory of those months on the Continent clouding his thoughts.

Orlando reached over, took Jonty's hand, and squeezed it; he didn't say anything else except, "Go on. Good strategy so far."

"I'll also say that Papa knew Peter back when he was a lad—by which I mean my father was a lad. It might well be true, given how many people the old geezer was acquainted with. And even if it isn't, Rosalind Priestland won't necessarily know that."

"Shall I come along to offer the Artigiano del Rames' condolences too?" Orlando kept rubbing his lover's knuckles.

Jonty wondered whether Orlando was upset that he hadn't been invited along from the start. Something was evidently still bugging him. "Much as I'd like to have you at my side, it would look a bit mob-handed if we both turned up. And too much risk of her putting our names together and then putting two and two together on top of that." Plenty of people had come across the names Coppersmith and Stewart in newspaper stories over the years. Or "Stewart and Coppersmith" when it had been Jonty's father writing the articles, paternal pride overriding alphabetical order. They didn't want to risk unsettling their quarry right from the start. "And anyway, when time's been short in the past, we've always split up to maximise our resources. You could find plenty of people in Downlea to work your charm on. Ladies from the church, ladies at the post office."

"I notice it's always the ladies getting a mention here."

"Oh, come on. I don't want you exercising your charm on the men, do I?" Jonty laughed. "Far too risky. It might lead to one of them wanting to steal you away, and then where would I be?" He freed himself from his lover's grip and ruffled Orlando's hair again, to the point that it resembled a bird's nest. "Stick to the ladies, and anyone else who'll be no threat to me." The stupidly smug smile Orlando was desperately trying to hide told Jonty he'd said exactly the right thing to reassure him. The daft beggar.

"So long as I don't have to do what Holmes did and get myself engaged to a parlour maid or something." Orlando tapped on his desk with a pencil, which looked like it was about to break under the weight of the man's loathing for the famous fictional detective. Probably because *he* never seemed to fail at anything.

"Any man who once posed as a professional dancing partner to solve a crime shouldn't sneer at something as lightweight as getting engaged to a maid." Jonty wandered over to a little table, found the last biscuit looking terribly forlorn on its plate, broke it in two and gave Orlando the slightly larger half. On such things was a loving partnership built. "Although maybe I shouldn't be so cocky. I don't want to have two wives like Watson did."

"Two wives? At the same time? That's plain greedy." Orlando had stalled halfway through the works of Conan Doyle, stating that the marvellous logic couldn't compensate for how much he hated Holmes.

"No. Serially or something. Doesn't quite hang together in the stories, but I don't think he was a bigamist. We do have one thing in common, though . . ." Jonty spoke wistfully. "The good doctor must have been driven mad at times. I wonder if he contemplated murder as often as I do. I suppose he must have kept that service revolver well-oiled, just in case."

"You *do* know they're not real, don't you?"

Jonty sighed. Orlando felt the need to keep reminding him about the line between his beloved literature and reality. The dark lady and lovely boy of the sonnets might well have been the genuine articles, but neither Inspector Bucket nor Fitzwilliam Darcy was. "Credit me with some sense!"

"This case. I suppose there *is* a realistic chance of us getting anywhere with it?"

Back there again. Orlando's tone twisted Jonty's heart; the great advances in confidence he'd made in the first few years he and Jonty were together had begun to retreat during the war, and the last year or so had been particularly hard on him. "We cracked the Woodville Ward case, didn't we? And Sarah Carter's murder. What's a few months when we've been able to tackle murders from years ago, if not hundreds of years, and get to the bottom of things?" Jonty tried to sound more enthusiastic than he felt. Orlando was right to have doubts, but he wasn't going to fuel them.

"I suppose so," Orlando sighed. "Well, I'd better get on with the self-torture." He bundled the case papers up, presented them to Jonty and drew a blank piece of paper—blank apart from the title "Inaugural Lecture"—towards him.

"You do that. I'll hang a sign on your door to make sure you're not disturbed." Jonty hovered by the desk. "Anything else bothering you?"

"No," Orlando said, too quickly and clearly lying. "It's just that meeting this morning. Wasn't as straightforward as I'd hoped."

"Would it help to discuss it?"

"Not at the moment. It would put a nasty gloss on the day. I'll channel my frustrations into this." Orlando tapped the paper.

"See you in the Senior Common Room for a sherry before high table." Jonty kissed the top of his friend's head. "Make sure you've earned it."

Whatever Orlando was brooding on would come out when he was good and ready. No point in forcing things.

Chapter 5

Having found a little stretch of sward that was level, clean, and almost made for the purpose of cosseting his metal pride and joy, Jonty parked his automobile on the outskirts of Downlea. He wished that Orlando had been driving; the height of amusement being listening to him complain about the difficulties of having to steer and change gears at the same time, not to mention the impossibility of focusing on the road when Jonty was sitting beside him. And then, perhaps five minutes later, see a face like thunder begin relaxing into what would eventually be a Mr. Toad-like expression of joy.

But, even though Orlando had been productive and earned himself a spot of investigating, he wasn't with Jonty today. Despite how much he'd been looking forward to it, his ambitions had been thwarted due to more of that wretched, and still mysterious, business with the plagiarist. While Jonty was heading off from Cambridge, Orlando was part of an early morning deputation to take the bounder's statement for the defence. Whatever the problem was, it was nagging away at Orlando, although he'd still bottled it up. If the man didn't let the secret out soon, Jonty was going to have to force it out of him. He couldn't live with those distant, tortured expressions much longer.

Orlando had arranged to catch the train as soon as he was done, and they'd agreed to meet for lunch at a local Downlea hostelry that one of the porters at St. Bride's had recommended. At that point, the bragging about who'd found out most so far could start.

Despite his worries, Jonty couldn't help grinning as he sauntered down towards the village green. With any luck, he'd be able to steal a march on his lover, which always got right up Orlando's nose. He'd had fourteen years of perfecting the process.

Funny how since the war they'd fallen back into the same sort of roles they'd had when they first met—Orlando creeping back into his hell, keeping worries to himself, while calling Jonty illogical and scatty, even when he wasn't being particularly so. Jonty was happy to play both of those to the hilt for the moment, if it helped Orlando lose the baggage he'd acquired in France and on his return home. Please God they'd have plenty of time to reestablish the norm, but for the moment, they could enjoy a day's sleuthing.

Downlea was bigger than he had expected. He'd a memory of passing through it years ago, en route to a cricket match in the grounds of an estate lying to the north. He'd been on a coach then, and had been given the privilege of riding up next to the driver as his family was taken from the railway station to the house. Downlea had seemed a small place in those days, pretty and picturesque, though quaint (even to a boy of eleven, who was already developing a mature eye for the world).

It had expanded now, Edwardian villas having sprouted two by two along the road and in lanes leading off from the high street. The village shops looked as if they were thriving under the influx of business from the new houses and, while the place wasn't quite as pretty as his rose-tinted recollection had made it, it still had a genteel, tranquil appeal. No wonder Peter Priestland had chosen to live here as long as he had. The house where Peter died, the house his widow still lived in—and which, according to Bresnan, she showed no signs of moving from—lay on the other side of the village, but Jonty didn't mind the walk. He wanted to get a feel for the atmosphere of the place, as though in absorbing that atmosphere, he might begin to get a feeling for what had gone on. Orlando would sneer at such subjectivity, but Orlando could lump it.

Thorpe House was a Georgian villa, set back from the road along a gravelled drive, with gardens full of rhododendrons and azaleas that must have looked a picture in the spring and early summer. This time of year was clearly not their best, for the only patches of colour were clumps of autumn crocuses. In a few weeks, it would no doubt be a riot of colour again as the leaves donned their richest hues.

If the house and garden were just as he had pictured in his mind thanks to the excellent pen portrait from Bresnan, Rosalind

Priestland was not. He'd built up a mental picture of some flighty little thing, powdered and painted and dressed to the nines, but the lady who awaited him in the morning room was nothing like that. She was plump, pretty, dark haired, had a deep, attractive voice and wore the sort of clothes even his mother might have regarded as somewhat staid. No wonder most people, who no doubt put far too much importance on appearance, hadn't had a bad word for her. They'd look at her, see someone who appeared kind and nice—and possibly reminiscent of the sort of benevolent maiden aunts who'd had a string of admirers but lost the one they really wanted—therefore kind and nice she must be.

Nor was the housekeeper quite what Jonty expected, either. Tall, slim, with an impressive bearing and hair tied back in a bun, Mrs. Hamilton looked more like a governess to a ducal family than the keeper of the pantry keys. She'd opened the door herself, which was surprising, welcoming Jonty with a brief smile and a nod before ushering him in.

"Dr. Stewart, thank you for calling. I really do appreciate you making the effort." Rosalind rose to meet him, offering her hand and indicating a seat in the sunlight. A small table was laid with cups and biscuits, awaiting the arrival of the tea or coffeepot.

"It seems a bit tactless to say 'my pleasure,' given the circumstances, but I hope you'll understand." He took his appointed place. "I've felt as if my father has been nudging me to do this from beyond the grave, or at least respect for his memory has. Or something." He tried his best to sound slightly muddled and totally appealing. Rosalind's kindly smile showed that he seemed to be succeeding.

"I have to confess I only vaguely remember Peter mentioning your father. Ah, Glenys, thank you." Mrs. Hamilton had entered with a steaming silver coffeepot, and the next few minutes were lost to pouring, sugaring, and creaming. Jonty wondered whether his hostess was dissembling as much as he was, with her "vaguely remember."

"Although," Rosalind continued, "I do recall him telling me a wonderful story about your mother. I hope you're not offended if I say it's the one about her knocking out a chap who proposed to her?"

"Not offended at all. It's one of my favourite stories, although I only found out about it when I was nearly thirty." So Peter Priestland *had* known the Stewarts, or at least had known of them; another bow drawn at a venture had hit its mark. Funny how often they did, especially where the Stewarts and their extended web of social contacts were concerned. Many of the breakthroughs they'd had in investigations had been more a matter of luck than judgement, although he wasn't going to get into that discussion with Orlando. Not until maybe 1928. "Did your husband often talk of the old times? Perhaps he knew some more tales about my parents that they'd managed to keep secret from their offspring."

"That's the only one I can recall. It's a shame you never got to meet Peter, as he might have been able to turf all sorts of skeletons out of closets. He had such a zest for life, right up to the end." She breathed deeply, as if holding back tears. Either Rosalind felt genuine affection for Peter Priestland or she was a *very* accomplished actress.

"My mother and father were the same. This wretched influenza robbed us of so many good, decent people." Jonty thought he might shed a tear himself, if he wasn't careful. Generating some sympathy in Rosalind's maternal-looking bosom might help the investigation, although he didn't want to risk being held there for comfort.

"Did your parents die recently?"

"Last year, although it feels like yesterday." Even though so much had happened in between, the loss still felt raw. "I don't actually know if it was the Spanish flu, as some people say it was too early to have been, but I'm convinced in my heart that was what took them. It was all so quick."

"I hope they didn't suffer. Peter seemed to be getting well, you know. We had such optimism that he'd make a full recovery." A hint of a tear again. "He looked so peaceful sitting out in the conservatory, where we found him. It truly seemed like he was just sleeping, tucked under his blanket in the middle of some lovely dream. Maybe he was, maybe he'd seen his mother again, just at the moment he . . ." Jonty proffered his handkerchief, but Rosalind shook her head and produced her own. "Thank you, no. I don't want to mess up your linen." She suddenly smiled. "I'm being a silly old thing."

"No, you're not. If it still hurts, then you're right to cry. You must do as your feelings dictate." He looked away to give her time to compose herself. Plenty of people might have said Rosalind should hide her grief. They'd have said that a stiff upper lip and repression of any outward show of emotion was appropriate, especially in front of a stranger.

Mrs. Stewart wouldn't have agreed. *Let it out, dear*, she'd have said. *Let it all flow away and then move on. Better than dwelling on it or hiding it away. Won't do you any good.*

Jonty had wiped away plenty of Orlando's tears these last few months, when the man had woken in a muck sweat, dreaming he was back in the trenches. Mrs. Stewart wouldn't have seen those tears as a sign of weakness nor Jonty's tenderness in dealing with them as anything effeminate or unsuitable. He cast a sidelong, surreptitious glance at his hostess, and caught her doing the same to him before looking away again, nervously. Was that heartfelt grief real, or part of some skilful act?

"I do miss him, that's the problem. I suppose I'm young enough to find another husband, but I'm not sure I want one." Rosalind blew her nose demurely. "Not if I can't have my Peter."

He was at a bit of a loss about how to proceed. The young widow sounded believable, those tears seemed real enough, but he couldn't forget that suspicious look he'd just seen. "Have you any family to help you through?"

"No, I'm afraid not. My parents died when I was quite young and I was an only child. Mrs. Hamilton, my housekeeper, has been a great help, as has the vicar, Reverend Mitchell." Rosalind wiped the last tear away, folding her handkerchief in her hand.

"Mrs. Hamilton was with you when you found your husband, I believe? At least you weren't alone to face the ordeal."

Rosalind nodded. "Oh, yes. I often wonder what it would have been like if I'd been here on my own. I might have been, you know, because Mrs. Hamilton was due to go out that afternoon to buy some material for curtains, but we had this terrible infestation of ladybirds and had to call someone out to deal with them. Afterwards, we went around the house making sure they'd all gone. You can never be sure workmen do a proper job, and I couldn't stand the thought of the things still lingering in the joints of the sash windows."

A stray thought about whether something used in the fumigation process—what was it Mrs. Ward swore by, Keating's Powder?—had been a contributory factor in Peter's death demanded attention. He'd have to consider the possibility or else Orlando was bound to upbraid him for casting aside the investigator's strict neutrality. And yet . . . call it intuition, or hearing what he wanted to hear, but there was definitely something in what his hostess had said that sounded like she'd been setting up her own alibi in advance. Not the words so much as an intonation of voice or a resonance of implication. He had no evidence for it, of course, except his natural, completely illogical (and much scorned by Orlando) scepticism towards alibis. He'd actually have been much *less* suspicious if Rosalind had been on her own in the house when her husband had died.

"No, that's very true. About slapdash workmen." Jonty cast around to find exactly the right, incisive question to follow up. He couldn't. *I must be losing my touch; too far out of practice.* "This might sound a bit odd, but if you could clarify something, it would put my mind at rest . . ."

"I'm sorry?" The wary note in Rosalind's voice matched her earlier guarded look. "Put your mind at rest about what?"

"Mrs. Priestland, I should be the one to apologise. My mother always said I was a terrible one not just for woolgathering but for voicing my thoughts out loud and making little sense in the process. I tend to just blurt out what I'm thinking and then nobody knows what I'm going on about." He hoped his brightest smile might lull his hostess back into a less wary state. "I was thinking about your husband and hoping that it was *you* who'd found he was dead. Silly, I know, but it would be sort of comforting if it had been a loved one and not, well, one of the domestic household. Does that sound too snobby?"

"No." Rosalind sounded relieved. "No, I quite understand. Yes, it was me who found Peter, and you're right. No matter how much it hurt, it was better that way than Mrs. Hamilton discovering him. More fitting. She went to call for the doctor, just in case we were wrong, and I held his hand even though he was gone." She sounded tearful again. "I've heard people say that the spirit lingers on for a while. Maybe Peter knew I was there and was grateful."

"I'm sure he did." Jonty felt the need to go and gather his thoughts, but it was too soon to stop the interview and not appear impolite. Best fill the breach with chitchat. "I may have got this wrong, but I heard that your husband was a St. Bride's man." It was worth drawing another bow at a venture.

Rosalind laughed. "Oh no, that's not right at all. He was at Apostles'. Not quite your archenemies but not said to be your greatest friends."

"You've got the measure of us, Mrs. Priestland. Still, I won't sneer at an Apostles' man. My brother-in-law's brother went there, and he's not a *total* disgrace." Jonty smiled.

"Peter and I visited the college last summer. He said it didn't seem to have changed at all."

"I'm not sure Apostles' has changed since Oliver Cromwell used to take his catapult and fling stones at the windows."

The conversation drifted onto Cambridge and its inability to embrace the nineteenth, let alone the twentieth, century. Jonty didn't feel inclined to pull it back in. He'd learned as much as he was going to learn at the moment, he guessed, so he concluded the interview and took his leave, his hostess showing him to the door herself. He'd wondered if the housekeeper would return to perform that task, but she was busy down by the front gate to the property, talking to a tall, reed-slim young man who appeared to be the grocer's boy.

There was something about errand lads, some combination of innocence and enthusiasm, that had always touched Jonty, and that affected him even more given his experiences of the last few years. He took a deep breath and strode along the path. Thorpe House wasn't a property in the same league of any of the Stewarts' homes, but it wasn't small, and the expanse of garden and sweep of the drive meant the road was a reasonable walk from the front door. Or, more appropriately in the case of Mrs. Hamilton and the other servants, from the tradesman's entrance. If this lad was making his deliveries, there seemed no logical reason why the housekeeper should have accompanied him all the way to the gate. Unless she was escorting him off the premises with her rolling pin at her side because of improprieties committed with the maid, but that was surely a hypothesis too far.

"Good morning again." He raised his hat. It *was* still morning—just.

"Dr. Stewart." Mrs. Hamilton spun round at the sound of his voice and performed a little bob. "What a stroke of luck."

"That's not what my students say when they see me coming." He grinned, even more intrigued now about what was going on. "What's lucky about it?"

"You coming along just as young Billy here was delivering the groceries." The housekeeper nodded for emphasis, her tight bun of grey hair hardly moving as she did so. Perhaps it had been threatened with a seeing-to from the hairbrush if any strand dared loose itself. "I thought he'd gone without you being able to catch him, but he was dawdling here at the gate, as usual."

"I wasn't dawdling, ma'am." Billy was a gangly, spotty streak of lad, maybe eighteen or nineteen, who'd have made a slice of bacon look solid.

"Don't mumble, Billy. Dr. Stewart needs to hear every word."

Jonty wasn't aware that Billy *had* been mumbling, but he smiled encouragingly.

"I said I wasn't dawdling, Mrs. Hamilton. There's a red kite over Mr. Norris's fields and I was watching it. It's looking for its prey." The last few words sounded as if they'd been overheard, remembered, and reused.

"Red kite, indeed." The housekeeper sniffed, loudly and with emphasis.

"Ah now, Mrs. Hamilton, I'm going to have to stand up for this young lad, here. There was a red kite around. I saw it as I came down the drive." Jonty gestured vaguely in the direction of where the bird might have been, taking pleasure in the *I told you so* look on the delivery lad's face. He'd not seen any such thing, of course, but he was determined to get Billy on his side. "Now, why should I want to catch this budding young ornithologist? I was actually hoping to have a word with you before I went."

Mrs. Hamilton pulled herself up to her full, impressive height. "I'm not sure there's anything I can add to what Mrs. Priestland has told you. Unlike Billy, who was also here the day the master died. He'd been lent by the grocer to help Fred Houseman kill those ladybirds."

I'm sure he was, but why are you so keen for me *to talk to him? And why him and not the scourge of flying things, Mr. Houseman himself? Or yourself?*

Jonty had been careful not to give the impression he was deliberately probing into the events of that day, yet here they were, being thrust at him. Either he'd been less subtle than he thought or the women had been on the watch for him, somehow. Although there was a simpler explanation: that Mrs. Hamilton had been listening at the door while he spoke to her mistress. That was more satisfying than the nagging thought that they *were* losing their touch . . . although it could even be just another case of his name, even without the "and Coppersmith" bit, being recognised from reports of their cases in the newspapers.

"I like ladybirds. It was sad to have to get rid of the little things." Billy earned himself a dirty look from the housekeeper. She seemed like she was about to give him a tongue-lashing to go with it and had to hold herself in check.

"An ornithologist *and* an entomologist." Jonty felt inclined to pull the bumbling Cambridge don card, even if his initial cover story had been blown. Billy didn't look the brightest thing on two legs, yet Jonty had taken an immediate shine to him. He'd had lads like this out in France, lads just the right side of being a little too dim for the King's shilling, doing their bit for England. All of them had seemed to appreciate their commanding officer for the fact his undoubted intellect hadn't elevated him out of the sphere of his fellow men.

"Billy wants to tell you what he saw that day." Mrs. Hamilton was determined to press on.

"Was it another red kite?" He didn't like the way Mrs. Hamilton seemed to both look down her nose at Billy and press him forward as a witness, maybe in her stead. "Here, Billy, I'm going back into the village. We can saunter along together and you can tell me everything. That way you won't be in trouble for hanging about when you should be working." He raised his hat to the housekeeper and started to walk, tipping his head to the delivery boy to follow. Billy hesitated for a moment and then fell into step beside him, wheeling the bicycle and peering anxiously over his shoulder at Mrs. Hamilton, whose face resembled Orlando's when he was in one of his darker moods.

When they were out of earshot, Billy continued. "People say there aren't any red kites round here, you know."

"Do they indeed?" Jonty suspected those "people," whoever they were, happened to be right.

"They say it's just buzzards I've seen. They attack newborn lambs, you know. Nasty, vicious things."

Jonty didn't want to ask whether it was the lambs or the buzzards or the red kites who were vicious. Even *he* could tell a kite from a buzzard, and he'd expect any country boy to be able to do the same. Maybe Billy would be just as unreliable about the day Peter Priestland died. Time to find out. "That morning Mr. Priestland died. What did you see?"

"A man. I saw a man in the grounds here, when we was just finishing off fu-mi-ga-ting the ladybirds." Billy spoke the long word carefully.

"Was he acting suspiciously, that you remember him so well after all this time?" He kept his voice airy, not wanting to frighten or confuse the lad.

"Suspiciously?" Billy gave his interlocutor a sidelong, puzzled glance.

"Acting odd."

"A bit. Around and about the bushes. I pointed him out to Mr. Houseman, but he told me to keep my mind on my work. So I did." Billy nodded, to emphasise the point. "I'm a good worker."

"I bet you are. I wonder how Mrs. Hamilton knew about this man, then?" Jonty had a feeling this meeting had all been set up to throw him off the scent. It was like being part of a conjuror's trick and knowing your attention was being diverted while the magician produced his piece of prestidigitation. Yet Billy struck him as being fundamentally honest, clearly believing in all that he said. If he was putting on part of the show, then he was a marvellous actor, so good it was impossible to tell where the act started and ended.

"She must have been told by Mr. Houseman. I didn't say anything to her." The bicycle bobbled over a rut, Billy checking it with a volley of colourful oaths and a hurried, "Pardon my French, sir."

"No need to apologise. I've heard worse." Said worse too, but Jonty wasn't admitting that at present. "She seemed very keen for me to meet you."

Billy nodded. "Keen as mustard. Only just now she almost chased me down the drive and said there was a gentleman—that'll be you, sir—wanted to know what had happened the day Mr. Priestland died."

"That's odd. It's even odder than the bit about the man lurking around the grounds. I don't think I want to know what had happened that day. Peter Priestland was an old friend of the family, and I just came to pay my belated respects. I was out in France when he died, so I couldn't have done it then." From Billy's nod and look of comprehension, that explanation made entire sense. "I didn't realise there was anything *to* discover. I thought he'd just suffered complications following the flu. Am I wrong?"

"Not at all, sir. Nasty stuff, that Spanish flu. It took my two young cousins and my granny, not long after old Mr. Priestland. I kept clear of it, but plenty of folk weren't as lucky. I was expecting them to cover granny's face after she was dead, but they didn't. She looked lovely and peaceful." Billy shook his head. "I wouldn't worry about that man I saw, though. I bet he was at Thorpe House just looking for rabbits or something else to put in the pot. People was still a bit short back then. Maybe he'd come up from the city for a nice bit of meat."

"Maybe." It was as good an explanation as any. Jonty wasn't sure he was going to get a lot else from Billy, not without the lad twigging that he really *was* prying into the affairs of that October day. Lads like Billy might not have a lot of book learning, but they often possessed common sense in spades. He wasn't yet sure that applied in this case. "Did you see him from the room Mr. Priestland was found in?"

"No, sir. We didn't do that room at all. None of the little varmints in there. Upstairs."

So accidental poisoning seemed unlikely. "Of course."

"You saw action, sir?" Billy asked as they came to a crossroads. It was clear he had to turn left while Jonty went straight on. The boy stopped, propping his bike against a post and fiddling with the handlebars while making a point of not looking at Jonty directly. "Might I ask if you got your scar out there?"

The question may have been blunt, but Jonty wasn't offended. Plenty of people made a point of not mentioning or looking at the scar; somehow that was even worse than when they asked directly or stared. "I did and it was. I got this almost a year ago." He fingered his cheek. "About the time it was all coming to an end."

"I wanted to enlist, sir, but my old ma wouldn't let me. She says my heart's weak, although I don't believe her. Maybe I'll get my chance one day."

"Maybe." Jonty sincerely hoped that would never come about.

"Everyone says there was a fair heap of young lads killed. It must have been a sore trial."

Funny how those simple words had the power to cut Jonty to the quick. "It was."

Billy held out his hand. "May I shake hands with a real hero, sir?"

"I was hardly a hero, but it would be an honour to shake your hand, Billy. You're the sort of lad we fought on behalf of. To keep you free." It sounded stupid, the sort of sentimental talk that might have been essentially insincere, yet Jonty meant every word of it. He'd have fought for innocent lads like Billy any day; he'd fought alongside plenty just like him. It would take a lot to make him feel inclined to fight for the Mrs. Hamiltons of this world.

Jonty lingered awhile, watching the delivery boy, whistling happily, cycle along the lane to his next stop. It had certainly been an enlightening little conversation, although not necessarily in the way the housekeeper—and perhaps her mistress—had intended.

Chapter 6

The lady at Downlea Post Office favoured Orlando with a smile and a deferential bob of the head as he entered the shop. He guessed she was in her early twenties, and observed that she was neatly dressed, with a huge dimple in her left cheek that appeared and disappeared as she spoke. He also supposed she'd be counted as pretty by those who were inclined that way, and perhaps a touch flirtatious, given the glint in her eye.

Orlando laid three letters on the counter—he'd brought some from home as a necessary prop—and asked for the stamps. "And I'll take some spare twopennies and a two-shilling one, thank you."

"Always best to top up supplies. Half a dozen?" The young woman seemed efficient, dealing with Orlando's post quickly and neatly, sticking on the stamps so they lined up exactly with the corner of the envelope, just as he liked them to be. Jonty could stick his on haphazardly, but Orlando sometimes felt he wouldn't be able to sleep if he knew he'd put something in the postbox that looked so askew.

"Thank you." He paid for the stamps and slowly put the spare ones in his wallet. "May I ask what is bound to seem a very silly question?"

"Of course. So long as you don't mind if I can't answer it." The woman had spirit, as well as a neat way with a stamp. The fact that she could flirt for a while with her handsome customer (Orlando had at last got it into his head he could be legitimately regarded as handsome and that it was a positive aid in his investigations) clearly amused her. Maybe nice men were as scarce a quantity in Downlea as they seemed to be everywhere else, the flower of a generation laid waste in Flanders Fields and other such places.

"I'd got it into my mind that the postmistress here was the wife of an old friend. He died earlier this year and I wasn't here to pay my respects." Orlando didn't elaborate on where he was. Ladling on too much unnecessary detail always looked a bit suspicious, and if the girl had any sense, she'd realise where he might have been and why he couldn't get back.

"Well, I'm the postmistress, and I've never been married to anyone. Alice Huddlestone I was born and Alice Huddlestone I've remained until now." The amplified twinkle in her eye suggested to Orlando that she was hoping this state of affairs might be rectified if nice men like him came along more often.

"Then I do seem to have got myself into a muddle." Orlando took off his hat and scratched his head; Jonty had often said the gesture made him look helpless and appealing. "Peter Priestland certainly lived here in Downlea, unless he'd moved during the war years and never told me. My Christmas cards always seemed to get through, but I suppose they may have been redirected . . ." Orlando carried on with his impression of an absentminded professor. *Professor.* He had to hide a smile at the thought of the prestigious title, a title that was all his.

"Oh yes, he does live here. Sorry, did. Thorpe House. The big place you can see among the elms from the platform of the up line." Miss Huddlestone spoke as if that made everything clear. "His wife would *never* be a postmistress."

Orlando waited for the catty remark he was sure would follow from this bald statement. Was this one of the small pockets of unkindness the Reverend Ian Bresnan had found? "Why would that be?"

"Because your friend wouldn't let her. I took over this post, if you'll excuse the pun, just three years ago." She beamed. "You may think I'm rather young to be trusted, but they were delighted to take me on."

Orlando thought she was rather on the coquettish side for such an important position but held his tongue, settling for an encouraging smile.

"Not long afterwards, Mrs. Priestland came in to get a postal order. We were chatting about how I was getting on, and she confided that she'd always wanted to be a postmistress, ever since she was a little girl.

Fascinated by the stamps and the parcels, the postal orders and the telegrams. All of it." Miss Huddlestone rolled her eyes at such childish enthusiasm. "She said she'd contemplated applying for the vacancy, but her husband had insisted she shouldn't. I don't think he went as far as saying 'No wife of *mine* is going to demean herself by working in a shop,' but it must have been something quite unpleasant. I could tell by the way she was making light of it. Covering up her distress."

"Sad how set in their ways some people are." *He'd* never be so hidebound by convention. Not now. No matter what Jonty might have to say on the matter. "And now she's free, but the position isn't."

Miss Huddlestone nodded. "I don't think her heart would be in it, anyway. Although she comes in here quite regularly to get her stamps or collect some stationery, rather than leaving it all up to the servants like some of them do around here. I suspect she gets a bit more freedom now that she doesn't have to always mind what her husband says." She leaned forward, lowering her voice. "He was a lot older than her, you know. Such a nice man, a real gentleman, but very correct and old-fashioned. It couldn't have been much fun for her. Oh! I didn't mean any slur on your friend, sir. I've let my tongue run on with me there."

"No offence taken." Orlando inclined his head, in a gesture he hoped would represent magnanimity. "Peter *was* rather an old stick-in-the-mud at times, even if his heart was in the right place. I just hope, for his sake, that they were a happy couple. I'd hate to think of his last few years as being in any way unhappy."

"He always seemed happy as far as I could see, sir. I'd have called him besotted with his wife, even though—or maybe because—she was so much younger." A dreamy expression came over the postmistress's face. "The way he looked at her over evensong in church. Proper romantic."

Orlando decided it was time to get away before the looks he was receiving became any more *proper romantic*. He scooped up his purchases, thanked Miss Huddlestone for all her help, then scurried out the door to have a quick reconnoitre of the countryside before meeting the only person he wanted to exchange romantic glances with. At least he had something to report about the case, even if it seemed very flimsy. It was interesting to have found some note of discord between husband and wife, but was not being allowed to work in a post office sufficient motive for murder?

English villages have a habit of putting the important things together. The shops are rarely far from the village green, and the pub is usually by the church, as if those emerging from matins or evensong might well feel the need of something fortifying as they make their way home.

Jonty had intended to call at the butcher's shop—always a source of good quality gossip—but he had to pass the churchyard en route, which led to a change of plans. As another assimilation of local flavour, he stopped to look at the notice board. You could learn a lot from what churches chose to display, although he hardly expected to see "Rosalind Priestland is a murdering wench" writ large there; that would have made life far too easy. She'd mentioned a Reverend Mitchell, though, and, as Jonty had expected, the name *Reverend Francis Mitchell* was at the bottom of various notices.

Would it be more worthwhile dropping into the vicarage to pick the vicar's brains on the postbereavement state of Rosalind's mind, or to pursue a speculative conversation over a pork chop? The idea of talking to Mitchell appealed, but how on earth was he going to wangle a valid excuse for doing so? Knock on the door and say, "Excuse me, we've never met, but can you tell me if Rosalind Priestland ever gave you the impression that she'd just murdered her husband?"

Still, it would be worth trying to make contact. The vicarage was set back from the road, and he could always at the very least pretend he wanted to see the brasses in the church. Maybe Mitchell would be sufficiently old and doddery to be conned into giving all sorts of things away. Maybe even, glorious thought, he might have been in love with Jonty's mother at some point in the past and would bend over backwards to help her son. It wasn't such a long shot; if all the men who'd fancied Helena Forster had been laid end to end, they'd have stretched to Edinburgh.

The man who answered the vicarage door was in his early thirties, clad in tennis flannels and wearing a towel around his neck. He was tall and dark, as handsome as Orlando, and had a healthy glow on his face from recently taken exercise.

"Can I help you?" He favoured Jonty with a wonderful smile.

If this was the Reverend Mitchell's son, he was a real eye-catcher. Not that Jonty wanted his eye caught, but you couldn't help admire at times—like when you looked at Greek and Roman statues, happened to find yourself staring at one of Antinous, and had to fight to keep the libidinous thoughts at bay.

"I was looking for the Reverend Mitchell."

"You've found him!"

"Oh." Jonty had been so sure he was looking for some white-haired dodderer that he was temporarily at a loss for what to say. "I was wondering if you could help me. I wanted to visit the grave of Peter Priestland, and I wasn't sure where to find it . . ." That sounded truly pathetic; he daren't own up to Orlando about how feckless he was being.

"I'm afraid you're miles off course. He's buried down in Hampshire, near Romsey. The family plot, you know." Mitchell smiled. "I'm sorry if you've come here on a wild-goose chase. Please, come in and have a cup of tea. I'll get my housekeeper. Mary!"

If Jonty had wanted to refuse the invitation, he couldn't. Mary was summoned and asked to produce some refreshments, leaving Jonty afraid he'd begin to dissolve with the volume of liquid he'd consumed. He was ushered into a comfortable, bachelor-type study, reminiscent of Cambridge sets and earnest discussions about esoteric areas of study over late-night port or cocoa. The familiarity allowed him to relax a little and gather together his befuddled thoughts.

"I should have checked before I set out." Why on earth hadn't someone, the grieving widow, or even Ian Bresnan himself, mentioned that Peter had been buried where his family had lived?

"Hindsight is a wonderful commodity." Mitchell looked suddenly serious. "I wish we'd been able to take what we knew in 1918 and exercise it four years earlier."

Jonty wondered what had occasioned the change of tack. Had Mitchell noticed the great scar that graced his guest's cheek, the livid mark of honour that had cost so much more in the earning of it than either Military Medal or Military Cross? Mitchell himself had a tracery of lines on the back of his hand that suggested old wounds. He'd have been the right age to serve.

"Were you out there?"

"I was. With the Cambridgeshires, from early 1915." He rose, fetching a photograph from the mantelpiece. "This is me, with my boys." The pride in the vicar's voice was palpable.

"They look a wonderful bunch." Jonty fought back the lump in his throat. The lads all appeared so fresh faced and young, barely more than boys, just as his own platoon had been. At times, he'd felt more like a nursemaid than an officer. "I won't ask you how many of them made it back as it'll upset both of us to have the answer. Please God, that *was* the war to end all wars, although I'm not optimistic." He glanced up, aware of the potential faux pas. "I don't mean I've no optimism in the powers of the Almighty. It's men I don't trust anymore."

"I can't help but agree with you." Mitchell took back the photo, taking one last long look at it before returning it to its place of honour. "Now, about this grave."

"Yes. I can't help wondering why he's been buried in Romsey. I suppose it's a case of a family plot?" The Stewarts had one in Sussex that had seen generation upon generation interred, some of them miles away from where they'd counted as home.

"I believe so, although it's not in Romsey itself. I forget the name of the parish, although I could find that out for you."

"Thank you, that would be most helpful." Jonty knew the answer, of course, assuming it was the same place that Simon Priestland had been buried.

"Don't go before I've written it down for you. Strange story about the Priestlands. Interesting, though. Mysteries seem to run in that family. I suppose he wanted to be near his twin brother, Simon." Mitchell smiled.

"Nice choice of names for them." Jonty returned the smile. "Any fishermen in the family?"

"Several who've taken a fly to catch a trout on the river Test, but none who set out on small seas in smaller boats."

"And none who've fished for men, either, I suppose?" Jonty warmed to his theme; Orlando didn't really appreciate this sort of

Biblical wit. "I take your point about the twin brother, as I understand they were very close, but what you said about mysteries intrigues me."

"How much of the family history do you know? And how much time have you available to spend hearing about it?" Mitchell seemed intelligent and was certainly appealing to talk to. It was easy to imagine what a consolation he'd have been to Rosalind Priestland, who didn't seem the sort of woman to suffer boring company. Jonty wondered how interesting Peter had been, particularly as he'd grown older. He also wondered whether a man as handsome as Mitchell would have raised any romantic feelings in Rosalind's breast, either pre- or post-becoming a widow.

"I know there were triplets, not twins. When Simon and Peter were born." It was a safe enough thing to say, proving that he wasn't a total stranger to the Priestlands but not even hinting he knew about the more unsavoury things the family might have to hide.

"That's right. The firstborn who didn't survive more than a few days, then Peter, and then Simon. Their mother was terribly ill afterwards. It seems to have cast a blight on the whole family." Mitchell sighed. "A horribly cruel process, I always feel, childbirth. All too often, I've seen the brutal side of it. Mothers and children in the same grave." He shuddered.

Bresnan's notes flitted through Jonty's brain. "This may sound very unimportant, but is that the order in which they were born? I always understood Simon was the eldest. His birthday was the day before his brothers'."

"Was it?" Mitchell ran his hand through his hair, appearing momentarily flustered. "Perhaps I'm the one who has the details wrong."

"It doesn't matter." It didn't at the moment, certainly, although Jonty made a mental note to see if they could confirm what Bresnan had told them. It was just possible *he* hadn't got his facts right.

"At least we can be certain that Andrew was born first. He was terribly sickly, I understand. The old man used to say it was a blessing he hadn't survived, so the estate wouldn't have been in the hands of a weakling." Mitchell shook his head.

"What a horrible thing to say of your own child."

"From what Peter told me, old Andrew Priestland was a horrible man."

Jonty wondered what secrets had been poured out over postprandial port and whether he could subtly dig up any about Rosalind. "Is the order of birth the mystery you alluded to?"

"Not that I was aware of until now, although what happened to the mother is. The story the sons had been told since childhood was that she'd been unwell, but survived almost until the boys were toddling. She then sickened and died, the effects of the birth still preying on her. Peter believed that until after his father passed away in 1873."

"Ah. And at that point he heard another variation on the tale?" The inflection in Mitchell's tone had been unmistakable; even rusty as he was at investigating, Jonty couldn't have missed it.

"Indeed. Some well-meaning person or other—so well-meaning and virtuous that they didn't bother to sign the letters—wrote to both him and Simon to say their mother had been alive and well up until the previous year. Allegedly she'd died at sea, when a pleasure yacht went aground off the Scilly Isles." Mitchell leaned forwards, elbows on knees and chin resting on steepled hands. "The yacht was said to belong to her paramour."

"So who's buried in the family plot? I mean, Mrs. Priestland the elder must have had a grave." Jonty stopped. He *was* losing his touch, being as thick as the proverbial two short planks. "Or are there two graves? Assuming the body wasn't lost at sea?"

"It appears it was, just to add another macabre twist to the story. So only one grave—the one where, for years, they'd believed she'd rested."

"Peter wasn't daft." Jonty hoped he wasn't making one assumption too many in front of someone who'd actually known the man. "Nor was Simon." At least he knew that for a fact. Everything they'd encountered in the case had shown the signs of an active mind, something that his nephew Bresnan also had. "They'd have wanted to know the truth."

Funny how this case was going, so quickly, the way that all their previous ones had. Tendrils of storylines reaching out, twisting and grabbing to attach themselves to all sorts of things, only some of which would be relevant to the vine as a whole.

"There is a headstone for Alice Priestland at the same plot where old Mr. Priestland is buried. As I said, he died before all the rumours came out, so they never got the chance to question him." Mitchell rubbed his chin. "One day I was brave enough to ask Peter whether they'd ever tried to verify any of the story."

"To have the grave opened, do you mean?" Jonty narrowed his eyes. "It would have been opened when the father was buried, of course. Did no one notice anything amiss then?"

"Not at all, apparently. That's one of the odd things. When he prepared the grave, the verger uncovered the first coffin and even made a point about saying he remembered the funeral." Mitchell rubbed his chin again. "His father had been verger before him, and he'd assisted at Alice Priestland's interment. He gave no impression that anything had been wrong with it or that he'd entertained any suspicions."

"And was there no further move to find out if that first coffin had been empty? Or if not empty, who it contained?" This was more like it. Now he was thinking more incisively, getting into his investigational stride again. Dear God, Orlando hadn't been the only one who'd missed the thrill of the chase.

"It's funny you say that, because it's exactly what Peter wanted to do, but Simon wouldn't let him. Desecration, he called it, although I can see both sides of the argument. The potential violation of their parents' grave versus the need to establish whether they'd been lied to all these years." Mitchell spread his hands, as if appealing to a judge and jury. "Alas, there are too many cases in life where there is no absolute right or wrong, despite what some of my more traditional colleagues might say."

"Amen to that." Jonty could think of plenty of his own examples of the grey shades of morality, but kept his counsel. He had another bright idea. "Did the brothers fall out over it?"

"Not to the extent that they severed all relations, if that's what you mean. I know these family feuds can start over relatively trivial things and escalate beyond all imagining, but in this case, they still remained good friends. Never stopped arguing over it, though, right until the end." Mitchell considered his teacup, clearly weighing his words. "Literally, I think."

"I'm sorry, I don't follow."

"Simon was here to visit his brother when he had the flu. Neither of them were in their first flush of youth—Simon's words, not mine—and there was always the risk that any meeting might be a last one."

"You said they were Simon's words. Were they used at the time? Did you see him when he visited?" He wished he'd got his trusty old notebook on his knee so he could keep an accurate record and not rely on memory. Sometimes the exact words that people used, rather than the impression they created, and vice versa, were the key to a case.

"I did. I'd met him on occasions before, over dinner at the Priestlands' house. He seemed very concerned that this time he might not see his brother again. Terrible business, this Spanish flu. It took a number of my parishioners." Mitchell rested his chin on his hands.

Jonty wondered whether the gesture was one he habitually used when talking of mortality. Men of the cloth were often good actors; did Mitchell have a repertoire of such actions that he employed to impress and comfort his flock? Still, the mere mention of the flu was enough to make Jonty shudder.

"I don't suppose he was actually here when his brother died?" He just stopped himself from adding that Simon couldn't have been in the actual room, given that the papers he'd left for his nephew had bewailed that fact. If he'd been present, he might have had the evidence he needed to incriminate his sister-in-law.

"Now, that's a peculiar thing. I understood that he'd left for home the day before, only returning after Mrs. Priestland informed him that Peter had died." Mitchell leaned forward; witnesses often seemed to do that before imparting some crucial piece of information. Jonty was convinced the more somebody leaned, the less likely they were to be telling the truth. What did Orlando call it? Negative correlation or some such mathematical nonsense. "But I was sure I saw him here in Downlea that very morning."

"The day that his brother died?" Was this Billy's "man in the trees"? Jonty had suspected that man was no more real than the red kite *he'd* pretended to have seen in order to make friends with Billy. And to get Mrs. Hamilton's goat, which was even better.

"The very same. Although that's not the only thing I've wondered about that day. I thought—" Mitchell stopped abruptly. "Do you know, I put subtle messages into my sermons to warn my parishioners about the perils of idle gossip, and here I am chattering away like the worst sort of old maid. You'll forgive me, please."

"Of course." Jonty forgave the gossiping, even if he was cross about it coming to an end just when it was getting interesting. Maybe it had been Mitchell's stern injunctions from the pulpit that had inhibited the parish gossip about Rosalind Priestland. Most of the women and some of the men would have been highly susceptible to the vicar's undoubted charms.

"If you want information rather than gossip, you could do worse than talk to Billy Waller, who delivers the groceries." Mitchell sounded a touch too airy. "He was at Thorpe House that day, helping out with some fumigation."

"Not flushing out red kites, I hope?" And why did people keep thrusting Billy at him?

"Ah, you've already met him. He's rather obsessed with them, isn't he?" The vicar produced an avuncular smile.

"I've assumed the things were extinct in England." Indeed, the only one Jonty had ever seen had been stuffed and in a case.

"They are. But I had a parish assistant from Wales who regaled Billy and some of the other lads with gruesome tales of what these birds could do to a lamb. Now every harrier or buzzard is a kite, in Billy's eyes."

"He has a wild imagination?"

"No," Mitchell said, maybe a bit too eager to protest. "He's a touch gullible, and I suspect one of the other lads told him he'd seen one, so he wants to see them too. But he's fundamentally honest, I believe."

"I hope so." Jonty wasn't convinced. "I'll talk to him again, though."

"Splendid." Mitchell rubbed his hands together. "Now, we have some very remarkable brasses in the church. Would you like to see them?"

Jonty paid for information received with ten minutes of admiring tombs in the church, only one of which fell into the "very remarkable" category because it contained a man and his three wives, whom everyone said he'd married sequentially but everyone suspected he'd wed concurrently. People in Downlea had always had fuel for gossip, it seemed.

They stopped for a moment at the door of the church, although Jonty was eager to be away as he was already running late. He was also fairly sure he wasn't going to hear anything about Rosalind, no matter how much he'd hinted while they'd looked at the monuments. However, he'd underestimated his luck, or the interference from his guardian angel, whichever of the two was on duty.

"Might I ask you a favour?" Mitchell might have been asking, but he couldn't look Jonty in the eye. "As you're a friend of the family, I should warn you that you might hear stories about Rosalind Priestland's past. Stories that might upset you."

Jonty could barely get an answer out. Hear stories? Ones that might upset him? He couldn't wait. "I've been lucky to avoid such things," he said, immediately cursing himself for possibly having turned off the informational tap.

"I'm pleased to hear it. You see, when Rosalind was very young, she did something silly, taking some jewellery that didn't belong to her. From a gentleman she was friendly with. The theft was discovered and brought to her door, but charges were never pressed, given the affection she was held in. She returned everything. She saw the error of her ways and made peace with God. Peter knew and he forgave her entirely." Mitchell stopped looking at the ceiling and addressed Jonty directly, spreading his hands. "There but for the grace of God go any of us."

"Indeed." Jonty waited for more to be added. There was a look in Mitchell's eye, as if some inner debate was being held between two opposing parts of his conscience.

"There are times when my profession is a delight, Dr. Stewart, and others when it is extremely difficult." That was written plainly on his face. "One hears things one cannot repeat. You'll surely understand that?"

"I do indeed." Again, Jonty waited, but nothing more was forthcoming.

"Thank you," Mitchell said, shaking Jonty's hand and ushering them into saying their good-byes.

Jonty, intrigued at the last little scene, scurried off to meet Orlando at the pub, likely to be forgiven any tardiness if it had occurred in the cause of investigating. Being late because he'd been pontificating about *The Merchant of Venice* would never be viewed with so much tolerance, even if he'd been discussing the true nature of Antonio and Bassanio's relationship. But arriving bearing a headful of interesting stuff would win him lots of merit points.

It was all very exciting to have stumbled over an array of leads so easily. Were the family stories some of the blind alleys Bresnan had spoken of? It would explain why he'd kept quiet about them, not wanting to rake up scandal, anchoring the case firmly in the present day. Jonty was becoming sure some part of the solution to this mystery lay in what had occurred eighty years ago and how it still resonated now.

Best of all was the titbit from Mitchell about Rosalind Priestland, although something about it continued to nag. If there were stories about her that might relate to the case, why hadn't Bresnan heard them? Or had he heard them and for some reason not bothered to repeat them? And why had Mitchell evidently gone out of his way to give Jonty chapter and verse about not repeating things he'd been told, when he'd done just that with the story of the theft?

More importantly, what else was it that Mitchell knew and couldn't possibly tell?

Chapter 7

"Got the beer in?" Jonty appeared at Orlando's side, making him almost spill his pint over the bar.

"Where did you spring from? Have you taken to sneaking up on me?" Orlando could imagine how much Jonty would enjoy the subterfuge involved in making a silent entrance to the pub and moving noiselessly across the floor.

"Hardly sneaking up. Didn't you hear me nearly go arse over tip crossing the front door step? You must be getting deaf."

"I am not deaf," Orlando said, in slightly too loud a voice, giving the lie to his protestations. He lowered the volume. "I was listening to what the landlord was saying over the other side of the bar. Or I was *trying* to, before a bull in a china shop appeared."

"Sorry," Jonty whispered. "Anything of interest?"

"I've no idea, seeing as some flaming idiot came in and interrupted my concentration. I thought I heard—"

Whatever he'd heard, or tried to hear, got interrupted in the telling as the landlord came over to see what Jonty wanted. He settled for beer too, alongside a plate of cheese and ham rolls to serve the pair for lunch. After they'd found a table by a bow window, Orlando resumed the discussion. "I thought he was talking about Simon and Peter."

"*Our* Simon and Peter?"

"As I said, I haven't the foggiest. Pest." Orlando spoke the last word affectionately. It was one of his favourite pet names for the love of his life and one he could legitimately use in public without arousing anyone's suspicions.

"You know, you might have imagined the 'and' and been simply overhearing part of some deeply religious conversation about the rock upon which the church was founded." Jonty pulled out his notepad, then took a long draught of ale and smiled with contentment. "Lovely. I've masses to write up. Thought I'd do it as I updated you. Unless you want to go first?"

Orlando appreciated the offer of precedence. "I will, thank you, although I've not a lot to report." He related the tale of frustrated ambition at the post office. "You've met the brokenhearted wife, or I assume you have. Did Rosalind Priestland strike you as someone whose ambitions had been thwarted?"

"She didn't strike me as anything but a typical grieving widow, if there is such a thing." Jonty shrugged. "No hint of lurking unease caused by frustrated desires, although I wasn't looking for that, was I?"

"So nothing to report on that front, either?" Orlando felt just slightly smug. Jonty might be the all-consuming love of his life, but he wasn't to be allowed to get the advantage of him in the investigative stakes.

"I wouldn't go so far as to say nothing. One fact worth following up, some lingering puzzles, and a bit of a feeling. Want the subjective or the objective first?" Jonty took another deep draught of beer.

"Art before science, I think."

The arrival of the rolls displaced both art and science in favour of gastronomy, although not even the excellent cheddar, the soft, doughy bread, and a couple of late tomatoes could stop the flow of Jonty's chatter.

"I had a feeling there was something contrived about that day Peter died. As if I was being put off the scent. Whatever's at the root of it, Rosalind's uneasy about being questioned too closely about the exact *who was doing what, where, when, and why*. Although it could be simple unease at having a stranger poking around." Jonty managed to eat, talk, and scribble at the same time. He explained the circumstances of Peter's death, as the widow had described them. "Odd thing, though. When I approached the topic, I put on my dim act— Excuse me, I heard that snort."

"You play dim very well. Please continue."

"Hmm. Well, I asked her to set my mind at rest about something. That put her on her guard, but she relaxed again when I asked her if she'd found the body. As though she was expecting a different question. Then there was an oddly contrived encounter with Billy, the grocer's lad."

"Billy?" Orlando wished, not for the first time, that Jonty could relate a story sensibly.

"Yes." Jonty produced a convoluted tail of red kites and housekeepers and ladybirds. "I'm sure Mrs. Hamilton had arranged for Billy to tell me his story, which raises the question of whether Rosalind asked her to do so."

"A mysterious man in the garden, eh? I wouldn't have believed a word of it, no matter how fundamentally honest your delivery boy appeared."

"The funny thing is I *did* believe him. And not just because he seemed such a nice lad. Maybe he'd been persuaded that he *had* seen someone. Like he's got it in his head about the birds." Jonty scratched his head, lodging some breadcrumbs there. "Anyway, I decided he'd been put up to say it and maintained that belief for all of the next fifteen minutes or so. Until I met the vicar."

"The vicar?" Orlando's mind, which had only just stopped spinning, was set gyrating again. "You've found out a lot more than I gave you credit for, haven't you? You've got your cat-with-the-cream face on." A particularly annoying, if handsome, one. Especially annoying when the person on the receiving end didn't have anything much to gloat about.

"I'd better explain that too. It's why I was a bit late. I'd been talking to the Reverend Mitchell, incumbent of this parish." Jonty had swopped the cat-with-the-cream look for one of innocence, suitable for talking to or about the clergy. It wouldn't have fooled anyone. "He told me a very interesting story. Two of them. Did you have any idea that Simon and Peter's mother didn't die when she was supposed to have done? That she went off with someone else and lies buried with him, not in the familial plot that bears her name, but in a wreck on the ocean bed off the Scilly Isles?"

"Blimey!"

Both men took a reviving swig of beer.

"Blimey indeed. She's got a headstone at the family plot and apparently there was a proper burial for her, coffin and all. Down in Hampshire somewhere, the same churchyard as Simon's buried in. If only stones could speak."

"If the ones at St. Bride's could talk, you'd be in deep, deep trouble by now."

The landlord came to take their plates, passing the time of day and letting Orlando get his mental breath back. Clues were coming in a bit too thick and fast.

"The man in the woods. How does this all link up to him?" Orlando said, when they could talk again without fear of being overheard.

"Mitchell said Simon was here on the day his brother died, even though he told everyone he'd gone home and come back again. He *also* was keen for me to talk to Billy, as he's supposed to be trustworthy, if a little gullible in the matter of raptors."

"Now you've lost me. Say that again slowly and sensibly." Orlando swallowed the last of his beer and prepared to make more detailed notes; *someone* had to approach this sequentially and mathematically and not dash about everywhere in the story. Logic, maths, making notes: all of them were a great comfort to a man trying to take his mind off the events concerning plagiarism.

"Simon was here when his brother caught the flu. He's supposed to have returned home on Thursday and then turned straight around and made his way back here at the weekend, when he heard about his brother's death. Only, the vicar saw him here on Friday, the day Peter departed this earth." Jonty looked up from his notes with an expression of glee. "I'm not sure he told any of that to the Reverend Bresnan. I suspect this is going to turn out to be a lot more interesting than a case of a young wife bumping off her hubby to get the lolly."

"Your mother would have whacked you for talking so coarsely. Maybe I should take her part and carry on the tradition." Orlando scribbled in his notebook, neatly folded the page, and ripped out a slip of paper. He'd not forgotten a similar threat to him, what now seemed weeks ago.

Owed to Jonathan Stewart. Six of the best for vulgar language.

Jonty read the note, but not aloud. "Can I keep this for a time when I'd fully appreciate it? Thank you." He grinned, tucking it away in his pocket. "There's more. Mitchell told me that Rosalind had done some thieving in the past, from another man she'd been involved with. She's said to have repented of that particular sin."

"Has she, indeed?" There had to be more, given the glint in Jonty's eye.

"Yes. Apparently Peter knew and forgave her. Now, that's interesting enough, but Mitchell knows more. Things that he can't possibly tell us, he said, although he made sure that I knew they existed."

"It pains me to say so, but it seems like you win hands down on information discovered. That knocks my rivalry over a job in the post office into a cocked hat."

"It should do, if I didn't still have this nagging feeling that I was being pulled along by the nose like a bull by just about everyone I've met today, except Billy, who simply struck me as being in a world of his own. If they made a point of telling me about the man, perhaps they made a point of telling me about Simon. And about Rosalind." Jonty eyed his pint, as if he'd find all the interpretation of people's machinations there.

"They? Are you saying all three are in collusion?"

"Maybe not. Mesdames Priestland and Hamilton couldn't have known I was going to divert to the vicarage. It leaves a strange taste in the mouth, anyway. Unlike this beer." Jonty downed the rest of his pint. "I can only think that Mitchell has heard something from somebody or other under the cover of the confessional. Although in that case, why mention it at all?"

Orlando shrugged. "It's a hare not worth coursing, whatever the confession or whoever made it. That door's closed."

"Hmm." Jonty picked up his empty glass, then set it down again. "Maybe the Apostles' one is open. Rosalind Priestland's brother went there, as did Peter, and we've plenty of connections to the place."

That was more like it. "Are you thinking either Ralph or Dr. Sheridan might know him? It's a long shot."

"Very long. Still, we've been lucky with this sort of thing before, so I hope we will be again."

"Maybe we've been too lucky." Orlando stared at his own empty glass ruefully. "Got to the answer by chance rather than reasoning."

"Does that matter? Ralph always says that the more he practices at golf, the luckier he seems to get. Maybe the two are related."

"Hmm." Orlando wasn't convinced. For all their successes and all their commissions, he couldn't help feel they'd got away with things. Although maybe that was just the effects of the last few years talking. He couldn't remember feeling like this in the summer of 1914.

"Back to Apostles'. If one of our contacts from there knew the brother, and knew of Rosalind as well, he might be happy to dish the dirt."

"Ah, but are you sure there's dirt to be dished?"

"Absolutely positive." Jonty nodded, emphasising his words. "Even if she didn't actually murder her husband, I think she's hiding something. There was just one occasion when I caught a look in her eye that reminded me of a dunderhead trying to work out if I've fallen for his story about the college cat eating his essay. And I'm not sure it was to do with this ancient theft, if Mitchell was so free and easy with the story."

"If there are deeds of darkness to be brought into the light, you'll find a way of hauling them there." Orlando gazed out of the window, herding his thoughts. "Were there no charges pressed for those thefts?"

"Apparently not."

"Another man who was smitten with her, do you think?"

"How can I possibly tell without any evidence? I'm not a dunderhead. Although I'd like to know if the real reason she didn't apply to be postmistress was her history of larceny. Didn't want to be led into temptation or something?" Orlando studied his glass. "I shouldn't be saying this, but do we really have time to follow up every little loose end?"

"Are postmistresses counted with the loose ends?"

"I think so. And maybe men in the shrubbery too."

Jonty looked up from his beer, shocked. "You can't mean that. Where's the Coppersmith spirit of assessing every piece of information?"

"Abandoned due to pressure of time. I've been thinking. Our brief was to prove Rosalind committed murder, and we have precious few available days to do it in." Orlando steadily held his friend's gaze. "We should concentrate on looking for any evidence that she did the deed."

"Which doesn't include proving that someone else did?"

Orlando shrugged. "I have no idea. Just like I have no idea what to do next."

"Nonsense." Jonty put down his empty glass. "We take the next step and then the one after. Put that notebook away and we'll tackle the landlord, together. Synergy."

"Synergy," Orlando echoed, unconvinced. They returned to the bar bearing empty glasses, hopeful expressions, and a handful of change.

"Another pint of the same, sir?" The landlord said, beaming over his pumps.

"Just the half for me, please." Jonty shook his head. "Too much beer at lunchtime and I'm out for the count."

"A half for me too. And one for yourself." Orlando had seen Jonty after a predominantly liquid lunch, and it wasn't the prettiest of sights. Or sounds, given the man's propensity to snore when he'd been on the ale. "And can we pick your brains?"

"Pick away, sir." The landlord deftly pulled the beer as he spoke, producing a nice, clear brew with just the right amount of head. "Mind you, I can't guarantee the quality of the answers like I can guarantee the quality of my ale."

"I don't think it's anything too taxing." Jonty held his beer to the light. "Lovely. It's just about an old friend—well, more a friend of the family—who lived here. Peter Priestland. I suppose you knew him?" He kept up the same story he'd used at Thorpe House. People talked in villages and he didn't want to risk suspicion by floating away on a raft of inconsistencies. Things were going to be tricky enough.

"I knew him to pass the time of day with, as you might say. In fact, I was only talking about him just now, with my wife, Dolly." The landlord held his own beer up to the light, seemed pleased enough with the colour and clarity to nod approval, then took a swig.

Orlando shot a fleeting look of victory in Jonty's direction. What he'd overheard *had* been relevant to the case. "I was hoping to pay my respects at his grave, but Dr. Stewart here says he's heard that the man's not buried in the churchyard in the village."

"And Dr. Stewart's right. Mr. Priestland came of foreign stock, if you'll pardon the expression. He was from Hampshire, and that's where his family are all buried, or so the vicar says. He's laid in his long bed with his parents and brother."

"He's from near Romsey." Dolly popped her head around the door at the back of the bar. "I hope he didn't spend too much time in the place."

Orlando and Jonty looked blankly at the landlord, then at each other, and then at the landlord's wife. "I beg your pardon?" they said in unison, sounding like something out of a Gilbert and Sullivan operetta.

"My mother hails from Southampton and that's what they say down there. 'So drunk he could have been to Romsey.'" Dolly airily waved what seemed to be a duster, emphasising her point. "Heathen lot. Anyway, drunk or sober, that's where your friend's buried."

"I told you." Jonty rapped his hand on the bar counter, as if upbraiding Orlando for doubting him. "That's going to be a day trip if we want to visit the grave. I wonder what happened to his sister, though. Is she buried there too?" Although Bresnan's mother didn't yet seem relevant to their case, nothing could be eliminated at this point. They'd turned up enough odds and ends to be wary, even this early in an investigation. "I don't suppose there's any chance you could tell us if she's in the same place? My parents were great friends of all of the Priestland clan."

"Ah, there's a thing." The landlord appeared delighted at the challenge he'd been set. "I can answer that easy as pie, better than I could answer my questions about the times tables in school. She's not there, just the parents, the babe that died at birth, and the two brothers who died in old age. You know, of course, that Simon Priestland followed his brother this year?"

"We do," Orlando said, nodding. "And I stand in awe of your knowledge. I wish we'd been aware of all this before we set out."

"Knowing that was more luck than brains, sir. I was sitting next to Mr. Priestland's widow at our harvest supper last week, and she told me all about it. She feels more than a bit put out that she hasn't got her old boy to hand, where she can keep an eye on him and see he's all right. I got told the whole tale of the family and the mother dying when them boys were young. Tragic." He shook his head, in the slightly overdramatic fashion some landlords favoured.

Clearly he hadn't got the whole story, then. "Aye, it is that." Tragic for two boys to be told their mother was dead when all the time she'd been alive. Orlando had taken a serious dislike to old Mr. Priestland, the father of the twins.

"And that's why I was talking about them with my Dolly. Her niece is expecting, and Dolly says she looks like she's carrying twins, the size of her."

"Dan, don't be so common with these gentlemen. They don't want to know about women's business." Dolly waved her duster again.

"Never mind us, ma'am. I've a host of nieces and nephews and have seen it all second hand." Jonty smiled. "And I'm forgetting my manners. We've stood your husband a drink. Will you join us?"

"No, thank you, sir. I've got jobs I should be doing." Although it had to be said that the landlord's wife didn't seem to be in any hurry to be getting on with her household tasks.

"Dolly was saying her niece has a hankering to call the children Mary and Ann if they're girls and Peter and Simon if they're boys. I said I'd find that pairing unlucky, after what I'd heard about the Priestland family."

There was a sort of logic to that, a lot of store being put into the power of names. "Maybe that's wise. And maybe the children will be one of each and solve the problem." Nodding, Orlando finished his drink and put on his hat. There seemed nothing more to be gained here. He'd counted without Jonty.

"My mother will be most concerned to hear that Mrs. Priestland is still feeling her loss so strongly. Such a lively woman. Mrs. Priestland, not my mother. Well, both of them, really." Jonty produced his waffling academic expression. "Mama would be much relieved to hear that she was taking an interest in the world again, so I'll tell her about the harvest supper, although I suppose I'll have to tell her there's no new suitor in the offing, to relieve Mrs. Priestland's grieving."

Dolly exchanged a look with her husband then smiled, knowingly. "She was a good wife and I daresay she's a good widow, but she's always had someone to ease her through her grief."

"Dolly!" The landlord looked horrified. "These gentlemen don't want to hear your gossip."

"It isn't gossip. It's no more than his job, to minister to his flock when they're in distress. Although . . ." Dolly stopped after another horrified look from her husband. "I'll have to get on with my work. Nice to have met you."

Jonty smiled gravely, bowed and said, "The feeling is mutual."

Outside the pub, the air was mild, the afternoon having turned out hazy but pleasant. Jonty yawned and stretched, the effects of imbibing at lunchtime starting to show. "I'm not sure you were too wise in there." He patted his friend's arm and began to stroll along the street, in the direction of the metal monster.

"What have I done now?"

"You called me Dr. Stewart. You know how people gossip. If they hear a man called Stewart has been asking questions, with another man in tow, there's a chance someone will put two and two together. Especially with your inauguration as professor being in the local papers. Both your name and your face are back in the news again."

"Maybe it will help. If people think they're being investigated, they might start to do all sorts of silly things." Orlando wagged his finger, as if Jonty were a particularly obtuse dunderhead. "In that case of plagiarism, the person concerned had done nothing to arouse distrust until someone quite innocently asked some questions related to the originator of the work. Then our plagiarist started to burn the midnight oil down at the department, and not just that, he burned documents while he was about it. One of the other dons noticed, and the game was afoot." He jabbed the same finger into Jonty's arm. "Anyway, you'll have given your name to both Rosalind Priestland and the Reverend Mitchell. Won't they have twigged?"

"Not necessarily, if I was on my own. Did Dr. Watson's patients always assume he was on a case?" Jonty nodded as if that settled the argument. "I'm glad we talked to the landlord, though."

"Why? What enlightenment did you gain from Dolly's niece's twins?"

"The fact that the story about Peter's mother isn't general knowledge, and that the landlord was told the official version. How did Mitchell get to know the truth?" Jonty paused, a gleam in his eye. "Assuming it *is* the truth, of course."

"Either he heard it over the dinner table, as he seems to imply, or Mrs. Priestland told him while she was being comforted. In the course of a vicar's duty," Orlando said, in an imitation of Dolly's voice. "He's young and attractive?"

"Oh yes. And charming with it. No, don't look so huffy. He's not so charming that I'd want to go picking petunias with him, or whatever they get up to in these villages when they're a-courting." They carried on walking. "Rosalind Priestland might have done, though, as Dolly hinted. If she'd taken a fancy to him prior to her husband's death, it would give her a motive for hastening the man's demise."

"And it would explain how everyone seemed keen to tell you about the mysterious man in the woods. That suggests other things. For a start, they must have known you were playing at detective." Orlando increased his pace, as he often did if he was mulling over a problem when out walking. It aided thinking. "Maybe part of the business with Billy was to delay you, so they could get a message down to the vicarage, just in case you dropped by."

"Does that mean we should take everything they said with a hefty pinch of salt? The shipwreck and all?"

"I think we should independently verify as much as we can."

"Of course. That's the Cambridge way. Now, you said 'other things.' Plural. What else does it hint at, Professor Pulchritude?" Jonty swerved, avoiding any chance of a shin-whacking with as neat a sidestep as he'd ever used on the rugby pitch.

Orlando sighed. "In my innocence, I thought I'd never tire of hearing the title professor, but if the remaining years of my life are to be filled up with variations on a theme, all from your ridiculous noddle, I may have to retire to a monastery. It also suggests, Doctor Irritation, that there certainly is something suspicious about Peter's death for us to turn up, murder or not."

"I wonder if Bresnan knows about Rosalind Priestland's past? I bet Simon did," Jonty said, almost dancing along the road. "That's why he had his suspicions. Where next, then? Coming straight back here and digging further doesn't feel right. Not yet, not until we have different questions to ask."

"Down to Hampshire, I'd have said. To see what we can dig up—excuse the pun—about the Priestlands."

"It would certainly be useful to get a complete picture of where the money goes, or has gone, in that family." Jonty stopped beside the little, rush-lined brook that trickled from the village pond. It was an idyllic scene. Dragonflies were quartering the water and ducks dabbling; it was hard to believe that any village as pretty as this could hide dark secrets. "The disposition of money didn't strike me as important, apart from the simple case of whether Bresnan gets Peter's lolly or Rosalind Priestland does."

"You mean Bresnan getting Simon's money. Or maybe you don't." Orlando rubbed his brow. "You're right. If Rosalind Priestland's inheritance becomes defaulted should she be proved a murderess, then Bresnan gets that portion as well."

"I'm convinced this case is going to turn out more complicated than just, 'Did A kill B?' Or 'R kill P,' in this case." There were reeds by the water; Jonty grabbed a stem, fashioning it into a little canoe to launch. "I wonder if Peter and Simon's mother had anything to leave . . . and what happened to it, if she did."

"I could try to get onto that as soon as I've earned myself another bit of sleuthing by getting some more words down on my lecture. Maybe our friend Collingwood has the right connections; he must owe us a favour or two by now."

"I don't think we should wait for you being in credit at the investigational bank. I'll have a shufti this afternoon at those figures Bresnan left us—and don't look at me like that! I may not be a mathematician, but I can count to ten and I can understand if 'money in' equals 'money out.'" Jonty slapped his friend's shoulder; they set off again. "It'll make a change for me to handle that sort of thing. I'll glean what I can from them and then I'll write another list of what we still need to find out. I'll make a start by seeing if I can verify the shipwreck tale. Not sure I'll be able to access any answers direct tomorrow, it being Sunday, but I can get on the telephone and pick people's brains."

"Does that mean I'm going to have to be the one trotting down to Hampshire and rummaging about there?" Orlando didn't relish the prospect. He might just have to stay overdrawn on his detective account. "I don't even know what I'd be trying to find out."

"You will by the time you get there." Jonty waved his hands airily, as he often did when he didn't really know the answer to something but wanted to pretend otherwise. "Maybe you'll find a handsome man of the cloth to help you."

"Like your friend Mitchell? Maybe if he's as handsome as you make out, ladies tell him all sorts of secrets, in the confessional or out."

"Maybe." Jonty laughed. "I did like that saying about Romsey. We should use it in St. Bride's SCR. So drunk he could have been in the college next door."

Orlando had to smile. Jonty was always optimistic that whatever problem faced them, they'd solve it. Maybe he should mention the other matter now, but Jonty looked so happy, strolling along in the weak sunshine, pulling on his driving gloves and smiling away at some private delight, that he didn't have the heart to enlighten him.

Jonty suddenly stopped, took Orlando's arm, and asked, "Now, what egg of worry are you incubating?"

"I beg your pardon?"

"Since Thursday you've been like a man who's lost his dissertation within days of handing it in. A problem shared is a problem halved and all that."

"Am I that obvious?"

"Only to me. Come on, tell Uncle Jonty everything." Jonty waited for an answer. Orlando was going to have to give it to him.

"That meeting, about the plagiarism. There was an . . ." Orlando strove for the right words. "An unforeseen consequence."

"Hmm. And the way you've been since then, it must be terrible news for someone. The department?" Jonty gently, encouragingly, squeezed Orlando's arm.

"Possibly. For us, possibly, as well. Owens has stuck his nose in." Orlando didn't have to add anything to emphasise the wickedness of the scoundrel. "He's not daft, whatever else we may think of him, and he's got a knack for diplomacy. Somehow, he's managing to both castigate his man and stick up for him at the same time. We all know that plagiarism has occurred, we've even got proof, but getting it sorted without an almighty stink is going to be a hell of a challenge."

"You said it could be bad news for us, as well. He's never forgiven St. Bride's for solving the Woodville Ward case, has he?" Jonty fished a couple of mints out of his pocket and offered Orlando one, which he took gratefully. After all, men needed extra nourishment in times of stress. "Us in particular."

"No. I don't think he's the forgiving type. I may be worrying about nothing . . . and don't you dare say, 'That's not like you, Orlando.'" He prodded Jonty's arm. "But Owens caught me on the way out of the meeting—he'd been invited to act as counsel for his colleague—and asked if you were well. And if we were working on any cases."

Jonty peered searchingly into Orlando's face. "You're not a man to react to nothing, not now. There must be more to it than that."

Orlando shut his eyes, picturing the scene exactly as it had happened, every word and nuance. "Owens said he hoped I wasn't the sort of man who lacked the milk of human kindness and that I'd show magnanimity when it was called for. He said it would do neither of our colleges any good to have our dirty linen washed in public. His parting words were 'Judge not that ye be not judged.'"

"I didn't think Owens was much of a man for quoting the gospel," Jonty sighed. "You think it's a direct threat? That he's got wind of exactly the sort of life we're living and he's going to expose us if you judge against his plagiarist?"

"Exactly that. It wasn't just his words. I didn't like the look in his eye."

"I've *never* liked the look in his eye." Jonty shivered, even though the day was still warm. "What would happen to this chap if you found him guilty?"

"Well he won't be hung, drawn, and quartered. More's the pity." Orlando tipped his head along the road, and they walked on. It was easier to think on the hoof. "It would be a case of public and professional disgrace. He might lose his position and the stigma would follow him wherever he went. Same as us, if *we* were exposed."

"But without the two years' hard labour." Jonty closed ranks with Orlando, walking so close their arms brushed against each other. "The decision's not yours entirely, though, is it? How many people are on your specially convened committee?"

"Six of us. And we're all convinced that this chap Gordon, Owens's little sycophant, is guilty. We're just waiting to check out his counter-accusation that the other man was copying *his* work.

Even if I wanted to convince the other people on the committee to let the matter drop, I don't think I could." Orlando patted Jonty's arm, briefly. "All this time we've managed to keep our heads below the parapet. And now, just when things were looking so bright . . ."

"They *are* bright." Jonty returned the pat.

"Really? I can't help feeling we've ridden our luck too long and now it's unsaddled us."

Jonty stopped, turned Orlando to face him. "We survived France. We've survived threats much worse than Owens. We'll survive him too, you'll see."

"You have a plan of action?" Orlando leaned into his friend's embrace.

"Not yet. But I will soon. That'll be my challenge, just like your lecture is yours." Jonty smiled. "And talking of challenges," he added, "you can drive home."

Chapter 8

Jonty settled back in his comfortable chair at his desk in his study. Neither too warm in summer nor too cold in winter, this was Jonty's favourite spot in the cottage—apart from the bedrooms, of course. He had an extension to the telephone on his desk (of which Orlando didn't approve, naturally), so that he could keep up with the doings of his nephew, his niece, and their scabrous friends in comfort. Lavinia's George held a special place in his heart, as he alone of all the family had persisted in believing, against all the evidence but in line with the facts, that his uncle had survived the war.

He picked up the phone and was put through to the Reverend Ian Bresnan's vicarage. The telephone rang for so long without answer that Jonty had begun to suspect the entire household was off gallivanting somewhere or singing a sly and rather early evensong. Just as he was about to replace the earpiece, an out-of-breath voice answered. "The rectory. Hello?"

"Dr. Bresnan? It's Jonty Stewart. I don't like ringing on a Sunday," he lied, surreptitiously crossing his fingers, "but it's about the case."

"Ah, Dr. Stewart," Bresnan said, when he at last had recovered a bit. "I'm sorry. I was at the door talking to one of my parishioners, and it was proving highly difficult to get them to go."

"No need to apologise. I just wanted to pick your brains."

"Oh." Bresnan sounded disappointed. "No news, then?"

"Plenty of it, but not what you want to hear, not yet. No solution, I mean." Jonty tried to sound encouraging. "Plenty of leads, though. Enough to make us think we're onto something. And you can help us with one of them. We need some more Priestland family history."

"You've uncovered the family's dark secret, then?"

"If you're referring to your grandmother, then yes. Is there another skeleton in your closet you'd like to enlighten me about?" Jonty wasn't sure that their client had told them the whole truth and nothing but the truth. Not yet.

"That's the only one I know of." Bresnan sighed. "I know what you're going to say. If I knew, I should have told you, but I truly wanted you to come to the case with no preconceptions. I tried to give you a clue in those riddles about my uncles' birth."

Jonty resisted the temptation to give him a sharp answer. Clue? If it was, it was a pretty obscure one. Bresnan was a sight too fond of puzzles and riddles to make this case at all easy. "Well, let's just make sure we're talking about the same thing. Your grandmother didn't die when your uncles were a year old."

"Ah, that's not exactly true. We *believe* she might not have died then. The theory hasn't been proven."

Jonty wondered how many times he'd have to say the Paternoster for entertaining thoughts about thumping vicars, and on the Lord's Day as well. "Let's look at the possibility that the theory is true. If she didn't die then, perhaps she left your grandfather." Or he could have thrown her out on her ear for any number of unpleasant reasons. But one possibility at a time. "Would she do something like that? And if so, why?"

"The old story, Dr. Stewart. She was said to have found another man. Maybe I *should* condemn her." He sounded convinced; Jonty wondered where the element of doubt had gone.

"But it's a case of 'Let he who is without sin cast the first stone'?"

"Ye-es. But also a case of 'I'm not sure I can blame her.' From everything I've heard, my grandfather was hardly the easiest man in the world to get on with." Bresnan sighed again, making Jonty wonder what ancestral stories lay in that simple remark. He couldn't have been old enough to remember the man *that* well, could he?

"I didn't realise you'd known him so well."

"We saw him two or three times a year when I was a boy. And I was thirteen when he died, which was time enough to make an impression one way or the other." No more seemed to be forthcoming, and there was no point in pursuing things further. They had enough alleys to explore.

"Did your mother ever suspect that things hadn't quite happened as she'd been told? She was older than the boys, so surely a five-year-old would know more about what had gone on?" Jonty would have done. He'd been inquisitive right from the cradle.

"She might well have had her suspicions, although she kept the fact to herself until her own deathbed, when she voiced them to me."

"When was that?"

"Bless me, didn't I put that in my notes? Just before the Christmas of 1872."

That year again. Was it possible that Mrs. Bresnan had known of her mother's death and died of shock?

"What did she say?" Jonty scribbled yet another note, determined to get all the points written down in some semblance of order.

"Not a lot that's worth repeating. I thought she was just rambling, of course. There was some rather distressing nonsense about how she'd had triplets and someone had lost one of them. She hadn't, of course. Just the one child, which was me. I suppose it was a regression to childhood and her brothers, naturally. When she said her mother had run away with a sailor, I just ignored it. Then the next year, when the letter came . . ." Bresnan didn't need to say any more. "I truly think my grandfather regarded her as dead, once she'd left the house. Perhaps he even thought he was telling his children and grandchild the truth. Certainly none of them doubted it until they were much older."

"The headstone on the grave would have helped keep up the illusion." Jonty felt a rising loathing for old Mr. Priestland. "At what point did they find out that it might all have been a lie? Did your grandmother try to get in touch with her children after the old man's death?"

"Never a word, as far as I can tell." Bresnan sounded tired. "Is there anything more I can tell you?"

"Just two things. The first is a touch delicate, but have you ever had any suspicions that Rosalind might be, or have been, romantically involved with the local vicar?"

"The chap who fought for the Cambridgeshires? Hmm."

Jonty liked the sound of the *Hmm*. "That's the one."

"It wouldn't surprise me at all. She has always spoken very highly of him."

Jonty waited, but nothing more substantial seemed to be forthcoming. "Ah well. Onto the second question. Could you, if you'll excuse the expression, take a comfy pew and tell me all about the Priestlands, the Bresnans, and the disposition of their goods and chattels?"

"Are you ready to compare notes?" Jonty poked his head around Orlando's study door. At four o'clock on Sunday afternoon with the prospect of a cup of tea on the horizon, even professors of applied mathematics could put aside their work and take some time to play. They'd not discussed the case since returning from Downlea; instead, Orlando had been getting his head down, not just over his lecture, but college and departmental work as well.

He'd come to bed late on Saturday, with Jonty already asleep. They'd risen early so Orlando could clear another part of his decks before morning service down at the college chapel. He'd probably have cried off that, except Lumley the chaplain was preaching about who the pharaoh of the exodus really was, which happened to be one of the few subjects Orlando actually enjoyed.

A glorious piece of roast beef, adorned with parsnips and Yorkshire puddings (but no roast potatoes as Mrs. Ward had decided there was a risk of her lads getting a bit tubby around the waist if they ate in the same quantities they'd done when they were mere striplings), had crowned lunchtime. Jonty had taken a brief nap before making his phone call, while Orlando retreated to his study again and cut himself off from the doings of the rest of his household.

"Compare notes? Oh, yes. Good timing." Orlando neatly stacked a pile of papers. "Over a pot of tea?"

Jonty grinned. "I'm sure I heard the kettle boiling, and as we forwent a dessert at lunchtime, I daresay a cake will make its appearance too. Things get better and better."

Orlando started to speak, then stopped.

Jonty spotted the tension in his lover's bearing. "Don't tell me there's another problem brewing on top of the lecture and Owens."

"Nothing new. It's just your saying things were getting better. All I could think of was Owens's smug mug."

The fire was banked low, fitting for a day that seemed, as Mrs. Ward put it, warmer outside than in. The tea was excellent, the Dundee cake was better and even the thought of Owens couldn't dampen Jonty's spirits. "You'll have nightmares. Forget about him."

"I'm trying to, but it isn't easy." The fire needed stoking, as the sun was sinking low in the sky and the evening chill setting in. Orlando knelt down to add a log and some old pine cones, warming his hands against the bright eruption of flame. "Maybe if we concentrated on more pleasant things, we could chase the ogre away."

Jonty slipped off the sofa, snuggling against Orlando on the hearthrug as if they were a pair of undergraduates engaged in some earnest late-night discussion. "I've been working hard on our case, and I'd love the chance to brag a bit about what I've done."

"Of course. Boast away." Orlando rested his head on his knees, hugging his legs.

Jonty smiled. Whatever happened, departmental problems or personal indignity, they'd see this through together. And they had a case to solve, which would help keep Orlando's mind off things.

He reached behind him for the folder that he'd laid on the floor earlier. "I've drawn a rather splendid diagram." He spread it out on the rug, out of range of anything but the most daring spark from the fire. "What I couldn't get from Bresnan's notes, I got from the man himself."

"You rang him?"

"Well, clearly I didn't fly down there in one of Dr. Panesar's time machines. He seemed slightly shocked to be receiving a telephone call on the Lord's Day, but I dragged his mind from things rectorial—and if that's not a word, it should be—to matters familial." He tapped the diagram. "Although, before I get to them, I'll cover the other bit. Bresnan had heard the story about Rosalind Priestland from Simon. Who got it from Peter. Her sin, penitence, and absolution seem to be common family knowledge."

"And were they the cause of Simon's doubts concerning his brother's death?"

"They were. Especially because, as maybe you can guess, the 'victim' of the theft was an older gentleman to whom she used to read. More secrets." Jonty sprawled over the floor, smoothing his beloved drawing. After a few moments of silence, he looked up to see Orlando start suddenly, clearly coming back from some labyrinthine passage of thought. "You've not heard a word of what I've just said, have you?"

"No, sorry." Orlando didn't even attempt to lie; he'd have been seen straight through. "I was thinking about you lying in front of the fire. Romantic memories. Could you bear to repeat it?"

Back then, both their bodies had been immaculate, apart from the odd mark from a rugby boot. Now they bore the signs of combat, although Jonty averred that the scar on Orlando's chest was one of the most erotically stimulating things he'd ever seen.

"What we did in front of the fire, or my little speech?" Jonty grinned. "I said it was a complicated old business. Only I used more words than that."

"I bet you did. Wasn't Bresnan surprised you were digging into the past?"

"Not especially. I insisted that it all linked to the case." Jonty ran his hands through his hair, reinforcing the impression of a wayward schoolboy. "I may have said we had an important clue."

"Lying. And on a Sunday too." Orlando shook his head.

"I wasn't lying, just stretching the truth a bit. Anyway, Bresnan hasn't always been candid, either. He's known a lot of the family history all along but didn't choose to share it with us." Jonty jabbed his finger at the place where the Reverend Bresnan's name appeared on the chart. "He knew about the grandmother not necessarily being dead. And we thought we'd rooted out some real scandal."

"Sounds like he deserves to be lied to—so long as you haven't stretched the truth so far that it pings back at you." Orlando pointed at old Mr. Bresnan's name. "Right. How did the money trickle through the branches of the family?"

"Will you *listen* this time? Good." Jonty traced through the lines of the fiscal family tree as he spoke. "Luckily there are no titles here, just good old-fashioned lucre and a bit of property. Old Andrew Priestland left each of his sons a healthy inheritance. Money was split fifty-fifty, but the house went to Simon, him being the elder by a few minutes."

"Hold on. Mitchell said that Peter was the elder, after the child who died."

"Exactly." Jonty smiled gleefully. "And it contradicted what Bresnan told us. If we assume our client's got it right, then Mitchell must have heard the story from either Rosalind Priestland or Peter himself. Why should they all lie to him? They must have known, even the grieving widow, or else she'd have been curious about why the *younger* of the two had been the one to inherit the house, rather than the elder."

"I can't think what they'd have had to gain by lying."

"Neither can I, at present. Maybe it was a genuine mistake on his part."

"Hmm. Perhaps. Did the daughter get anything?" Orlando circled her name with his finger.

"A small bequest, not in the same league as her brothers'. Presumably Mr. Priestland expected her husband to look after her. Although as I understand it, while the Bresnans weren't exactly poor, they weren't as comfortable as the rest of the family." Jonty wrinkled his nose. "Our poor old reverend seemed more and more embarrassed talking about it. No wonder he'd like to get his hands on Uncle Simon's estate. And no wonder Rosalind wants to sit tight and get her hands on her dear departed's lolly."

"What's this small scrawly thing here? The one in red?" Orlando traced a spidery line along the chart. "The one that looks like some small creature has clambered through the inkwell and progressed along the paper while your mind was, as so often, elsewhere."

"That, old thing, is the inheritance in the maternal line. Oh yes, Simon's mother had property of her own, tied up so tightly, the twins' father couldn't get his paws on it. Intended for her children at her death, irrespective of their gender and, again, in proportion to their primogeniture." Jonty poked his lover's knee. "Want me to explain that last word?"

"No, thank you. I don't think you used it properly, anyway." Orlando put on his *one up to the mathematical boy* smile. "The first-born child got a bigger proportion of the loot. But when *did* they get it? That's the thing."

"*Not* when they were barely out of swaddling clothes. They didn't even realise there might be any money due to them, not until the kind and thoughtful letters came, explaining the truth about their mother's disappearance and hinting that there was a financial implication." Jonty doodled on the chart with his fingers, circling the names. "Bresnan's pretty upset about that too. His mother would have been well-provided for."

"I don't think I follow." Orlando traced the red lines again. "Is this where the money went or not?"

"It's where the money was *supposed* to go, only it didn't. Obviously not when her husband said she was dead, as she was probably still alive. And not when she actually died, assuming she was the same woman who took the ill-fated yachting trip."

Orlando peered at the minute writing to ascertain the Christian names. "Now I'm completely lost. Is there some doubt that it was . . . Alice Priestland on the boat? And who on earth's *this*?" He pointed to the name Helen Phillips.

"That's the woman who died at sea. Or what she called herself. Helen was Alice Priestland's middle name, apparently, which argues for a link between the two. But you're right about there being some doubt." Jonty put on a suitably smug grin. "You can bet there is. She'd clearly changed her name, to hide the shame and scandal. Her husband wouldn't give her a divorce, so she was living in sin, or so the letters said. Nasty things, those letters. I'd love to know whose hand was behind them."

"Why didn't Bresnan tell us all this beforehand?"

"I think he's mortified to have to expose so many of the skeletons in the family closet. I suspect that's why he tried solving this problem on his own and then came to us rather than a private detective. Wants to keep it all as quiet as possible." Jonty stretched, taking in the fire's warmth. Orlando had said he often thought of him as a great ginger cat that he kept as a pet. Well, cats deserved their place of honour on the familial hearth. "And he's a sight too fond of riddles and showing off his clever way with them. Would it make you feel any happier to know that Bresnan was very impressed that we'd located so many of his blind alleys so quickly? I didn't say we'd simply stumbled across them."

"I should hope not. Or that we seem to have been handed a map marking them all." Orlando looked worried again.

"I wish we had those letters to look at." Jonty rubbed his forehead, forgetting his fingers were inky.

"Look at the state of you. You've covered your face with smudges." Orlando took out his handkerchief, wetted the edge, and got to work tidying his friend up. "I bet those letters were burned. And anyway, what good would seeing them do? It's not like we could recognise the writing."

"I'm sure we couldn't. Ow. Do be careful." Jonty swatted his lover's hand away. "I just feel they'd give off something rather nebulous and subjective. Stop snorting, these things happen. They might give us an inkling of who wrote them, by the style or something."

Orlando snorted again, probably at the wooliness of the average fellow of Tudor literature's thinking, although even his own precise logic wasn't helping much. "I still can't get a feel for this case, why information is being withheld and then offered or, in the case of the interviews at Downlea, thrust upon us. Back to the money."

"As usual, my genius boy, you've come to what seems to be the whole crux of the matter. It's why Peter wanted the grave opened and Simon didn't. It wasn't just a matter of establishing whether it was empty and if the woman who'd died at sea might have been their mother. Apparently, they had people telling them that she couldn't have been Alice Priestland and that the letters were just malicious, so there was a reasonable element of doubt. It was also about what had happened to their rightful inheritance. The fact that they were due something had never been in doubt. They found her will."

"When? Where?"

"With the old nurse who'd looked after them when they were babies. It had been left in her safekeeping, as Alice Priestland didn't trust her husband. Simon and Peter got in touch with the nurse after the letters started to arrive, in case she could throw any light on the matter. Bresnan says he'll send us a copy." Jonty slowly folded up his chart, then settled in front of the fire, hugging his knees like one of the dunderheads. The early evening was becoming cool and the fire was enticing.

"Don't hog all the heat." Orlando whacked his friend's backside, making him budge up so they could range together, like a pair of attractive firedogs, gracing the hearth. "And don't hog all the information, either. What did the nurse say? If she had the will, why didn't she make it public when Alice Priestland supposedly died? Or *did* die, if you're of that opinion."

"Because the nurse was one of those who suspected she wasn't dead. Alice Priestland was very low after the babies were born and had spoken to her, in confidence, about wanting to leave her husband."

"Blimey."

"Save that blimey for the last little bit I have to share with you. There may even be the need for some language a touch stronger. Talking of which, do you fancy a small libation of sherry?" Jonty made to rise from the rug, only to be restrained by Orlando's firm grip on his leg.

"You'll get no libation of any sort until you tell me every last morsel of this story."

Jonty grinned, leaning into the viselike grip. "The nurse told the twins that their mother had converted all her worldly wealth into jewels."

"Not *that* again. It's becoming old hat, women dispensing money by means of gewgaws and jewellery, especially when they want to avoid their husbands knowing about it."

"You should be jolly grateful that they do it. You've done pretty well out of Grandmother Forster's jewellery."

"I stand corrected."

Prior to meeting Jonty, Orlando had been, if not in a state of penury, then at least financially constrained. Perhaps like Bresnan was now. Some clever and imaginative use of the jewellery Jonty's grandmother had left him to bestow on his bride had made the Coppersmith coffers healthy. If he couldn't match Jonty's riches, at least he could pay his way now and not feel like a kept man.

"I suppose," he continued, "that she'd found some sort of means of wangling it, if the money was in trust. What happened to these jewels?"

"Nobody knows. Maybe they financed her running off with her paramour, if run off she did. Maybe they even bought that fatal, faltering yacht." Jonty stretched again, snuggling against his lover once more and counting off points on his fingers. "They weren't in the house, not unless old Mr. Priestland got his hands on them. And the nurse insists he didn't. Not with the family solicitor or at the family bank."

"What about in Helen Phillips's house? Or *her* bank?"

"Search me. Maybe they went to Davy Jones's locker with their original owner." Jonty pursed his lips in thought. "Apparently Simon and Peter didn't try to find out, or if they did, they played the fact so close to their chests that their nephew wasn't aware. I just don't understand it."

"What, where the jewellery went?"

"No, idiot. Why the brothers didn't dig deeper. If someone had written to me last week to say that Mama had escaped the flu and run away with the gardener or something, I wouldn't rest until I knew the truth. You understand that, don't you?"

"Of course." Just as it had been for Orlando and uncovering the facts about his family name. No peace until they were established without doubt. "Did you ask Bresnan?"

"Yes, and he was none the wiser. Maybe Rosalind Priestland knows, but I'm not sure I can see, as yet, how we can ask her. Unless the answer lies down in Hampshire."

Orlando sighed. "If I go down to this place near Romsey and manage to avoid all the pubs, who is there left to talk to? The nurse must have died, surely?"

"She has. But the verger who buried old Mr. Priestland is still there, apparently. Bresnan keeps in touch with him."

"Hmm. I'm not sure anything is to be gained from talking to somebody who, knowing our present luck, will turn out to be some senile old man who probably doesn't know what day of the week it is." Orlando stared into the fire, eyes unreadable. "And isn't all of this getting away from the point? We're supposed to be finding out if Rosalind Priestland killed her husband."

Jonty watched the flames dance. "I know. And I'm convinced that the key to it's here." He lovingly tapped his folded-up chart. "Knit all these strands into a credible tapestry and we'll have the solution in our grasp."

"Are you saying you think that Simon *was* there? And that he sneaked in and killed his brother because of something to do with their mother?"

"I'm not saying anything so definite. But the solution to everything is in here." Jonty tapped the paper again. "I bet you ten quid."

A dinner, a glass of port, and a game of cribbage later, Jonty sat in his bed, spectacles perched on his nose and a tired, contented smile on his face. Orlando felt for a moment like saying no to carnal desires—it had been a long day, going through what had seemed a ton of paperwork left by his predecessor—but there was something in the twinkle of those blue eyes that drove him to nod his head. Maybe Delilah had blue eyes like that, and she'd flashed them at Samson en route to the hairdresser's. Or Cleopatra had pointed her cornflower-blue gaze on poor old Anthony and changed the destiny of two nations. Alexander surely had blue eyes. When Hephaistion saw them, he'd been driven to . . .

"You're too quiet. I don't like it." Jonty's spectacles were perched on his head now, while he rubbed his brow and looked like a particularly obtuse dunderhead.

"I was thinking." Orlando hung his jacket on a coat hanger and then began to undo his cuffs. He wasn't prepared to admit what he'd been thinking. He could illustrate that much more clearly in gestures once they'd touched on this business with Owens. Funny how often they'd punctuated deep, intricate conversations, whether about other people's murder cases or their own personal challenges, with bouts of lovemaking.

"Is that all you were doing, thinking? Couldn't hear the cogs of your brain grinding, so I couldn't be sure."

Orlando didn't grace the remark with more than a snort. There'd been plenty of jokes these past fourteen years about his habit of thinking everything through to the nth degree. "You reassure me about our friendly blackmailer while I get into my pyjamas. Give me a plan of campaign."

"Plan? All I seem to have is a random jumble of ideas about too many things. I need to sleep on his horrible threats, just as I need to sleep on the horribly complicated family business with the Priestlands and the Bresnans." Jonty gently disentangled his spectacles from a stray lock of hair, removed them, and placed them carefully in their case. "Maybe I'll wake in the morning with inspiration on both fronts."

"Chance would be a fine thing." Orlando's pyjamas seemed to be fighting back, the buttons wanting to inveigle themselves into the wrong holes.

"I don't know why you're bothering with those. That jacket will be off in a minute."

"It's to annoy you, of course. Or maybe to excite you. I know how fond you are of stripping me. I'm just getting everything as you like it." Orlando twitched back the covers, sliding into a bed nicely warmed by both a hot water bottle and his lover's body.

"Well, that takes some beating. I've had chocolates from you—and flowers on one notable occasion—but never a love token so amusing as a perfectly presented row of buttons." Jonty took the book he'd been reading earlier and laid it with much care on the bedside table, an act that had come to mean, *Lights out, time for love.* "I know you've been hard at work over a hot slide rule or sets of tables most of the day, but I hope you've got enough energy left for . . ." He didn't finish the sentence, choosing instead to run his fingers along his lover's thigh.

"Are professors allowed to do this sort of thing?" They hadn't made love since Orlando had been given his title properly, what with lectures and paperwork and investigating. It felt like years.

"I'd have thought it would be de rigueur for professors. Or should be, at least. Even for mathematicians. Their bodies aren't just a means of conveying their brains from point A to point B." Jonty proved his theorem by moving his fingers up from Orlando's thigh to his crotch. "See? This isn't designed for calculating, even if it's as rigid as a set of Napier's bones."

Orlando wasn't sure he was capable of calculating anything at the moment, not even the likely interval between now and the inevitable explosion of ecstasy that always followed Jonty's fingers, or any other part of Jonty, making contact down there. "Well, what is it designed to do, then?" When they'd first been partners, in bed as well as in investigating, Orlando had found it hard enough to even think of a word to describe the act of intercourse, let alone say it out loud. Now he enjoyed talking smutty on occasions, and getting Jonty to do the same, not that the imp needed much prompting.

"I'll resist the temptation to say, 'If you need to ask the question, you won't understand the answer.'" Jonty carried on stroking his target. "This thing was especially made for pleasing me, of course. In a variety of ways."

"Not for pleasing *me*?" Orlando's voice was hoarse, now. Anybody's voice would have been hoarse with *that* being done to them.

"You as well, of course, but not without me being involved somewhere. Solitary pleasures are never quite as satisfying."

They kissed gently, then eagerly, tongues exploring and tasting. This was a joy that never dulled with repetition: a simple kiss as exciting a prelude to the main event as a man could wish for. It was more than a dozen years since they'd first shared a sexual experience. Orlando often wondered how he had survived his empty and unfulfilled life before Jonty had come along and opened his eyes to a world of delights that were neither numerical nor logical.

"Have I not broken you of that desperate habit yet?" Jonty had made his way down to Orlando's chest, trailing kisses all the way, but he came back up to eye level to remonstrate.

"What habit?" Orlando tried hard to think of some little nasty practice that he might have fallen into, particularly when the war had kept them apart.

"Thinking too hard when we're supposed to be concentrating on the flesh, not the intellect. I can almost hear your brain cells clashing together." Jonty dived down again, edging the line of kisses southwards.

"I shall try my hardest to clear my brain, but as I've told you a million . . . oh." There was no chance of Orlando speaking or even thinking now, not with Jonty doing *that*, *there*.

Normally Orlando was the methodical one, ensuring that every inch of skin on Jonty's chest was tasted. Ensuring each process on

Jonty's backbone had been caressed and stimulated before letting his fingers make their way before, behind, and between in search of their ultimate goal.

But now Jonty was inching kisses all over Orlando's chest, across his flanks, and onto his back. This reversal of their usual roles was proving both unsettling and wildly exciting. When Jonty's tongue reached the little place just above Orlando's hip bone, where the great scar on his chest ended, it felt like he might just go berserk.

"It's remarkable how well you've kept your shape." Jonty sat back for a moment, all the better to admire his lover's fine lean frame. "Like a man twenty years younger."

"Oh, hush." Orlando was secretly pleased, of course he was, but it didn't do to confess the fact. It was exactly the sort of evidence of vanity that might be kept and used against him on a later occasion. "And it's remarkable how you've never lost the ability to prattle on and on, even at the most intimate of moments. One day I'll insist on rogering in silence, and then where will you be?"

"I seem to recall we've done it before, and I'm sure we could do it again. Is that a challenge?" It seemed so daft, the pair of them lying naked now and greatly aroused, talking instead of doing, but that had often been the way of things. At least some element of sex was, for both of them, cerebral rather than just carnal.

"It wasn't, but it is now." Orlando drew Jonty towards him, silencing him in the best way he knew: with deep urgent kisses. This was going to be a test for both of them. They'd managed hush before, whispers as opposed to talking aloud, but utter silence they'd rarely succeeded in. How would they know if it was to be "turn" or "turnabout" or any other of the coded terms they used to describe their preference of the night? How would they know when it was the moment for proper union?

Jonty pulled out of the kiss. "If I'm to keep silent then your brain is to stop processing stuff, as well. I can hear it whirring and chugging away in there. Whatever's exercising it now?"

Orlando hoped he hadn't turned too deep a shade of crimson. It was rare for him to blush now, so rare that Jonty always made a special point of mentioning it and being impertinent. "If we're completely silent from now on, how will I know what you want to do?"

"Turn or turnabout, you mean? Turnabout." Jonty grinned, running his fingers along his lover's chest and down to the field of ultimate engagement. "Anything else to clarify before we go into action? There'll be no calling out then."

Orlando could barely raise his voice above a whisper. It was all very well discussing these things in the heat of passion, but to be planning them in advance like a military strategy was . . . actually, it was rather exciting. "We'll take it nice and slowly. Just, you know, to get the feel of things. Oh, do stop laughing. You're worse than one of the dunderheads."

"I'll be sensible." Jonty crossed his heart and raised his hand. "Actually, I'll say it for you as you can't manage the words: You'll go once more into the breach, or whatever euphemism you want to use for partial rogering, then we'll calm down a bit before we go for the big finish. Make the moment last."

Orlando nodded, glad that Jonty understood him so well and the conversation could cease. They might have thirteen years of experience with each other, but every new engagement was to be regarded as something significant, sacred, precious. And after their separation during the war and the confusion and heartbreak that had followed the end of hostilities, intimacy with each other was something they'd never take for granted again. "One last thing. Can I say 'I love you' now, if I'm not allowed to say it *then*? You know, at the moment of . . . um . . . crisis?"

"You never need to say it out loud, although I'll never tire of hearing it. I've known it for so long." Jonty caressed Orlando's face, then let his hand wander lower again. The time for action had come. "So, so long . . ."

Orlando wasn't sure if the last remark had been intended as a pun and, frankly, he'd gone past the point of caring. He focussed his mind, at last, on the pleasures of the flesh.

"Are you asleep?" Orlando realised it was a stupid question as soon as it was out of his mouth. He'd be jolly lucky not to get a clout in response if he woke his light-of-love. He hoped he'd judged the signs right; Jonty had a certain tenor to his breath when asleep, and that note had been missing these last ten minutes.

"Sex has obviously affected your powers of logic again. How can you expect a sensible answer to that question?" Jonty turned over, snuggling up against his lover. "Talking of sex, you're not after a second helping are you? Because I feel absolutely shattered."

"No, of course not." Orlando wasn't lying for once; neither of them was getting any younger. Even if the spirit had been willing, the flesh felt a bit drooping. "I just wanted to talk about the case."

"Have you been lying awake worrying about it? I could feel you tossing and turning."

"Did I wake you? Sorry." When they were younger, and their bodies weren't quite so wilted, they'd have lain in each other's arms after the act of love, discussing the case they were working on. Strange how often they'd made some sudden leap of deduction in a haze of postcoital bliss. Now sleep usually overtook them too quickly for such luxuries. "No, I haven't been lying awake. Well, only this last half an hour." Worrying about Owens too, although he wasn't going to admit that. "Something about Mitchell doesn't quite ring true. It's been gnawing at me since we were in the pub. Of course now I've twigged it, the thing's entirely obvious."

"Well, it may be to a professor of mathematics, but a humble student of the Bard is struggling to get what's going on." Jonty arranged the covers around himself, making a little nest. "Especially at two o'clock in the morning, or whatever it is. Please enlighten me, if that's not beneath your dignity."

"He says he served out with the Cambridgeshires. How did he have time to get home at the end of the war *and* find a parish *and* get to know the Priestlands before Peter's death when the man was already dead before the Armistice?"

"Eh? Can you say that again slowly?"

"We . . . must . . . assume . . . Ow!" Orlando rubbed his shin. It was a low blow to give a man a kick while sharing a bed with him. And not just low, dextrous with it. He moved his legs out of range.

"Not as slowly as all that, for goodness sake. You clearly haven't had enough shin whacks recently and are getting into bad habits again." Jonty jiggled his foot as a warning.

Orlando mustered all the dignity that his sore shin would allow. "We must assume that he's been in the parish since earlier last year to have come to know the Priestlands reasonably well. Unless he was there prewar, of course, or knew them from somewhere else."

"I didn't get that impression from what he'd said, so while I have no definite evidence one way or the other, I feel—don't roll your eyes, I saw that, even in the dark—it's unlikely to be so. I can offer some nice objective evidence about the first part, because when I got dragged round the church, I saw the painted board with the list of vicars." Jonty yawned. "The previous vicar had served until October 1917. I remember because his name was Sheridan and I couldn't help wondering if he was related to Dr. Sheridan, although apparently he isn't. Then there must have been an interregnum, because your man Mitchell didn't take up the post until March of last year."

"He's not *my* man."

"More's the pity, if you saw him. Very nicely turned out lad. I bet he has all the old maids' hearts aflutter."

"As you keep saying. Behave. Irrespective of all that, what was he doing back in Blighty in early 1918, or late 1917, I suppose, to be interviewed or whatever it is they do to prospective parish priests?" Orlando pulled the covers tighter around him; the night was reaching its coldest point.

"They make them meet three old maids of the parish in a locked room and see if they can avoid being molested over a period of one hour. Any handsome young priest who passes through the fire of that ordeal must be the one for the job."

"Can you never be serious?"

"Not after the events of a few hours ago. And anyway, I've seen enough of being serious over the last few years. I think it's my duty to be frivolous for the rest of my life. Except in our bed, of course." Jonty laughed. "I bet you're blushing. Shame I can't see it."

Orlando deliberately ignored the remark, resolving to make his friend pay amends in that same bed, whenever they were both up to it again. "Mitchell. Did he seem like he'd got an injury that would have sent him home?"

Jonty, suddenly serious despite all his earlier protestations, became quiet while he considered, his steady breathing reflecting his depth of thought. "Not that I was aware of. I suppose he might have been sent home with trench fever or a bit gaga, and then recovered sufficiently to take up light duties in his parish. Might even have had a wooden leg under his tweed trousers, and was so adept at using it that I didn't notice."

"Is there any chance that it wasn't him in the photo? That all the bit about being an officer was just a pretence? A nice convenient lie to impress the ladies?" It seemed like a long shot, but loose ends and inconsistencies always nagged at Orlando. He hated everything that didn't coincide with his mathematically logical view of the world. Except, of course, the gloriously subjective, annoying, messy, and irrational Jonty Stewart.

"It certainly looked like him, although I suppose it might have been a twin brother. I hope there aren't two sets of twins in this case, like Shakespeare had. That would drive me mad." Jonty sighed, the sigh turning into another yawn. "Sorry, I need my beauty sleep. Is this important?"

"I don't know. It niggles, and I'm always wary of things in a case that niggle. Like why he said that Peter was the elder," Orlando said, fidgeting to get comfortable, as unsettled physically as mentally.

"Maybe Rosalind lied to him."

"But why?"

"To impress him? To make him think she was richer than she was? Because she likes to lie and knows she can get away with it? My head's spinning." Jonty yawned. "Right. Then who can we contact to have Mitchell's war record confirmed?"

"Willshire." The name was dropped into the conversation with finality, like a bombardment sweeping away all opposition.

"Of course, the very man." Willshire had been their boss at Room 40 and had maintained a spider's web of information gathering, both within official channels and without. People said he could have found out anything, from the name of the next derby winner to what Baron von Richthofen had been having for breakfast. He probably kept the web in active service. "Will you do the honours or me?"

"Me. Tomorrow."

"Today, you mean." Jonty yawned again, leaned over to give Orlando a kiss, then snuggled down. "Get some sleep. Professors need all they can get their grubby mitts on."

"Sleep or rogering?" Orlando shot his legs across the bed before they could be attacked again.

Chapter 9

Jonty had always lauded the power of the subconscious brain to solve problems or to mull over facts and rearrange them into a surprising order. He said it was like squinting at a faint star; if you looked at it straight on, you couldn't see it, but gaze slightly to one side and it was there, on the edge of your field of vision. Orlando, when consulted, had always been prosaic about the matter. Even Dr. Panesar—what right had he to be so boring?—had put it down to nothing more than the construction of the eye, an arrangement of cells in the middle of the retina that gave a lack of clarity or some such twaddle.

Jonty didn't doubt the truth of the anatomical explanation, but he preferred his own: That some ideas, like faint stars, were too nebulous to be fixed straight on. That to pin them down under intense scrutiny was to lose them. Better to look at something else and let the thoughts come to fruition in peace. After all, how many great notions had come to inventors and philosophers when they'd been doing something else entirely rather than inventing, often something mundane, as if the conscious body needed to be occupied so the rest of the brain could get on with important things?

In their own experience, the solutions to cases had been found in dreams, or when they'd awoken in a clarity of mind that had driven them towards a solution. Not via Orlando's beloved logic, much as "himself" would have liked that. This time, Jonty had awakened with Orlando snuggled up to him, gently purring and looking beatific. And while Jonty's brain might not have laid out the entire solution to the Priestland case, it *had* given him the next step.

Historically, if he'd wanted to get some inside information on someone from the past, Jonty would have been straight in touch with his parents. By telephone, preferably, striking while the iron was hot. While he no longer had the option of accessing the powerful weapon that was the combined Stewart parental brain, he could still make use of something almost as potent. While Jonty's brothers seemed only to have inherited the family looks, his sister Lavinia was heir to the Stewart intelligence and the Forster native wit. Maybe *she* could get onto the scent over the next few days, while he and Orlando were kept in Cambridge by college and university duties?

"Hmhphm." The susurration of gentle snores emanating from the other occupant of the bed had turned into speech, albeit incoherent.

"Good morning, Orlando. Lovely to see you." How many times had Jonty spoken those words on waking? They'd become as important and iconic to them now as "That sir, is my chair," and a half a dozen other little phrases. A secret language they could even speak in the presence of others, the only public acknowledgement they could ever make of their love.

"Hmm." Orlando snuggled further into Jonty's embrace, seeming still a bit befuddled, either from last night's satiation or from the lack of sleep caused by airing investigational thoughts long into the night. "Sleep well?"

At last the emanations from the man's mouth were beginning to make sense.

"Excellent. I now know my next step on the Priestland case. And I have another idea. About tackling Owens."

"Really?" Any absence of clarity in Orlando's brain had evidently dissipated; he was fully alert now.

"Thought that might wake you up. Now, you'll have to suspend your moralising, as this is hardly the most Christian of suggestions. Not exactly a case of turning the other cheek."

"Are you suggesting we use one of my foolproof methods of murder? The ones that could never be detected?" Orlando reached over, curling his hand to better twiddle with his lover's hair. "The ones I was saving for when I get tired of you?"

"So your sleeping mind's been mulling it over too?" Jonty ignored the remark; that particular one was becoming old hat. "I wasn't thinking of going as far as murder. Just a bit of his own medicine. Who's the most formidable female you can think of, now that Mama no longer walks this earth? If that's too hard, I'll give your poor befuddled brain a clue: she has no great love for Owens, either."

"Mrs. Sheridan."

"Exactly. I think we should tell our Ariadne what the bounder's about and see whether she's got any muck to rake up on *him*." Jonty stretched, yawned, and rolled out of the bed, almost as easily as he'd done a dozen years before. "I'm sure if there's a whiff of scandal to be traced in the air, then she can sniff it out."

"Fight fire with fire?" Orlando looked worried. "Doesn't that risk the whole conflagration getting out of hand?"

"It may be the only thing that sort of man understands. With any luck, she'll turn over a stone and out will crawl a secret marriage or an act of such despicability that no one would believe a word he had to say against us." Jonty nodded, as if the whole matter were signed and sealed. "They'd think he was just trying to get his own back."

"They won't think that anyway, by any marvellous chance? You know, him making a parry at the slur to his college's reputation? And getting his revenge in for us having whipped the Woodville Ward from under his snotty nose?" Orlando sounded hopeful, although not convinced.

"That would be asking for too much, I fear. I think we should prepare to get our retaliation in first, as my old rugby teacher at school always used to say." Jonty kissed his friend's brow and reached for their dressing gowns, slinging Orlando's onto the bed in an intentionally messy heap.

Orlando eased his frame from the comforts of mattress and eiderdown, stretching and scratching, the normal morning routine. The nights were getting nippy and they'd both slipped back into pyjamas after their romantic exertions; it was one of the occasions where practicality had to take precedence over romance. Now woolly and slightly pragmatic dressing gowns had to be worn, even for a trip to the toilet. They might delude themselves that it wasn't to frighten their housekeeper with the sight of a slightly underdressed male, but it was more a case of thinning blood and an increasing awareness of the cold.

"Tell me one thing and one thing only." Orlando caught Jonty's hand just as he was about to slip out of the door. "I trust you implicitly. Always have done. Things *will* be all right, won't they?"

"Absolutely fine." Jonty gave his friend a parting kiss and set off to perform his ablutions, trying to look more confident than he felt.

Orlando had barely left for the department, ready to give some impenetrable lecture, when Jonty took himself and a piece of toast to his study. Best to strike before duties down at St. Bride's started to eat the day away. He picked up the telephone receiver and asked to be put through to his sister, while he snaffled the last bite and wiped away the stray crumbs that always seemed to follow him about.

"Is that Forsythia Cottage?"

"Lavinia?" It had to be her, given the stentorian tones in which the question had been asked.

"Jonty!" His sister's voice was getting more and more like their mother's every day. "If you're after your partner in crime, he's not here. Surprisingly enough, we choose to send him to school on weekdays."

"Oh, ha-ha. I do understand the domestic requirements of the average household, old girl." It made a change for him to be ringing the Broads' home without the primary intention of speaking to Georgie, though. "I wanted to talk to you, actually."

"Hmm. I don't like the sound of that." Lavinia's choice of words may have sounded grumpy, but she was evidently in good humour, the sudden softness in tone giving that much away. "It takes me back to when you were just a boy, and were after a loan of five bob until pocket money day."

"You read me like a book." Jonty settled back in his chair. If it was going to be as easy as borrowing five bob, he could afford to relax. "As you guessed, I'm after a favour. Information, though, not money."

"Oh." Lavinia sounded as if that was a worse prospect. "Information about what?"

"About whom, actually. A lady called Helen Phillips who died in a yachting accident off the Scilly Isles in July 1872."

"Am I supposed to remember that far back in any sort of detail? I was only . . . well, never you mind how old I was. Just a child," Lavinia protested with a laugh.

Jonty knew exactly how old his sister had been then, but he didn't pursue the subject. He never used to tease her too much when he wanted five bob, so why change a winning stratagem? "I don't expect you to remember. I'd just like you to go and do some digging for me. I can't get away from Cambridge until next weekend to apply the spade myself."

"I'm surprised Orlando's letting you out of his sight before his lecture's written and given. Barely a fortnight away, isn't it?"

"And don't I know it. Got your frock sorted yet?"

"Of course. My milliner says it makes me look ten years younger." Lavinia giggled. "Don't you dare say anything, pest. Shall I bring the fruits of my investigative labours up to Cambridge with me?"

"The case is far too urgent for that, Mistress Mischief. Can you get amongst it and report back as soon as possible? I'll pay you back any half-crowns still owing."

"With interest, I hope." Lavinia sighed, the laughter gone from her voice, replaced by wistfulness. "This is where we miss Mama, isn't it? She'd have said straightaway, 'Oh, Helen Phillips. She left her husband and children for another man. Such a scandal.'"

Jonty almost dropped the earpiece. "Has the old girl been sending down angels to whisper in your ear? You have no idea how near the truth that is. Scary."

"You're making me shiver, you horrible boy. Tell me more."

"Helen Phillips might just have done that very thing. Only her children were kept in the dark about it for years, being told she'd died. They didn't find out until their father passed on. We think."

"You *think*? You and Orlando don't *know*? You're losing your touch. I'll have to report this to Georgie; he'll be most disappointed to think his uncle has feet of clay."

That was too close to the truth to be amusing. "Don't snitch on us just yet. The trouble is that the people in the case don't know—well, didn't know—and didn't want to take the appropriate steps to establish the truth once and for all. That's why we need you. Anything about Helen Phillips, especially about her background and whether she mysteriously appeared, as if wafted down from heaven, twenty years before she was killed. If the name Priestland turns up in connection to the case, we're on a winner."

"Don't want a lot, do you? Still, I think I have an inkling about what to do. There's a chap at *The Times* on the editorial team who had a big crush on me when I was eighteen. I heard that!" Lavinia almost pierced Jonty's eardrums. "How dare you snigger? I have a good mind not to do your dirty work for you."

"Georgie would be terribly disappointed if you had the chance to be in on a case and didn't take it." Getting retaliation in first; it worked on the rugby pitch and it appeared to work off it.

"Hmm. This is going to cost you more than my son's good will. A dozen roses at least."

"Done. Now, about your paramour at *The Times*. Does your husband know you have a fancy man?"

"Oh hush. You know I've never had eyes for anyone but Ralph. Been smitten with him ever since we were seven and he used to throw frogs at me. Poor Freddie, that's the editor, was heartbroken that he couldn't win me away, no matter how many small amphibians he waggled in my direction."

Jonty resisted making any sort of saucy pun about what people waggled at each other when courting and how he'd never heard them called "small amphibians" before. One had to be careful with Lavinia, given that her marriage hadn't started on the best of notes, and the consummation of the same had only happened after many years of frustration. And the intervention of a dollop of wisdom from Ariadne Sheridan. Even though Lavinia was now a mother of two, no one wanted to bring memories of earlier days to the surface.

"Anyway," Lavinia rattled on, not having inherited her mother's telepathic skill at identifying when Jonty was having smutty thoughts, "he can probably find the back issues of the paper and see if the story's reported there. He's got a nose for scandal and if he can't produce something there and then, he'll no doubt have an idea about how he can give me more solid verification."

I bet he will, Jonty thought, but didn't dare say that either. He'd have to see how he could work the words "solid verification" into the conversation next time he and Orlando were in bed. "Whatever you turn up may well be vital."

"Are you going to tell me what this is about?"

"When you come up for Orlando's lecture. I'd rather tell you face-to-face, as parts of the case border on the slanderous and I'm never sure the operator isn't listening in. All will be revealed."

"I'll be in touch. Love to Signor Artigiano del Rame." Lavinia put the phone down abruptly.

Maybe the editor chappie at *The Times* would turn out to have improved with age; Jonty just hoped he wouldn't prove so attractive that he gave Lavinia any ideas. She was at a funny age, but then again, she'd always been at a funny age. So long as this Freddie bloke didn't shake any small amphibians at her, then all should be well.

Potential murderesses, twins, triplets, vicars, and shipwrecks had to take second place to *Othello* and vector analysis for the rest of the day. Man couldn't live by investigation alone. Either their usual work or their sleuthing would have felt wrong as a lifetime's sole occupation, the former too prosaic and the latter too hedonistic. And a pleasant discussion of developments and ideas—mathematical, literary, and investigatory—over dinner made for the best of entertainment.

Once they'd disposed of whether Iago was envious of Othello or of Desdemona, whether vector analysis had any practical application to the Isle of Wight ferry, and whether Mrs. Ward's rabbit with prunes had been better than the Sunday roast, they turned to Bresnan's commission.

"Did you contact Willshire?" Jonty ate the last of his fruit salad, slightly lifted the bowl, as though he was about to lick out the last of the cream, then clearly resisted the temptation. Perhaps he thought his mother was still watching from some heavenly height.

"Of course I did." Orlando had saved a small piece of pear, with which he scooped out the last soupçon of creamy, fruity liquid. "If I say I'll do something, I do it."

"One seems a little touchy, does one not?" Jonty rose, gestured for Orlando to come to the drawing room where they could sit together on the sofa, then put his arm around his shoulders. "Tell Uncle Jonty all. Handkerchiefs fresh and ready to be supplied."

"Idiot." Orlando sighed. "It's nothing, really. Just some talk down at the department about how the counterclaim for Owens's protégé is unlikely to succeed unless he can produce a darn sight more evidence that *he* was stolen from. I think hoping that the miserable swine would have no cause to put pressure on us is a vain hope."

"We definitely need some nice little juicy bit of something or other we can hold over Owens's head. His own sword of Damocles."

"And have you made any progress on locating such a miraculous thing?" Orlando resisted the temptation to say that the more he thought about it, the more it seemed that such an eye-for-an-eye approach was hardly in keeping with Jonty's principles. They could argue the toss on that front after the business was sorted, and absolution found. A man had to be pragmatic at times like this.

"I've taken step one. We're having lunch with Ariadne Sheridan tomorrow. Don't worry, I've checked your Tuesday commitments and you have time for both food *and* gossip. We'll throw ourselves on her mercy. And I've set another hound running too, if I can be so crude about my own sister."

"I'll tell her. Then she'll have your guts for garters." It was an idle threat; Orlando might have snitched to Lavinia when they were younger, but not now that she'd become the matriarchal Stewart figure. Jonty would know that. "What job have you asked the poor girl to do?"

"She's on the trail of Helen Phillips and whether she's who we think she is. I have enormous confidence that she'll be a bobby-dazzler and come back with a hatful of information."

"Brilliant idea!" Orlando gave Jonty a huge, smacking kiss. "I should have thought of that myself, but you've outfoxed me. Well done."

"Thank you. If that's what I get for ringing my sister, what reward will I qualify for if I make a real breakthrough?"

"Make one and you might find out."

"And do you have something to report that requires comparable recompense?" Jonty puckered up his lips but only met thin air.

"I hardly think my poor piece of progress deserves even holding hands, let alone a kiss. Willshire said he'd find out about Mitchell and get back to me."

"That's a start. At least you can be sure he'll come back and with the correct answer, too. Reliable, like my Lavinia." Jonty kissed Orlando's cheek anyway. "Now, if I want to play 'throwing ourselves on Mrs. Sheridan's mercy' tomorrow, and then detectives on the weekend, I need to prepare some work on *Twelfth Night*."

"I should be glad you said that. I've been worrying about how I could get time off from matters domestic to get on with my lecture this evening." Orlando sighed. "Now I don't have to bother."

"It sounds like you were hoping I wouldn't let you go and do your work." Jonty pulled Orlando towards the dining room door. "Come on. I'll ask Mrs. Ward to serve coffee in our studies, so you can get your head down. An hour, that's what we'll confine ourselves to, and then we'll have an early night."

"Early night?"

"No, not *early night*. Really, can you think of nothing but sex? A *proper* early night, and I'll read to you from one of those long-winded textbooks you so love. It's been a long time since I did that."

"Ah." Orlando beamed. "That's a positive incentive to get another page or two written."

"Just don't refer to the delights of the double bed in your lecture. The vice-chancellor would faint."

Chapter 10

Ariadne Sheridan would never have been described as beautiful, or even pretty, even in her youth; her attractiveness lay in her formidable intellect and her warmth of heart. She'd been surrogate mother to many a lost and lonely St. Bride's undergraduate, Jonty included, and had created a happy and purposeful life. Especially now that she'd managed to astonish the whole university by marrying—for love, no less—in her late forties.

She'd taken to the role of wife and hostess with the same calm competency she'd applied to every other part of her life. She'd been chatelaine of the St. Bride's lodge for years, of course, looking after her brother when he'd been master, up until her marriage to Dr. Sheridan, when she'd temporarily deserted the place in favour of gracing Apostles' college. When, during the war, her brother, then master of St. Bride's, succumbed to the aftereffects of a fall down a college staircase, the vacancy at the master's lodge had created a gulf at the heart of the college and in Ariadne's breast. Both of them had been as inconsolable in grief as any wife who'd lost her man on the front.

Jonty admired the way in which Robert Sheridan had comforted his wife and filled the gap at St. Bride's, restoring order and bringing consolation and healing to his adopted institution. Not least because he'd brought Ariadne back with him. Now she was as much a part of St. Bride's again as the choir stalls in the chapel and the black currant stains on the wainscoting in the hall. And now that the postwar pieces were being picked up, she had time to catch, dig for, poke at, or in any other way generally annoy any planarian worms which took her fancy.

Today she had two less vermiform creatures at her dinner table and was plying them with lemonade, pie, salad, and Bakewell tarts.

Ariadne had always taken the denizens of St. Bride's under her wing, even if her interest, always officially maternal, was more so now that she had her very own red-blooded male to frolic with.

Still, no doubt the contrast of light and dark, solemn and capricious, logical and intuitive, at either side of her would be something an intelligent woman would appreciate.

"Thank you for arranging all this at short notice." Orlando, glass of lemonade in hand, looked as awkward as an undergraduate.

"You make me sound like the family solicitor or something equally stuffy. You're old friends. You could knock on my door in the middle of the night, and I'd find a cup of tea for you. *And* cake." Mrs. Sheridan offered one of the succulent little tarts to Jonty, who rarely refused fodder.

"Thank you, but I'll take one when I've had my salad. Have to earn the privilege." He considered the pastries, debating whether he could break all rules of proper Stewart meal etiquette and take pudding first. "And maybe they'll have to wait until after we've explained what we've come about. It's rather a delicate, not to say awkward, matter, isn't it, Professor Coppersmith?"

Orlando looked longingly at the cakes on the plate. Maybe he thought the answer to the question lay among the egg and jam? "If I say it concerns Dr. Owens, I think that shows just how difficult it is."

"Owens?" Mrs. Sheridan almost upset the lemonade jug in her consternation. "That—that—don't tell the chaplain I used these words, but that filthy, lecherous, grubby, plagiaristic *swine*?"

"That's a mild way of putting it." Jonty grinned. "The very same."

"What's he done now? Is it this plagiarism case? It's the talk of the university."

"I'm afraid so," Orlando said, laying down knife and fork. He gave a précis of what had gone on at his meeting, conveniently ignoring the fact that most of it was supposed to be strictly confidential. He didn't skimp on the details of the conversation he'd had with Owens afterwards. Words used and meanings implied.

"But it isn't just you on the committee, is it? There must be other members with as much influence in considering the evidence as you."

"I sit as chairman of the six of us. Therefore, I would have the casting vote." Orlando still couldn't raise his eyes from contemplation of a piece of lettuce.

"And a chairman less fair-minded than Professor Coppersmith could use his influence to sway the rest of his conclave whichever way he wanted them to go. It happens." Jonty sighed. "Probably Owens thinks we're all as corrupt as he is and imagines that if he can pressure our professor here into doing his bidding, then he'll have the whole committee in the palm of his hand and his man will get away with this skulduggery."

"The absolute bounder. I've a good mind to go round to the college next door right now and thrash the so-and-so." There was a native club hanging on the wall, courtesy of a previous master with a penchant for little-known tribes. The way Mrs. Sheridan eyed the weapon suggested her threat was deadly earnest. "Would the disgrace of being beaten to a pulp by a middle-aged woman make him see some sense?"

"I doubt it. Being trampled by a stegosaurus wouldn't make Owens see sense." Orlando snorted, stabbing a piece of pie as if it were Owens himself. "And anyway, he's only made the most veiled of threats, if threats they really are. He may be devious, but he isn't daft."

"So how can I help? Apart from lending a sympathetic ear?"

Orlando seemed suddenly to have lost the ability to speak, so Jonty leaped in. "What we could do with is a very large piece of artillery we could wheel out at a moment's notice to flatten him if he steps out of line. And the chances are that step he will, because things don't look good for his protégé."

"Right. Well, leave that to me." Ariadne nodded her head emphatically, as if she had the very thing already in her possession.

"You've got something in mind?" Remembering his manners, Orlando at last glanced up with an eager look in his eye.

"Not yet, but I will have, given a bit of time."

They ate in silence for a while, each of them following their own lines of thought, probably none of which were very complimentary to Owens. Ariadne broke the hush. "Is it possible he might be putting pressure on your colleagues as well? No chance that we can all form a wall of outraged resistance against him?"

"I doubt it. I made some subtle enquires—I saw that smirk, Dr. Stewart, and I *can* be subtle when the occasion demands—of a couple of them, this morning." Orlando produced as much of a self-satisfied smile as he could manage in the circumstances. "In anticipation of just such a question."

"That was brave of you. How did you manage it without arousing suspicion?" Jonty, for all the smirking and eye rolling, was full of admiration. "I never thought you'd have it in you."

"The old Coppersmith wouldn't," Ariadne murmured, earning her a smile from both her guests.

"I took the bull by the horns. Said I'd heard an extremely disturbing rumour that Owens was putting undue pressure on a member of the committee investigating the plagiarism, pressure that was not to be tolerated."

"Did you use those very words? The sheer length and complexity would have let them know you were serious." Jonty edged his leg back, just in case he'd overestimated the width of the dining table and had left his shin at risk of a kicking. "Watch him ignore me, Mrs. Sheridan. I'm distraught that he no longer rises to the bait."

"Oh, hush, you pest, and let the professor say his bit."

"Thank you." Orlando bowed his head towards his hostess. "I'm glad *someone* at this table has proper manners. I assured my colleagues that, if it were true, I wanted to offer the man my total support in standing up to the swine. I think I can detect a lie by now, and I'm sure they were telling me nothing but the truth when they said it wasn't any of them. They seemed genuinely perplexed."

"Impressive so far. Were you smart enough to give them a confidential chance of admitting they'd been approached?" Jonty eased a Bakewell tart onto his plate, picking off a crumb or two just to whet his appetite.

"Of course. I suggested a note in one of my pigeonholes, but nothing's been forthcoming."

"So we eliminate that option, at least for the moment." Ariadne picked up the plate and offered Orlando the largest of the Bakewells. "Well done. I shall endeavour to be as efficient with my little commission. And now for important matters. Have either of you room for a small, sweet sherry?"

Jonty had come home after lunch and got on so well with *Twelfth Night* that he'd cleared his decks entirely of everything that needed to be done for his next lecture—one to be delivered only to dunderheads and not, like Orlando's inaugural one, before Uncle Tom Cobley and all. One day he'd have to write a paper on whatever must have been going on in the Bard's brain that he seemed to have an obsession with men called Antonio who were in love with other men, ones who didn't deserve, or adequately return, their affection. Although whether such a paper would ever be published without causing a national scandal, he wasn't sure. Not even in these slightly more enlightened days.

Such industry deserved a reward, and he'd taken it sitting in his favourite chair and musing, most definitely musing and not dreaming, on his favourite topic.

He answered the phone at its sixth ring, leaping from his comfy chair where he'd most definitely *not* been dozing off in front of the fire. "Forsythia Cottage. Stewart speaking."

"Hello, stinker." Hardly the sort of greeting Jonty had expected for an august fellow of a revered Cambridge institution, but sisters were no respecters of personage. Even if Jonty were ever given a Chair of some sort, Lavinia would always address him as her snotty little brother.

"Hello, spotty." If nursery names were being traded, Jonty could do business with the best of them. "How are things in Broad land?"

"Fine, if you ignore the fact that Alexandra knocked one of her teeth out falling from a tree. Only a milk one. Tooth, that is."

"I always said she took after her grandmother. Apparently Mama was a great one for climbing and other tomboy activities in her younger days." It would explain the formidable right hook she'd wielded as a young lady. "There's a smug tone to your voice. You come bearing news?"

"I do. But I had to work hard for it."

"Nothing my conscience is going to prick me for?" Especially as it was so soon; Lavinia had clearly got her skates on. He only hoped she hadn't taken anything off in furtherance of her efforts.

"Wash your mouth out, you little toad!" Lavinia's voice had developed the same capacity of decibels as their mother's. "I had lunch, that was all. A long and quite boring one, actually. He must have gone and found the story in the archives within minutes of my first ringing him." She sighed. "I'm so pleased I was smitten with Ralph. If I'd settled down with Freddie, I'd have biffed him with the solid silver candlesticks by now. He's handsome, but he's awfully tedious."

Jonty resisted any temptation to make a remark about how a married woman didn't live by bed alone; it was both indelicate and could have been seen as an allusion to the early years of Lavinia's marriage. "I'll make it two dozen roses, as recompense. Colour of your choice."

"Hm. Puce, I think. To match Freddie's face after he'd finished lunch. Maybe it's reward enough to know that I'd not made an error all those years ago." Lavinia chuckled. "Anyway, Helen Phillips. She was lost at sea while on a yacht belonging to Sir Steven Marchant, baronet. Made a lot of money in the most ridiculous ventures. He did, not her." Lavinia's style of narrative resembled her brother's; Orlando would have had a fit. "His family sold warming pans in the West Indies. Don't laugh. Very popular for stirring molasses, so I'm told."

"I think you're making half of this up, but carry on."

"You may well *wish* I'd made it up by the time I get to the end of it. An acquaintance of Marchant's and his lady friend, whom Freddie reckons was an actress of the time, one of slightly shady reputation, were also on board. I don't know if 'actress' is euphemistic for . . ." Lavinia's bravado seemed to depart for a moment, but she rallied. "A fallen woman."

"Probably. I suspect Helen had a touch of that about her too." Although who was he to judge her, given what he'd heard about her husband?

"Be that as it may, everyone was lost, including the crew. Some bits of debris were washed up on Tresco, but the rest lies in Davy Jones's locker."

"Anything get rooted out about inheritances?" If it had, that would be two out of the three things Jonty had hoped for.

"Marchant's went to his son, although I suspect that's not what you meant. Freddie found a peculiar little announcement in the papers a week or so later, about how heirs of Helen Phillips should contact her solicitor to find something to their advantage." Lavinia's voice sounded smugger than ever. "You'll never in a million years guess whose firm it was."

At least Lavinia's puzzles didn't involve twins and triplets. "It has to be someone we know. Our solicitors?"

"No, but you're on the right lines. Your old pal Collingwood."

"Blimey." Jonty and Orlando had crossed paths with Collingwood on a couple of occasions, each time to their mutual advantage. Although no longer officially active, the solicitor kept an interest in his firm and, it was rumoured, a matronly mistress in St. John's Wood. He was possibly the sprightliest seventy-year-old Jonty could think of. "That's a stroke of luck. I'll get onto him right away."

"No need." The smugness had reached new heights. "I called in to see him myself. Such a charming man, even at his age. We were soon knee-deep in old files."

Jonty resisted asking whether that was all they'd been knee-deep in. He hoped his sister wasn't turning into some femme fatale of the investigation world. "This game sounds just your cup of tea. We should recruit you again, old girl. Papa always used to be our man in London and you can inherit the mantle." Poor Mr. Stewart. He'd have lapped up this sort of case. "And talking of inheritances . . .?"

"It was never claimed. A large quantity of jewellery sits in a bank vault, awaiting someone coming forward."

"Jewels? I like the sound of that. Alice Priestland was said to have converted her wealth to gewgaws. Easier to arrange inheritance of, for one thing."

"Don't get overexcited. It could still be coincidence." Lavinia's voice sounded horribly reasonable. "I'm surprised it hasn't reverted to the Crown."

"So am I. Either they still hold out hope or Collingwood's wilier than I gave him credit for. I wonder how long it can go unclaimed?" Jonty pricked his ears, a veritable greyhound in the slips.

"Find that out for yourself. Must I do everything?"

"I'd love to, but I'm not sure I could cope with another deadline in the case. There are two other legacies already, both date-dependant and both reaching their crux over the next few weeks." Jonty had the urge to wax lyrical. "Like ships converging on the same part of the ocean for some great battle."

"Or chips converging on the same part of the roulette table? I'd forgotten how flowery your language can be at times. Even Georgie is picking it up now." Lavinia produced a heartfelt sigh. "Coming out with allusions and allegories and analogies at the drop of a hat."

"It could be worse. You'd rather I taught him flowery language than bad, surely?" Jonty could have taught the lad things that would have made his mother's hair stand on end; mercifully, he'd restrained himself. "So just let me clarify. Nobody's come forward to claim this stuff and been rebuffed?"

"Not at the time of her death. And not since. I'm glad Freddie gave me Collingwood's name."

"Freddie's done a lot of work for you, hasn't he? Above and beyond the call of duty. Shall I tell Ralph to prepare himself for some bad news?" Jonty might have been able to resist teaching his nephew inappropriate words, but winding up Georgie's mother was a different matter.

"Oh, for goodness sake, will you behave? Otherwise, I won't go and do any more of your dirty work for you." Lavinia's words were harsh but she sounded happy. Was she going to prove to be the latest member of the Stewart clan who'd caught the detecting bug? If Lavinia had discovered the thrill of the chase, and was always as efficient in pursuing a lead, then Jonty had better keep her sweet.

"I apologise profusely. Mea culpa and all that."

"I don't like it when you act contrite quite so readily. Makes me suspicious. What is it you're after now?"

The third of the three things on his list, of course. "Your aspiring and never-to-be-paramour Freddie didn't happen to mention anything that might have suggested Alice Priestland and Helen Phillips were one and the same? Apart from the jewels?"

"No, he did not. You'll have to get off what Mama used to call your fat, lazy bahookie and find that out for yourself as well." Lavinia's use of the expression sounded just like their mother's. "Love to the professor. Or maybe I should say, love to Saint Orlando. I don't know how any one man could have enough patience to put up with you."

"Give Ralph the same message from me. And pass their uncle's very best love onto my two small pals."

"Small? Georgie's almost as big as his father. Shooting up and out of his clothes. It's been too long since you've seen him." Lavinia invested the rebuke with about a paragraph's worth of meaning.

"It's only been about a month! Are you stretching him on a rack?" Jonty tried to hide his guilt; his nieces and nephews were the only children he'd ever have an investment in and he could do better by them than a telephone call. "I'll see him in the school holidays. Better still, he could come up here for a few days, and I'll drag him down to the museum to annoy the fossils. Living and dead."

"Go and ring Collingwood, annoying boy." Lavinia put the phone down.

Once Jonty had stopped grinning, he obeyed his sister's instruction, although not before deciding that *three* dozen roses might be a better amount and making a mental note that the partnership of Stewart and Coppersmith now had another fully fledged extra investigator and priceless source of information. Fortunately, they had a home number for Collingwood, which was just as well, as he wasn't in the office and the rather snooty secretary would no doubt have refused to divulge the private number for the man himself.

As the telephone rang, Jonty hoped that it wouldn't prove to be one of those days when Collingwood went off to visit his lady friend. They needed to start making some real progress in this case, and all they had at present were lots of ideas and very few facts. Good grief, he was starting to sound like Orlando, even in his thoughts.

"Kensington 4312." The voice wasn't Collingwood's. Probably his butler, or whoever in the household was the official keeper of the telephone. "May I ask who is calling?"

"Jonty Stewart, from Cambridge. Can I talk to Mr. Collingwood, please?" Jonty tried to strike the right note of businesslike affability to impress the haughty manservant.

"Is he expecting you?" The tone sounded even snootier.

"No, but if you tell him it's in connection with a possible murder, he'll get the picture."

Collingwood not only got the picture, he picked up the phone within what seemed a matter of seconds. "Dr. Stewart! Sleuthing again?" He sounded affable, hearty, and hale. Maybe his mistress was keeping him young in mind, spirit, and body.

"I'm afraid so."

"Well, I'd be delighted to help you. Investigations ancient or modern?" It had only been the up-to-date cases Collingwood had been involved with; perhaps he had a yearning to get his hands dirty on one of their long-dormant puzzles, like the Woodville Ward.

"Ancient *and* modern. Fairly modern, anyway. We're investigating a death that happened last year, but one of our tracks has taken us into what may be a siding or may be the route to the heart of the solution. Sorry. Waxing lyrical there." Jonty was pleased Orlando couldn't hear him and upbraid him for beating around the bush. "What I mean is that you might be able to give us some answers, and we could clear up one of your mysteries at the same time. Helen Phillips."

"Ah, yes." Collingwood sounded as if he was easing himself into a chair; perhaps this call was going to take a long time. "You're aware of the unclaimed jewellery?"

"Oh, yes. And I might just have found the people who should have inherited them."

"Splendid! I'd rather they went to the proper legatees rather than eventually becoming the property of the Crown, however much I admire Their Majesties." Collingwood didn't sound as if his 'however much' was very much at all. "Any idea why these people didn't come forward when we put our appeals out?"

"Because they didn't know. I mean, they suspected they might have been related to Helen Phillips, although not under that name. And I'm not sure they knew about her legacy at all, as the jewellery belonging to the woman they *thought* she was had vanished." Jonty stopped, breathless. "That seems awfully muddled, I'm sorry."

"No, I've got the gist. It's no more complicated than some of the things I have to deal with, I assure you. You can explain the rest to me in your own good time. Are you certain these two ladies are one and the same?"

"Not one hundred percent certain, I have to admit. There was some dispute between the two principals about whether they should try and clarify the facts." Jonty laughed. "I'm off on a tangent again. Let me elucidate. Are you sitting comfortably?"

"I am. Proceed."

Jonty told the story in all its complexity. Collingwood listened without interruption or questioning and at the end simply said, "We've not a lot of time, have we? All these dates converging and these jewels possibly forming part of the inheritances. Hmm."

Jonty liked the *Hmm*. Orlando often used the sound when he was thinking his deepest.

"Is there any record in the family of this Alice Priestland's jewellery?"

"They're itemised as part of her last will and testament. I'll send you a copy of the list."

"Splendid. If we can match the two up, I think we'll have our answer. Proof enough even for your friend Dr. Coppersmith."

"*Professor* Coppersmith he is now, so we all have to watch our p's and q's." Jonty laughed. "Shall I send you my list today?"

"If you would. And to this address, please, so it gets my immediate and personal attention." Collingwood dictated an address that was surprising in its distinction, one of the swankiest roads in that part of Kensington, unless it had gone severely downhill from when Jonty used to go and play with a friend who lived around the corner. "I may even have an answer for you tomorrow, if you're lucky."

"Splendid. Now, there's just one more thing, if I can push my luck so far."

"Ye-es?" Collingwood managed to convey politeness, puzzlement, and wariness all in one short word.

"Your team has proved remarkably able in the past at what I'd term legwork. Any chance they could do some discreet digging among some doctors and undertakers?"

"I'm sure they can." The wary tone had magically transformed to enthusiasm. "Tell me more."

Jonty did, laying out all the items to be double-checked in the process of verifying there really hadn't been any obvious reason for anyone to suspect foul play. "I'm sure your men would manage that with much more discretion than we could. Although maybe discretion isn't what we need. It would be nice for our suspect to get wind of official type enquiries and maybe begin to panic." Clutching at straws, although it was beginning to feel like that was all they had.

"I should advise you now that may be all you have to hope for. If there were signs of mischief, the chances are they'd have been noted by someone and acted on at the time. Young wife. Old husband. Inheritance. All grist to the suspicion mill. Although . . ."

"Yes?" Jonty asked, eagerly.

"Rosalind was in the best position to hide any evidence. Left alone when the housekeeper went to phone the doctor. Which suggests, just possibly, that there were no signs that anyone else had murdered him. She'd have drawn those to the housekeeper's attention, surely? So as to protect herself?"

"Our very thoughts," Jonty lied, kicking himself that *they* hadn't thought of it first. "Thank you very much."

Jonty went to his study and prepared his letter, sticking on a stamp and shoving the thing in his pocket to be taken down to the postbox. A pleasant saunter, enough to get the gastric juices going in anticipation of dinner and to get some ideas about ways to wind up Orlando when he got home.

A nice-looking lad passed him, heading in the other direction—a sailor home on leave, by his appearance. There'd been lots of nice-looking lads in Jonty's platoon, back in France, not that he'd ever felt anything towards them and not that he would have done even if there hadn't been Orlando to consider. It didn't do to foul your own doorstep. Still, a man could look; pastries in a window were there to be admired even if you didn't want to indulge.

Matthew Ainslie was easy on the eye, as was his partner. Mitchell, the vicar, was good-looking too, as Bresnan must have been in his youth. The pair of them were spinsters' delights, as Mrs. Stewart had termed good-looking clergymen. Or maybe the widows' delight, now that Bresnan was getting on a bit.

Jonty stopped, thoughts going back to Mitchell again. Widows' delight . . . *Wife's* delight? Wife's friend. Wife's confessor? For all their joking, what if the vicar was keeping Rosalind in Downlea, dreams of being a postmistress notwithstanding? Maybe that's what his pained speech, concerning things he'd heard but couldn't repeat, was really about. Deflecting attention from their relationship, but not actually putting it onto anybody else?

And who was going to confirm just how friendly the vicar and the widow were?

When Orlando got home, he had no need to ask whether Jonty had made progress in the case; the serenely smug look plastered all over his face gave that away. It seemed unfair, when he'd been so bound up with business and had nothing to report, that mere fellows in Tudor literature should have been having fun. Still, he patiently listened, over dinner, to the news from the London members of the Madingley Road Irregulars, as Jonty tended to refer to anyone who helped them out.

"So there's more money to be claimed in the case. Or will be when the two ladies are proven to be one and the same. Will Rosalind be allowed to keep her share come the end of October? Thank you." Orlando smiled at Mrs. Ward's granddaughter, who was clearing the plates. "That gravy was as good as anything your grandmother can produce, but don't tell her I said so."

"I'll keep quiet, Professor." She smiled. "Ready for pudding?"

"Please. And coffee in about half an hour." Orlando watched her leave the room. "And to think I dreaded her coming in and catering twice a week."

"You've never been one for change, have you?" Jonty stretched. "As for Rosalind, I'm not sure she gets any of it. Peter predeceased the claiming of the jewels so I suspect they all go to Bresnan. Crikey." He slapped the table. "Orlando, do you think there's any chance he's playing us like fish? That this whole thing has been less about Rosalind Priestland than finding Alice Priestland's missing jewels? For which he seems to be the only heir?"

"Then why make such a tarradiddle about things? Why not just ask us to find the jewels in the first place?" Orlando said, shrugging.

"Because he likes to make things complicated. Look at all the business with the riddles and his grandmother. I don't trust a word he says at the moment."

"His behaviour has certainly been odd." The aroma of Eve's pudding suddenly wafted through the door, borne by a descendant of Eve herself. But even the wonderful aroma of sponge and apple couldn't distract the detective instinct. "He's clearly a clever man. Do you think he's trying to be more than clever?" Orlando pointed with his spoon. "Could he actually have killed his uncle and be trying to divert the suspicion to his aunt?"

"It seems a bit far-fetched, although I wouldn't discount anything where murder and murderers are concerned." Jonty postulated, helping himself to a big spoon of pudding, evidently to aid his mental processes. "If Billy's telling the truth, maybe Bresnan's the mystery man in the shrubbery. He could have slipped into the house and done Peter in."

"When Rosalind and Mrs. Hamilton were pursuing ladybirds? It's possible. Peter would have let him in if he'd come to the conservatory door, and he wouldn't have been on his guard." Orlando nodded. "Actually, I doubt he needed to let him in. It might have been unlocked. Even if Peter had woken from his sleep, the sight of Bresnan at his side wouldn't have raised any alarms." He waggled his spoon again. "And the same could be said for either Simon or the Reverend Mitchell."

Jonty nodded enthusiastically, sending crumbs flying everywhere. "I suspect it would be easy to get away with murder, or just about anything, if you're a man of the cloth. You can go anywhere, be let in, have people turn their backs on you, and . . ." He made a gesture like wringing a chicken's neck.

"Thank you. Very subtly put." Orlando scraped up the penultimate mouthful of pudding. "What would his motive be, though? Or Simon's?" He stopped, disappointed. "Or Bresnan's? He would know Peter's money was going to go to Rosalind."

"That latter fact would be ample motivation for Mitchell, especially if he thought he was going to get his ecclesiastical boots under her bed at some point in the future. And, surprisingly, I have a possible reason for Simon to do the deed." Jonty began to work his bowl, to get every last little morsel onto his spoon. "He didn't want to see his mother's grave desecrated. Maybe Peter was becoming insistent that they should find out, while they had time."

"That's a lot of supposition. And it all seems far-fetched." Not enough to interrupt Orlando polishing off his pudding. Just as well it wasn't one of Mrs. Ward's cooking nights; she'd have made them eat fruit salad. "If you're going to indulge, so will I. Let's say that Bresnan knew about his grandmother's jewels and wanted to increase his share of them by ensuring that their discovery was after Peter's death. My assumption is that Helen Phillips's will only specifies that her children inherit and not their heirs."

"But that makes even less sense. Bresnan wouldn't get anything." Jonty pushed away his empty bowl, almost sending his water glass flying.

"Not necessarily. Alice Priestland's death was in 1872, so Bresnan was already alive. She might have named him specifically. Collingwood could get hold of all these wills and verify the details." Orlando rose. "I can smell coffee. Shall we repair to the sitting room?"

"Only when I have the answer to this. There's another big hole in your argument. Bresnan doesn't know where the jewels are."

Orlando grinned. "Maybe he does and he didn't dare admit it earlier as it would throw suspicion on him. That's why he's asked us in. Because he knew we'd turn his inheritance up, and then he'd have nothing to do but act surprised."

"You're a genius." Jonty took his friend's arm and accompanied him to the sitting room. "Either that, or totally daft."

Chapter 11

Wednesday dawned bright and breezy, blowing away the cobwebs literally and figuratively. Jonty always felt particularly chipper in the morning, when the day was brimful of new opportunities; often something that had seemed an insurmountable problem the previous evening felt manageable at daybreak. Even Orlando appeared to be in better humour, having had some sort of vision in the night that clarified one of the knottier points in his lecture. Breakfast was pleasant, the cycle ride down to St. Bride's invigorating, and the note awaiting Jonty in his pigeonhole—without a wasp in sight—was the cherry on the cake. Mrs. Sheridan required his presence when convenient, as she had news.

The only annoyance was that it *wasn't* convenient until three o'clock in the afternoon, although at least that meant there might be tea on the table and the last of the Bakewell tarts on offer.

Jonty had hardly wiped his feet on the lodge's doormat before he began interrogating his hostess. "Progress?"

"Oh yes. What one of your heroes might call a palpable hit. Tea?" Ariadne led him into the drawing room.

"Only if you elucidate while we wait." Jonty settled into a nice cosy chair just the right distance from the nice cosy fire.

"Of course. Although we won't have long to wait. I spotted you coming and put the order in."

Jonty didn't ask if she'd been watching and waiting at the window.

"You know there was all that trouble when Owens left here?"

"But of course." How could any decent Bride's man not have it permanently in mind, that perpetual blot on the collegiate escutcheon? The opinion of the Senior Common Room was that

Dr. Arthur Owens should have been strangled at birth, although that might have been too good for him. Even the chaplain, that good, truly Christian man, would have liked to see Owens hoist on his own petard, if he had a particularly explosive one, or thrown in the Cam with his possibly plagiarised papers to weigh down his pockets. When he'd left the college, he was said to have purloined several volumes from the library, although no one could prove the fact.

"He's proved a slippery, slimy thing to pin down." Jonty frowned. "Nobody could get to the bottom of the plagiarism, either. Not even the students from whom he nicked the work. I'll say this for him, he's clever."

"Not too clever for me. Or my beloved Robert. He'd like to get those books back for the college." The arrival of the tea and what looked like some more of those delicious tarts improved matters even further.

"Would he? Then maybe he'll succeed where your dear and much lamented brother failed."

"My Lemuel was far too noble for his own good at times. The present master is much more . . . let us say, pragmatic."

Did "pragmatic" translate as "willing to play dirty"? Jonty hid his grin behind his teacup.

Ariadne seemed so distressed about the missing books that she waved her spoon, sending droplets of tea flying all over her royal blue dress. "One of those books contained possibly the earliest known reference to Marsh's *Sphenacodon*."

"As if there were any other *Sphenaco*-whatsit."

"Behave. Robert has never seen the original, so he has a personal interest in getting the book back."

"Why would Owens take a thing like that? I thought he studied philosophy when he was here?"

"I think he took anything he could get his grubby mitts on." Ariadne leaned forward, conspiratorially. "Which, I sincerely hope, will be his downfall."

"I like the sound of that. Nice word, downfall, when it's applied to your enemies. Could I beg you to elucidate?"

"No need to beg, I'll do it gladly." Ariadne thrust the plate of cakes at him. "Eat up while I prattle. Yesterday afternoon, I went back through the old library archives. No, I must give Dr. Strauss some credit." Strauss was St. Bride's librarian, and probably had been since Noah came in to borrow some papyri about boat building and animal husbandry. "We went through the archives together. He was distraught about the thefts, as he believes it was all his fault."

"He shouldn't be. He wasn't even here." That was all part of St. Bride's lore, how Strauss had been in a convalescent home, getting over tuberculosis.

"That's one of the reasons for the guilt. He's convinced none of this would have happened if he'd been present. Swears he wouldn't have allowed the unctuous microbe alone with even a sheet of paper, let alone the Prince's favourite."

"The who's what?" Jonty made a grab for his Bakewell, which had decided to leap out of his hand.

"That's almost exactly what I said to Strauss. Want another cake? That one's looking a bit bashed." Ariadne proffered the pastry-laden plate. "No? Well, perhaps better not to. Mrs. Ward would kill me if you didn't eat your dinner." She placed the plate well out of Jonty's reach, as he was clearly only a boy of seven and not to be trusted. "Apparently one of the volumes that mysteriously disappeared had belonged to Prince Albert Victor. He'd donated it to the library here during his short sojourn at the university."

"But he wasn't at Bride's. Why not donate the book to Trinity?" Even the last bits of sticky pastry couldn't enable Jonty's brain to make sense of that conundrum.

"Services rendered. Strauss can be remarkably discreet in what he actually says, but if you combine the words with inflexion of tone and the twinkle in his eye, you get quite a picture. The picture I got was of a young man who'd got himself into a distinct spot of bother and needed to be rescued." Ariadne grinned; she must have seen a few of those down the years.

"Ah." Jonty had heard the rumours, although he wasn't sure he believed them. His father had been taken to play with the royal family as a boy, so he was in the best position to comment on the gossip, and he hadn't been sure either. "The old chestnut?"

Ariadne nodded. "College servant this time. Pair of them got caught. The Prince of Wales, as he then was, got wind and was livid.

The then master of St. Bride's had the old man's ear and saved the day by covering the scandal up."

Jonty couldn't resist cutting in. "Poor old Eddy. Sorry, Albert. Family nickname for him."

"Your father's royal connections coming out again?" Ariadne grinned. "Carry on."

"Whatever we call him, I bet he was immensely grateful, although I didn't know about the scandal. Not this one, or the book."

"Shame we don't have your father still with us." Ariadne didn't need to say more. Mr. Stewart would have been able to fill in any missing details.

"I know. I miss the old boy more than ever." Jonty shared a wistful smile with his hostess. "Now, back to the point. Cleveland Street is a well-known scandal—at least well-known in the greater scheme of things. How did the master manage to maintain such secrecy about *this* business?"

"*This* business was relatively minor. Much easier to keep secret than an entire establishment devoted to, um . . ."

Jonty waited to see what euphemism Ariadne would come up with for renters.

"To unfortunate boys. Don't grin. Besides, Dr. Stewart," she said, deftly side stepping the issue, "you've been in the Senior Common Room often enough. You've seen them close ranks."

"I have. But I've no experience of whether the same applies at Trinity."

Ariadne began to laugh in her deep, almost-manly chuckle. "I'm glad your professor isn't here to see you make such a mess of what should be an obvious bit of deduction. The servant worked *here*. The prince wasn't daft enough to make a mess in his own backyard. The lad in question was found a position elsewhere."

"With an emolument to oil the wheels of his going and help keep his trap shut?"

"Something like that. Prince Albert showed his gratitude by donating a particular book, one that had come to him from his grandmother. One we're now pretty sure Owens purloined when he got his sticky fingers on the other volumes."

"Has nobody confronted the despicable hog about it?" Jonty could imagine King Edward himself coming along and thrashing the truth out of the man.

"Apparently my brother did, when he accosted him about the other missing stuff. Of course, the lying toerag denied ever having had his hands on the things. Said the timing was merely coincidental." Ariadne sniffed. "Lemuel never believed a word of it. He even considered asking you two to break into Owens's set of rooms, locate the missing volumes and snaffle them. I wouldn't let him, of course."

"Spoilsport. I'd have fancied that. And if Professor Coppersmith felt it beneath his dignity, Papa would have lent a hand. He was a true Christian." Jonty grinned, sparking off another bout of the giggles from his hostess.

"One day a thunderbolt will strike you, and I hope it doesn't spark onto either me or Professor Coppersmith."

"Perhaps you should wear rubber boots when you're in my vicinity." Jonty sighed. "Lovely idea, even if I suspect larceny wouldn't have worked. Owens will have the thing hidden away in a bank vault or the like."

"Now there I think you're wrong. Of everyone in St. Bride's, I'm the one to have known the man best." Ariadne coloured as she spoke. Another part of college lore was how he'd tried to take advantage of her in the Fellows' Garden and ended up being kicked for his pains. The exact location of the kick was only ever referred to as *between the two small forsythias*. "He wouldn't hide those books away. He'd have them somewhere he could take them out and gloat over them. They're probably in the lodge now, so if anyone from Bride's dared to set foot over his threshold—you'd have to be inoculated first, of course—the books would be almost mocking them."

"Like the faint star you can only see out of the side of your eye and never straight on. So are we to go and liberate them? An old-fashioned cutting-out expedition?"

"You *are* losing your touch, aren't you? I knew Dr. Coppersmith's lecture was affecting *his* mental acuity, but I didn't realise it had affected *yours*. Have some more tea." She wrested another cup from the pot. "They'd be no use to us then, unless we offered them back to Owens as payment for shutting up and not making a nuisance of himself. We need to threaten him with exposure of his theft."

They sat for a moment, thinking the thing through.

"Unfortunately, I see a huge flaw in your plan." Jonty laid down his teacup. This was beyond the restorative powers of even that magnificent brew. "If it's true that book could be used to smear Eddy, because of what's in it or the circumstances in which it was donated, and through him St. Bride's, seeing as the servant was one of ours, then it's a powerful weapon. If Eddy's brother could be dragged in as well, then it's dynamite." That petard Jonty had wished for; but how could they hoist Owens on it? "Isn't it more likely he'd use it to break some sort of scandal, raise the whole Cleveland Street thing again, link it to St. Bride's, then sit back and watch us try to limit the damage?"

"You're right. I'm sorry." They sat in silence, contemplating a teapot that had turned cold and cakes that looked like they'd turn stale just to add further spite to the situation.

Jonty was glad Orlando wasn't there to hear talk of Cleveland Street and male brothels. He hadn't even realised the places existed when first they'd met. His eyes had been opened enough to fully understand the implications of the Pemberton-Billing libel case, though. Who could have missed them? The notorious and probably mythical Black Book . . .

"Treason!"

Ariadne almost leaped from her chair as the word ricocheted through the room. "I beg your pardon?"

"Treason. Subversion." Jonty swallowed hard, memories of the war bubbling up. "Cowardice. We were on edge for years, looking for spies around every corner. At least, some people were. If only we could find some way of bringing a similar charge to Owens's door."

"What chance is there of that? He'd have been too old for the draft and I'm not aware anyone made noises that he should volunteer. I have nothing to offer on that front. At least, not yet." She suddenly made two fists and brought them together. "No, he won't defeat us. There has to be a way; we've just not found it yet." She narrowed her eyes. "Don't tell your Professor C. He'll only mope. Say that matters are moving forward, which they are."

That was going to prove almost as difficult as defeating Owens. "I'll try, but I find it almost impossible to lie to him. At least about important things."

"Oh, that's easily sorted. I'll write a note and you can just hand it over." She rose, moving across the room to an elegant Jacobean writing desk. "We must keep him calm or he'll be unable to concentrate on his lecture."

Jonty wondered whether the lecture would ever get written and, given Orlando's state of mind, whether it would concern anything more complex than adding tens and units.

The note was shared before dinner, but before Orlando could interrogate further, the telephone rang and, in a move so out of character it must have reflected a state of some agitation, he went to answer it. Jonty tried not to listen, given that there was nothing more frustrating than half a conversation, and buried his nose in the newspaper.

"Who was that?" he asked, when Orlando eventually returned.

"King George himself. Offering me a knighthood." Orlando grinned.

At least there seemed to be some better news, then. Even if Jonty doubted the veracity of the honour. "On what grounds, may I ask?"

"Preserving the British public from your idiocy by keeping you busy."

"Oh, ha-ha. King George would never be daft enough to do such a thing. He used to pat my head when I was in my perambulator." Jonty budged up to let Orlando sit on the sofa.

"I shall have to work that out and see if it's possible." He would, Jonty knew; it was just the sort of loose end Orlando could never let dangle. "It was Willshire, with the lowdown on Mitchell."

"He works quickly. Anything of use?"

"His record says he was a model soldier. Signed up to fight, even though he was already ordained. Unlike the ones who stayed at home and urged people on from their pulpits."

"Steady on there." Just as well this scene was taking place in their own home, where it didn't matter if Jonty gave his friend a hug. "What else did Willshire say?"

"Mitchell could have made a good career soldier, if he'd been inclined, but he developed fits. They think it was due to the strain out there . . ." Orlando stopped. This was delicate ground, and not just because of the references to France. Jonty had suffered fits because of the sexual assaults he'd endured at school. There'd been a time, after the war, when those fits had returned, but that was when he was still out on the continent; they hadn't come back to Cambridge with him, thank God.

"I understand. So Mitchell returned to his original profession. I wonder if the living of Downlea is in someone's gift? I can imagine some crusty old colonel getting very excited at the prospect of an incumbent who'd been out and seen some action."

"Action and glory too. Willshire says he wished there'd been more like him."

"How disappointing. I feel like I want to wash my brain out and start again." Jonty closed his eyes. "Back to the start, ignoring all handsome vicars, grocery boys, and any other possible suspects, including the mythical red kites. The one and only thing we were asked to ascertain. Do we have any evidence that Rosalind Priestland killed her husband?"

"Ah, now that's interesting."

Jonty thought he'd never heard a lovelier phrase. "I knew you were pleased about something."

"Willshire said the only bad thing he'd heard about Mitchell was a bit of mess gossip. He'd got himself entangled, when still at theological college, with a young widow. A rich young widow, which was said to be the main part of the attraction."

"Maybe he has a soft spot for them. Or they have for him."

"Wedding bells were predicted to ring, until he called it all off. Luckily, no promise was actually made." Orlando smiled; Jonty guessed he was trying to look knowing. "Rumour had it she was under suspicion of having hastened her husband's demise."

"Aha. Not the sort of evidence that would stand up in court, but at least it's a start. Likes money, likes widows. Seems to have a liking for women who've blotted their copybooks." Jonty counted off the points on his fingers. "Mind you, I guess that acquainting oneself with repentant sinners is a bit of an occupational hazard."

"Should get on well with you, then," Orlando murmured.

Jonty ignored the jibe, continuing to enumerate points. "Given his war record, he's probably pretty fearless and not averse to taking lives, despite the clerical collar." Thin stuff, very thin, but the thought of Mitchell aiding and abetting Rosalind Priestland made sense. "I wonder if . . ."

A strident bell sounded from the hallway. "There's the bloody telephone again. It's like Paddy's Market around here." Orlando had reverted to his normal attitude towards modern communication, probably because it had interrupted a potentially fruitful train of thought.

"Oh, hush. You moan about it, but it makes our life easier. What if we'd had to keep going to London every two minutes to find this stuff out? We couldn't investigate anything."

"Just get a move on and answer the wretched thing before whoever it is hangs up." Orlando slapped his bottom in passing. Jonty closed the door behind him, aware that Orlando had no scruples about listening in and, even worse, sometimes asking questions as the conversation proceeded.

Whoever it is was Collingwood, bouncing with joy, or that was the impression his voice gave.

"Bingo!"

"I beg your pardon?"

"Bingo, Dr. Stewart. We have a match. Your Alice Priestland's inventory of jewellery matches the list I have for Helen Phillips. I would be satisfied to pass the inheritance on to her heirs so long as they can prove that they're entitled to it."

"Splendid." It *was*. Just the sort of cat to set among the pigeons and see whose feathers got ruffled the most. "If you don't mind, though, I'd rather hang fire on it for a while."

"I understand entirely. There's a small fortune here. If you've got a murderer, those jewels might just spur them into action."

"Just what I thought." Please God, it wasn't the sort of action where he or Orlando would end up getting whacked over the head.

Chapter 12

Orlando wished he'd asked Jonty to employ the metal monster to take them to All Saints' Church. It would have cost him dearly in a ragging about his finally having seen the error of his ways, but it would have been infinitely preferable to this. They were standing at Mottisfont Station, looking hither and yon for a cab, Orlando wondering whether they'd end up walking miles in the pouring rain to where the Priestlands were interred. There didn't even seem to be a porter or stationmaster to tell him what was going on, just an endless stream of drips off the station canopy, beating a martial music.

"Autumn's a lovely season, but the rain at this time of year seems worse than at any other." Jonty peered out from under his umbrella. In theory he shouldn't have needed it, but in practice it was vital, given the percentage of drops that penetrated the cover and seemed to aim themselves directly at them.

"I think the weather's deliberately punishing us for playing truant."

"Dr. Sheridan said we could go. Can't count as truancy." Jonty grinned; apparently not even the rain could dampen his spirits.

"Gentlemen! I'm sorry, gentlemen!" A flustered, out-of-breath voice sounded behind them, accompanied by running footsteps.

They turned to see a porter, a chubby-faced man who was clearly not designed for breaking into a brisk walk, trotting up from the end of the platform.

"We've had such a commotion. A lady in the waiting room here, she's . . . she's . . ." The porter didn't seem to be able to find the words to explain what the lady had done.

Orlando wondered just how scandalous it could be. "She's what?"

"She's—" The porter didn't lower his voice; he just cut it off completely, mouthing, "Having a baby!" His face displayed some strange mixture of pride and utter horror. "The stationmaster's gone off in the cab to fetch the—" He resorted to mime again. "Midwife."

"Um, yes. Well, don't let us bother you further." Orlando had dreadful visions of the midwife not appearing and himself getting roped in to boiling kettles, or doing even worse things. He turned to Jonty, who seemed to find this amusing rather than horrifying. "Please refrain from volunteering your help."

"Are you a doctor, sir?" The porter's face became transfused with hope.

"Not of medicine, alas. I was only going to offer moral support."

Orlando grabbed his friend's arm. "We'll find ourselves transport. Is there a garage in the village?" The sight of houses not far away filled him with the hope that they'd locate a conveyance before they caught their death of wet and cold.

"No need for that, sir. The stationmaster will be back soon and you can use his cab. Maybe you'd like to wait in the . . . ah." The porter took off his cap and scratched his head. "Better still, come and wait in our office. It's warm there. And dry."

"Sounds like a foretaste of heaven." Jonty grabbed Orlando's arm this time. "No debate about whether it would be appropriate to be in a railway employee's office. The rain overrides anything else."

They'd hardly had more than a few minutes to sample the heat and aridness when the stationmaster returned, and they were able to get into the cab—a motorised one—escaping any contact with the midwife in the process.

"Why are there babies everywhere in this case?" Orlando looked out the cab window at the rain. There seemed to be little chance of it clearing soon; at least they could meet the verger in the church, assuming there wasn't a wedding to add to the fun. "I hope the verger is as hale and hearty as he makes out."

"In his letter, he said he still had a mind as sharp as a pin."

Orlando wasn't convinced. He'd met an old don at St. Thomas's once who'd allegedly had a brain as sharp as a pin despite being nearly a hundred, and he'd turned out to be convinced that he was living in

Nineveh at the time of the lion hunts. And had mistaken Orlando for his charioteer, which had been distinctly unpleasant. "I hope that proves true."

"And I hope the lady at the station doesn't have triplets." Jonty cleared some condensation from his window.

"Amen to that."

The sun had chased away the rain by the time they reached the church, and the churchyard sparkled with autumnal loveliness. Mr. Cottar, the verger, was there to greet them, his hair a mop of white, but his eyes twinkling as brightly as the drops on the leaves. In their experience, vergers were either dour or slightly mischievous; this one seemed to come into the latter category.

"You're the gentlemen from Cambridge who want to see the Priestlands' plot."

"That's us." Jonty initiated the round of handshaking. "And pick your brains about the family."

"You can pick as much as you like, but what you'll glean, I can't guarantee." Cottar jerked his thumb over his shoulder, turned on his heel, and led them to the far end of the graveyard at a spritely lick for a man who must have been in his eighties. "You're the Woodville Ward men? The ones in the newspaper?"

"The very same." Orlando nodded; maybe there was a chance that Cottar was as astute as they needed him to be. "I'm surprised you remember from so long ago."

"Bless me, it was only a month or so back. They did a series about unsolved mysteries and the men who'd sorted them out." He stopped to pick up a fallen branch. "I do have a good memory, though. I certainly remember old Mr. Priestland's funeral fifty years back. My uncle was still verger then, but I helped dig the grave."

"And you said you were there for his wife's interment too? That must be another thirty years earlier."

"Eighteen-forty, that was. I was six, and I'd just started in the choir. I recollect it clearer than I remember last week."

"Professor Coppersmith is already showing signs of going the same way," Jonty said, grinning.

"We all had cakes with pink icing afterwards, as that was her favourite colour. I'd never had those before, which is why I remember it so well." They stopped at a fine row of memorials. "Here they are."

The headstones were in good condition, the grave well kept, not just to the impressive standard of the rest of the graveyard, but above and beyond it. Simon had probably done his part when alive, but someone else clearly looked after the plots now.

"Who keeps the graves so well? I thought none of the Priestlands lived here anymore?" Jonty ran his fingers along the grey marble that marked where Simon and Peter lay.

"The wet nurse's son." Cottar nodded vigorously.

"Excuse me?"

"The twins' wet nurse." Cottar pulled up some ivy that had dared to appear beside old Andrew's headstone. "Their mother couldn't really care for them, she was so ill after the birth, so Mary Gurney shared the nursing of them. She'd not long before had her own baby and lost it, and she'd been nursing a friend's who'd struggled to cope, so between her and the dairy, there was milk enough."

"And is it an older or younger son who comes and tends here?" If it was older, they bred them long-lasting along the valley of the river Test.

"An adopted one, about the same age as the twins were. She got Bartholomew when Alice Priestland died and the twins were put in charge of a 'proper' nurse. I suppose she felt a bit lost, having thought so much of those boys, so when her cousin died in childbirth, Mary adopted her older babe." Cottar scratched his head. "Bartholomew. Bit of a fancy name to be giving anyone, but she always had fancy ideas. I don't suppose that was what he was christened. Good woman, though . . ."

"Where's Andrew buried?" Jonty's question shot through the air like a bullet. "The baby that died. Is he with his mother?"

Cottar shook his head. "I think he's here, even if there's no stone for him. My uncle asked old Mr. Priestland, and he said his wife had pleaded with him not to have the grave marked. She was a bit superstitious and felt that, as he'd not been baptised, he should be slipped in here on the quiet. As if God would let a little harmless babe slip through His arms."

Jonty pursed his lips and poked out the tip of his tongue, as he habitually did when thinking something through or seeking for the right words. "It's an odd question, but can you remember anything peculiar about Alice Priestland's funeral? Your uncle didn't mention any . . . suspicions he might have had?"

"Suspicions?" Cottar smiled knowingly. "I was wondering if that was why you came."

"We've been given a commission by the one remaining member of the family." Orlando looked down at the headstones; if only they could speak and solve all the mysteries of the Priestland family's tortuous history at once.

"Mr. Bresnan? He's been here a few times to pay his respects, especially when his uncle was still alive. The uncle wanted the grave opened, but I'm sure you know that."

"We do." Although it was nice to have it confirmed by someone who didn't appear to have any other motive in the case.

"It's an old rumour. My uncle helped with the burial and he was convinced something wasn't quite right." Cottar looked down at old Mr. Priestland's grave. "Had his suspicions that *you'd* been up to something. And maybe you had."

"Why didn't he speak out?" Orlando asked.

"Because suspicions isn't proof," Cottar said emphatically, if ungrammatically. "The old vicar didn't seem to think anything was amiss, so he didn't say any more."

"And what *did* he suspect?" Orlando waited for a tale of a coffin that didn't seem heavy enough, or a mystery surrounding the laying out.

"That the old man had made up the story about his wife not wanting the baby to have a grave. It had been his idea, just to spite her. He wasn't a very nice man."

"I think we've worked that out for ourselves." Jonty eyed the grave with what seemed like disapproval. "But there must have been more than that, surely?"

"Oh yes, sir. My uncle believed that Andrew murdered her."

Orlando was aware of his mouth working up and down but no sound coming out; even Jonty was lost for words, although Cottar didn't seem to have noticed.

"Here he is now."

"Here's who?" Orlando imagined a mouldering spirit arising from the grave.

"The nurse's son." Cottar waved to a tweed-clad, bearded figure coming along the path with a posy of flowers. "Hello, Bartholomew. These gentlemen were just talking about you."

"Nothing too scandalous, I hope?" There was a round of pleasantries and hat raising. "Would you be the men from Cambridge? Mr. Cottar mentioned you'd be coming."

"We are. And we're delighted to meet you." Jonty had recovered his wits first. "Would you mind us asking a few questions?"

"About the Priestlands? That would be fine."

Had everyone guessed their business, or had their expected visit been the main village topic of discussion the last few days? "Yes, about the Priestlands. Your mother was a great support to Alice Priestland, I believe? So much so that she left her last will and testament in your mother's safekeeping?"

"That's right, sir. Poor Mrs. Priestland didn't have anyone else to turn to, not with that brute of a husband of hers keeping an eye on her every move, so she confided in her nurse. Excuse me a moment." Bartholomew laid his posy on Alice's grave, clearing away the damp leaves that had been blown there.

Cottar winked and nodded at Orlando as if to say, *See, he was a brute. My uncle was probably right.*

"Do you think it possible that Andrew Priestland might have murdered his wife?" Jonty got the question in before anyone else could.

"That old chestnut?" Bartholomew got slowly up from his knees, wiping his hands together. "If she had been dead, then I might have believed it. He certainly gave her a belt. I was always told that was the straw that broke the camel's back."

"And at that point she left?" Orlando wasn't going to be denied the fun of the chase.

"So I believe." Bartholomew addressed the verger like an advocate in the county court. "New name, new life. It may not have been a very Christian act, Mr. Cottar, but I don't think I can blame her."

Cottar looked confused. There was evidently going to have to be a lot of explaining to him about the real Priestland family history, probably over a beer or two.

"You've been very helpful, gentlemen." Jonty turned on his brightest smile, even though they hadn't really learned anything new, apart from the fact Alice Priestland's running away had been well-concealed. "Can you tell us anything at all about Peter Priestland's wife, Rosalind?"

Cottar beamed. "Pretty little thing. Quite a sense of humour. Bartholomew, do you remember her gulling the old choirmaster here?"

"That old stick-in-the-mud? I do." Bartholomew scratched his head. "She told him a tale about how she'd always wanted to be a church organist, but her husband wouldn't let her as it would harden her soft little hands. She almost had the choirmaster in tears."

"Didn't Peter object?"

"Object? He was in on the joke. Thought it was marvellous to have found someone so bright and lively to lighten up his days." Cottar looked down at Simon Priestland's gravestone. "Peter thought the world of his wife, although Simon wasn't so keen. Simon and Rosalind never saw eye to eye, although I suppose that's to be expected. The twins were close, and then she came along and upset the apple cart. Is there anything else we can help you with?"

"I do have one question, although I'm not sure you can answer it," Orlando said, glancing from the verger to the nurse's adopted son and back again. "Did Simon Priestland resent his brother for not wanting to open his mother's grave and confirm what the rumours had said? Rumours that haven't become general knowledge, if what Mr. Cottar told us is anything to go by."

"They argued, but I wouldn't say he resented it. He loved his brother without reserve, even if Rosalind got short shrift. And he'd have loved his other brother just as much if he'd had the chance." Bartholomew ran his hand over Simon Priestland's headstone.

"Simon told you that?" Or had Bresnan been down here with his enquiries, muddying the waters? Orlando wasn't sure he trusted the man as far as he could throw him.

"He did."

"And did he tell you whether he went back to Downlea the day his brother died? Even though he'd only just come home from visiting Peter?" Jonty asked. "Someone told us he was seen."

The question seemed to rattle Bartholomew. "You've been misled somewhere, sir."

"Have we?" Had Mitchell been stringing them along, just as Jonty had suspected?

"Oh, yes. Simon didn't go *back* to Downlea, as he never left the place. He was there from when he went to visit his brother to when he brought him back here to be buried. If you don't believe me, ask his nephew."

"The Reverend Bresnan?" Orlando hoped there wouldn't be another nephew turning up to befuddle the case.

"The very same. They were both there together."

Both there? Blimey. Had he and Jonty been taken for an almighty ride? Orlando looked at his friend, who shook his head, clearly warning against saying anything else for the moment.

"You wouldn't happen to know," Jonty said, neatly side stepping the awkward fact they'd had cast in their path, "the order in which the triplets were born?"

"Oh, yes. Andrew came first," Cottar said.

So Bresnan had lied about that as well.

"Then came Simon and then Peter."

"Are you sure?" Jonty scratched his head.

"Positive." Cottar looked at Bartholomew, who nodded. "You seem surprised."

"We are. That's the third different version we've heard."

"Well, are we any the wiser?" Jonty had a mug of beer in hand, a cheese and tomato sandwich on his plate, and his confidant opposite him over the pub table. They'd taken the train to Romsey to enjoy one of the many hostelries, and the short journey had been worth it. The beer wasn't just a poem, as he'd sometimes described the brew at the Mitre; it was a full-blown sonnet. He suspected they'd both end up with their eyes shut on the way home, having to rely on the guard to tip them off at the right station.

"We know we've been led a merry dance—*again*—by our beloved client." Orlando looked daggers into his beer.

"I've come to the conclusion that anything Bresnan tells us has to be externally verified."

"Hmm." Orlando took a draught of ale. "*If* we were told the truth here today, then we've cleared up some loose ends. Simon was in Downlea and could have killed his brother on the grounds of resenting *him* for not wanting an exhumation and resenting *Rosalind* for getting between them."

"That sounds more like it. Get some more beer inside you to further oil your brain cells." Jonty took some of the prescribed remedy himself. "At least we're further forward about the fair Rosalind. Sounds like the story she spun your postmistress was part of the normal range of charades."

"Yes," Orlando said after a long, slow draught of beer. "She seems to enjoy having people on, and she's clearly good at it, even with people who've known her long enough to see through an act. No wonder you thought her sincere."

"If all that 'poor sad widow' stuff at Downlea was Rosalind trying her acting wiles on me, I might just go and thump her with the postmistress's . . . whatever it is postmistresses have that would create a nice bruise." Jonty made light work of half of his sandwich. "Why did she do it, *if* she did it?"

"Wind people up? I have no idea."

"Not the acting. I'd put that down to original sin." Jonty grinned. "Why murder her husband? Just for the money? If she'd waited a year or two longer, chances are it would have come to her."

"Maybe. If she was involved with Mitchell, he wouldn't have waited that long." Orlando eyed his sandwich, as if the motive might be written in the butter. "And who'd have credited he'd be right about Andrew being born first?"

"As if that makes any difference. They're all three of them dead." Jonty looked depressed, as if not even the beer could hearten him. "I wish there was somebody we could trust to ask whether Mitchell and Rosalind were more than friends. Neither of them would tell us, Mrs. Hamilton would close ranks, and Bresnan's too biased. Although if he'd heard rumours, he'd have reported them back, surely."

"Try another tack. I suppose we know who wrote those 'helpful' anonymous letters about the twins' mother."

"Do we?" Jonty almost dropped the remains of his sandwich in surprise, but at least he looked momentarily happier.

"I'd have thought it obvious," Orlando said in his usual Jonty-you-can-be-surprisingly-dim-even-for-an-English-Fellow voice. "Although I won't share my theory until you promise not to smack me for basing it upon very little evidence."

"As you're not one of my dunderheads, you can be excused from academic rigour. I dare say it doesn't apply much in your department, anyway. Ow!" Jonty rubbed his arm. "That lack of whacking should apply both ways. Right, what's your earth-shattering theory?"

"It was the nurse. She's the best candidate we have in terms of knowledge and motive, and I bet old Andrew got rid of her when the boys were a year old because she knew too much." Orlando waved his ham roll dramatically. "I bet she'd have wanted the twins to get their birthright."

"I think you could be spot on, my genius boy. Like I said, if only we could see those letters and know whether they were as hurtful as Mitchell, by which we probably mean Rosalind, made out."

"So what now?"

"Back to Downlea." Jonty leaned closer. "I want to talk to Mrs. Hamilton."

"Why?"

"Isn't it obvious? To see what truth lies in the story about the man in the garden. I wouldn't trust Rosalind to give us a fair answer or us to be able to detect if she was lying. So we have to follow up with the housekeeper or young Billy. Maybe we can ask them about the vicar while we're at it."

"You think if there was a man there, it was Simon?" Orlando rubbed his temples. "And they're trying to cast suspicion onto him?"

"I do. At least the latter part. I wouldn't be surprised if the man was Bresnan himself. I'm not discounting him, Professor Coppersmith." The beer might not have been clearing Jonty's mind, but it was making him bullish. "I don't think we can discount any set of circumstances."

Chapter 13

In previous years, no journey through London would have been undertaken without a stopover—even if it were only for tea and cakes—at the Stewarts' house. But Clarence had that now and, while Jonty loved his elder brother, the two didn't share the same easy affection as Jonty'd had with his parents. And, of course, Clarence still thought that the baby of the family was merely a confirmed bachelor who shared a house with Orlando because nobody else would put up with either of them.

Now familial visits to the capital centred on Lavinia's household, which brought the added advantage of being able to join in Georgie's games and so relive the best parts of Jonty's childhood. As Orlando had suffered a pretty miserable upbringing, he was never averse to taking part and usually ended up being the happiest of all present.

On Friday late afternoon and evening, en route from Romsey to Downlea, Jonty was able to fulfil his avuncular duty. Georgie was in seventh heaven at having his two favourite uncles to indulge his every whim, and Orlando was once more declared king of all the board games. And Lavinia got the three dozen roses that she'd been promised, delivered to her door.

As a way of refreshing their mental powers, it was without compare. As the train headed north into Cambridgeshire the next morning, Jonty and Orlando felt ready to tackle anything the mystery could throw at them. In Jonty's case, it was Mrs. Hamilton, and in Orlando's, the grocer's lad, Billy.

Jonty made his way to Thorpe House by foot, the half hour's walk proving an excellent way of burning off at least part of the wonderful dinner Lavinia had provided the night before. He'd reached the gate, aiming to sidle up to the servants' entrance if possible and beard Mrs. H. in her own den, when a car sped past him and up the drive. He'd often wondered about guardian angels—having plenty of circumstantial evidence of their existence, given the number of times events had worked precisely in his favour—and suspected they were at it again.

He retreated into a clump of bushes, where he could observe the house through a convenient gap in the foliage. Sudden memories of doing exactly the same thing while observing a skirmish from a scrawny stand of trees in France were quickly dismissed; this was no time for a dose of the collywobbles. Luckily, he only needed glasses for reading. Unlike his "other half," he still had excellent distance vision, so he could clearly make out the lady of the house leaving her front door and entering the vehicle.

He waited, nestled in the bushes like a poacher waiting to spring his trap, until Rosalind's car was out of the gate. Feeling like a naughty child only added to the fun as he slipped along the wall and darted in and up the drive. Jonty was halfway to his destination when the sound of wheels on gravel and a female voice brought him to a halt.

"Dr. Stewart!"

A spike of horror shot up his spine. He thought he'd timed it to perfection, but Rosalind must have doubled back on herself—although whether at the sight of him or simply because she'd forgotten something, who knew?

"Ah, Mrs. Priestland." He beamed, took off his hat, and bowed, as the car pulled up alongside him. "So glad I caught you," he lied, with what he hoped was great aplomb.

"And I'm glad you've returned, Dr. Stewart. Might I be so bold as to ask if you're acting in your official capacity?" Rosalind leaned slightly out of the window.

"Official capacity? As Kildare fellow in Tudor literature?" Jonty knew damn well what she meant, but he needed to buy himself some thinking time.

"Perhaps I should rephrase my question. Your *unofficial* capacity. As an amateur investigator." She smiled, although her eyes were bright and cold.

"I'll be frank with you." Jonty hoped his father wasn't looking down from heaven, flapping his wings in horror at his youngest son's keenness to keep conversation flowing with the odd little lie here and there. And if he *was* looking down, Jonty hoped he'd understand that it was in the cause of getting at the truth. "When I first visited my purpose was twofold, to pay my respects and to make some preliminary enquiries regarding a case we'd been asked to look into. It concerns an old friend of ours, and trying to track down the beneficiaries for a peculiarly complicated inheritance. I hope you'll forgive me for not being entirely candid at the time, but I had to defer to the confidentiality I was entrusted with."

Jonty wasn't sure if his smile or the suggestion of inheritance had worked the trick, but something had softened Rosalind's attitude. If she'd known about Alice Priestland's jewels, then maybe she was putting two and two together. She got out of the car and ushered him away from the driver's earshot. "I accept your apology. I understand that you must have delicate cases to deal with and I'd be delighted to help you if I can. Can you enlighten me about this legacy?"

"I'm afraid not. I'm very grateful for the help you gave last time, though. Very valuable."

"Then I'm a bit confused. Why have you returned if it isn't to find out more concerning your case?"

Time to extemporise, and maybe flush some prey out of cover while he was at it. "I don't need to investigate any further, so I came to impart some news. While I can't give any details, I can confirm that your husband was almost certainly one of these legatees."

"Really?" Rosalind looked thoughtful. She came closer, smiled, and laid her gloved hand on Jonty's arm. "And you're sure you can't tell me any more about Peter's mysterious benefactor?"

"I could, but I'm not sure I'm allowed to." Jonty decided to give the impression she'd lured him into indiscretion. "All I'll say is that it's a close female relative."

"His mother! I knew they'd run those jewels to earth one day." Rosalind almost bounced.

Jonty beamed back at her. "It's a great day for the family."

"Such a shame Peter couldn't have been here to see them." She fished in her pocket for a handkerchief. "I'll have to put them on display, as another reminder of him. As if I needed more." She dabbed her eyes, but Jonty was no longer taken in by the playacting.

"I'm afraid that, as I understand it—and I may have got it wrong—you wouldn't be eligible to inherit, owing to the timing." Jonty was sure he'd got that right, even though the workings of the law were as befuddling to him as Boolean algebra. If Peter had died before the inheritance was claimed, then he couldn't pass it on to his widow.

"Really?" The tears, if there had been any, soon disappeared. "We'll have to see what the courts say about that!" Rosalind made as if to return to her cab, then turned back. "Maybe they'll have to think again when I tell them Mr. Bresnan was here the day my Peter died. I call that highly suspicious."

And having delivered a parting shot that left Jonty both speechless and with his brain about to implode, she got into the car and left.

He watched her go, momentarily so stunned he couldn't remember what he'd actually come to Thorpe House for. When he'd eventually knocked his brain back into shape, he strode up the drive once more, hoping that the housekeeper would be an easier prospect.

Mrs. Hamilton answered the door, saw who was calling, and looked down her nose; she was a tall woman and could give Jonty a good three inches, towering over him like the governess he'd imagined her as the first time they'd met. "I'm afraid you've just missed Mrs. Priestland."

"I was able to catch her on the drive, thank you," Jonty said, guessing that Mrs. Hamilton had probably witnessed the whole scene from the house. "We had family business to discuss."

"I'm not sure I can help you with anything like that." The housekeeper looked defiant, as if daring Jonty to ask her something impertinent so she could beat him with a broom.

"I appreciate that. But I hope you'd help me clarify something about the day Peter Priestland died." He lowered his voice. "It may be germane to an inheritance case."

Mrs. Hamilton looked puzzled. "German?"

"Ger*mane*."

"You'd better come in." She let Jonty through the door but no further than the hall. "I suppose you want me to confirm that his nephew was lurking about that day? I'm afraid I can't, as I didn't see him."

"Oh." Jonty had expected chapter and verse about witnessing the man acting suspiciously.

"I saw Simon, though, despite the fact he told everyone he didn't return here until he'd heard of Peter's death."

"And was that why you asked Billy to tell me about the man in the garden?"

"Yes. Although I suppose that might have been Mr. Bresnan, as everyone says he was here too."

Everyone? Was there some gossiping hotline between here and Hampshire, or did "everyone" just mean Mitchell and Rosalind herself? "Could either or both of them have come to see Peter? I mean, could they actually have spoken to him, when you were busy going through the house?"

"Not through the front door, as it was on the chain. The outside door to the conservatory was closed, although the windows were open. It was the only part of the house didn't need treating. But all doors throughout the house were shut. All part of the treatment to get rid of those wretched insects." She sniffed.

"The door was closed? Was it locked?"

Mrs. Hamilton stopped to think. "I don't know. It's usually locked because of the orchids, as we don't want anyone to steal them, although it might have been left unlocked because of the general hoo-ha that was going on."

Jonty remembered what he'd been told regarding the hoo-ha about the wasps in St. Bride's porters' lodge and could believe it. Maybe someone had seen it as an ideal time to cause chaos. But which someone? "Thank you. I'd appreciate your confidentiality in this matter. It's a very delicate case."

"You'll have it. I wouldn't want my mistress to be deprived of anything she's due. She could do with some happiness." Clearly the matter of Alice Priestland's jewels was another matter of Downlea gossip.

"She must miss her husband greatly." Jonty had become certain Mrs. Hamilton spoke in good faith. Unless, of course, he'd lost all ability to sniff out a lie. "You can tell her from me she's too young to mourn him forever."

"That's just what I've told her already, sir. And the vicar." Mrs. Hamilton's face softened in a smile at the mention of Mitchell. "He says it would be selfish of her not to consider marrying again."

"Sensible advice." Especially sensible on Mitchell's part if he was in the frame. "Mrs. Priestland's not taking it, I assume?"

"She says she'll reconsider come Christmas. That's a decent amount of time."

And by then all the hullabaloo about the wills would be cleared up. "That sounds reasonable. She'll have plenty of suitors, I'd warrant?"

"Bless you, sir, she won't have a man in the house, except on business. Except the vicar. On parish business," Mrs. Hamilton clarified, with a tone of voice implying he didn't quite count as a man.

"Most respectable." Jonty turned his hat in his hands but couldn't think of anything else to ask that wouldn't risk him being hit with one of the umbrellas in the hallstand. Maybe Orlando would be able to get some more tittle-tattle straight from the horse's mouth.

Orlando eyed the vicarage with suspicion. He wasn't happy in the vicinity of a church at the best of times, and even the thought of getting his detecting teeth stuck in wasn't a great incentive. He wasn't convinced he'd get much from Mitchell, although he had his list of questions. Had Mitchell seen either Simon or Bresnan on the day Peter died? Had *he* visited Thorpe House on that same day? Why did he think someone had lied to him about whether Peter or Simon was the eldest? Did he have so much of a liking for rich widows that he went around creating more? What did any of it matter?

It felt like they were missing something terribly obvious—maybe more than one thing—and nothing Mitchell was likely to tell them, short of a confession, would help.

In any event, Orlando only got a fraction of an answer. As he came up the path to the vicarage, somebody in a clerical collar, who had to be Mitchell given his resemblance to Jonty's description, came scurrying out of the door.

"Hello, can I help?" Mitchell asked, slowing down but not stopping. "If so, you'll have to walk with me. Got an urgent visit to make."

Orlando fell into step and got straight down to business. "I wanted to talk about Peter Priestland. We've been asked to clarify the circumstances of his death, as it's relevant to an inheritance."

"Dr. Coppersmith, is it? I had your colleague here recently and wondered when you'd follow."

Curse *The Times* and the notoriety those articles about them had brought.

"I'm here now. Anything you can tell us to clarify events that day would be useful." Orlando quickened his pace to keep up.

"As I told your colleague, there's little I can offer. Talk to Billy Waller, the grocer's lad. He saw things that day." Mitchell kept his eyes fixed straight ahead, down the road.

"Billy's on my list. But he isn't an intimate of the household, is he?"

Mitchell stopped, and turned on his heels. "What do you mean by that?"

"He's a delivery boy, not a friend of the mistress," Orlando said, innocently, fascinated at the reaction his choice of words had provoked. "I was hoping you might have some special insight you could share."

Mitchell worked his mouth up and down, maybe debating giving Orlando a mouthful. In the end he said, "Dr. Coppersmith, I don't need to tell you that I am bound by my vocation. There are things I can say and things I can't. Talk to Billy. I have to go." He span on his heels again and set off at a pace.

Orlando watched him go, then headed for Mr. Houseman's cottage, more convinced than ever that the insistence they talk to Billy was deflecting attention from the vicar's relationship with Mrs. Priestland.

He approached the killer of the ladybirds with a similar story to the one Jonty was using. They needed a consistent front, given the Downlea gossip network.

Houseman, helping to clarify the time of Priestland's death, confirmed that he and Billy had left Thorpe House before lunchtime, and that they'd both seen someone lurking around the shrubbery at the bottom of the garden around the time they were finishing off the job.

"And Peter Priestland was alive when you left?" Orlando wasn't sure how the answer to that would help, apart from neatening things up.

"Alive and well, if a bit wheezy," Houseman replied, nodding. "Up to making jokes, as well. He was teasing Billy that he'd seen a red kite over the house earlier that day. Poor Billy thinks every honey buzzard or the like he sees must be a red kite."

Orlando still couldn't hear mention of honey buzzards without shivering, but he smiled bravely. "If he was so full of beans, did his death surprise you?"

"Lor', no." Houseman shook his head. "Poor Mr. Priestland had barely got over the flu. He looked and sounded like a breath of wind would blow him over."

Orlando came out of the grocer's shop with half a pound of Peace Babies in lieu of answers. He'd never thought anything could replace liquorice allsorts in his affections, but these little blighters had. Just as well, seeing as he'd discovered that Billy was out on deliveries, so his original purpose for visiting the grocer had gone west. He popped one in his mouth and wondered how he was going to explain his lack of success to Jonty. He was on his third one (and feeling like he could do with scoffing the lot) when investigational deliverance appeared in the form of a shop boy on a bicycle. This had to be Billy, given the word picture Jonty had painted.

"Billy!" Orlando waved and smiled, standing to one side as the bicycle was brought to a stop next to him.

"Yes, sir?" Billy returned the smile, full of trust.

Orlando held out his hand. "My name's Doct . . . Professor Coppersmith." That still wouldn't stick in his mind. Maybe when the dreaded inaugural lecture was behind him, the title would flow more easily from his tongue.

"The detective?"

Orlando nearly dropped his bag of sweets. "Yes. How—"

"I thought Mrs. Hamilton was having me on. She said that officer I'd met up by Thorpe House, the one who'd seen the red kite same as I did, wasn't just a soldier and a teacher but helped the police as well." Billy puffed his chest up. "I'd love to help the police."

"That's a very patriotic attitude to take," Orlando replied, overcome with emotion. He'd had lads like that in his platoon. Many of them still lay under a French sky.

"Thank you. She told me to remember your name, which wasn't hard, it being such an odd one, in case you came to Downlea. You'll be wanting to hear about the man I saw in the bushes, I guess."

"If you can give me an accurate account of him, then yes."

"He looked just like Mr. Priestland."

Orlando wondered whether Billy had been primed to say just that, but the lad didn't seem as if he was repeating lines he'd been taught. Maybe he'd been persuaded he'd seen someone looking like Peter Priestland, just as he'd been persuaded he'd seen one of those wretched red kites. "How extraordinary. You must have got a good look at him, then."

"I did," Billy replied, seeming to swell with pride. "My mother always says I've got the best eyes in the family."

"Glad to hear it." So the problem lay in his perceptions rather than his eyesight? "Was he old or young?"

Billy considered for a moment. "Older than me but younger than Mr. Priestland."

Bresnan, then, rather than Simon? Assuming, Orlando reminded himself, that the man was more real than the red kite had been. "Thank you for clearing that up. Did you see anyone else around that day? Someone who shouldn't have been there?"

"No. I'd have remembered. I had to get away to do my deliveries. I had a lot to catch up on and I wasn't supposed to hang around skiving." Billy fiddled with his handlebars. "Is that all, sir?"

"Pretty well." Orlando smiled. "What do you think of the vicar?"

"Mr. Mitchell's a nice man, but he's not as much fun as Mr. Evans. He warned me about the red kites." Billy had looked puzzled, but seemed to relax as he got onto his favourite topic.

Orlando ploughed on, ignoring matters ornithological. "I suppose he's a great comfort to the ladies at Thorpe House?"

"I think so. My mother says he's dipping his bucket in the well, there. I didn't know they had a well, but I guess he's helping the ladies out."

Dipping his bucket in the well? Orlando bet Mitchell hadn't intended *that* to come out when he'd insisted they talk to Billy. But as the lad seemed to believe what he'd said, Orlando didn't seek to disabuse him. "It sounds like it."

Billy nodded, and worked the handlebars of his bike again. "Would you tell your friend I said hello? He must have been a real hero with a scar like that!"

"He was. He is. He always will be to me." That last bit was out before Orlando realised he'd given voice to his thoughts, but Billy hadn't seemed to notice how much emotion had been loaded into the phrase.

"Did you serve out there too?"

"I did." But Orlando wasn't going to go around displaying his scar. Not to anyone but Jonty.

Billy looked appropriately concerned. "I don't understand why some folk have to do it, cover the face of a dead body I mean, but I suppose they feel it's right. I've only seen it the once, but you must have seen loads of dead men. Did they cover the faces of the dead in France? It must have been a heap of work."

Was this another obsession, along with the red kites? Something to do with the gruesome tales the parish assistant had told?

"We . . . we couldn't always manage to do everything we wanted for them. Not the services they might have received at home." Orlando took a deep breath. He needed a pint and a bit of a think. "I'll let you get away to your lunch. Thank you."

"You look like you could do with a beer." Jonty was already drawing on a pint, in the garden of the pub they'd visited last time. "You sit down and I'll get one in. Enjoy what's left of this year's nice weather."

Orlando arranged himself to best benefit from the sunshine. Out of the breeze, it felt almost like a summer's day. So much so that he'd almost succumbed to a touch of great tiredness by the time Jonty returned bearing beer and rolls.

"Sorry it took so long. Dolly's niece has had her babies and yes, it was twins."

"Whose niece?" Orlando roused his brains. "Oh, yes. Dolly. The landlord's wife. What did they call them?"

"Jonty and Orlando, of course." Jonty steadied the glass in his friend's hand. "Only joking. Faith and Charity. Nice touch, seeing as the world always needs more of both."

"The world could do with a bit of clarity, at present." Orlando sipped his beer. "Is there a possibility that Ian Bresnan has been leading us on an even merrier dance than we'd considered?" He gave an account of his morning's discoveries.

"In terms of Billy? He may have been geared up to talking to us, but he strikes me as fundamentally honest. Or as honest as he can be. He tells us what he *believes* to be true."

"I agree. Unless he's one of the best actors it's been my privilege to see. There were far too many nuances about what he said to me, and what he said to the housekeeper. I know we've been taken in before by what seems to be innocence."

Jonty shivered. "That first case. Those other cases."

"I should say we've encountered the most unlikely of murderers at times." Orlando remembered them well.

"Well, if the last few years have done anything, they've knocked any vestiges of naïveté from me. The ladies of Thorpe House knew he'd seen someone, knew he could be trotted out as a witness independent of the household, knew he could be beguiled into thinking and saying it was a particular person, and pointed him in our direction. QED." Jonty grinned and took a bite from his roll.

"Don't be so hasty with your so-called proof. It's time we talked this through. Suspect number one." Orlando held up a solitary finger, just in case Jonty had forgotten what the number was. "Bresnan."

"Why's Bresnan suspect number one?"

"Cast in order of appearance. I'd have thought you'd appreciate that."

"I do. In that case, suspect number two is Rosalind, and three—"

"Can we not concentrate on one at a time?" Sometimes all Orlando's efforts to keep Jonty on one part of a discussion rather than fifteen at once came to nought. If it weren't for blind adoration of the man, he'd have given up by now. "This application of an entirely logical style may be alien to you dilettantes, but it's meat and drink to a scientific mind. You might learn something."

"I'm not sure that's anything I'd *like* to learn, thank you, but I'll undergo the experiment. Just for you." Either the sunshine or the beer was working its mellowing magic.

"Bresnan would stand to gain if he killed Peter, then fobbed the murder off on Rosalind. Assuming he knew about the convoluted wills beforehand. He could have copped the lot, Grandmother Priestland's jewels and all. He best matches the man Billy says he saw." Orlando tried to keep his mind focussed as the sun lit up his friend's hair; silver threads now among the gold, but no less fine.

"I suppose he does. Then he conveniently gets us in to prove Rosalind the killer? And locate those jewels at the same time?" Jonty smiled, which was even more distracting. "Do you honestly believe he thinks we're so thick we wouldn't consider him? In that case, he's either very clever—too clever for us, somehow—or very stupid, and I can't believe either."

"And what about the fact he's misled us consistently?"

"That I'll concede, but lying and murder are worlds apart."

Orlando laughed. "Very true. Think of the number of times you've wound me up with some cock-and-bull story that I've believed, only to find it *was* all cock-and-bull."

"And you call this logical thinking?" Jonty swigged back the remains of his beer. "I hope your inaugural lecture makes more sense, or people will start throwing rotten tomatoes or slide rules or whatever else august mathematicians keep under their gowns."

"Please don't say that, even in jest," Orlando said, feeling decidedly queasy.

"Then bypass your system and go onto *my* suspect number two: Uncle Simon." Jonty patted his lover's arm, briefly but with a wealth of affection. "He was said to be in the area, and could be the mysterious man if he looked better preserved than his brother. We know he, or anyone, could have got into the house—"

"Do we?"

"Oh, blimey. I've not brought you up-to-date." Jonty rectified his error, relating all his adventures up at Thorpe House.

"That open conservatory door is just annoying. A locked door would have implied that Peter knew his killer and let him in. Which might have brought us to suspect three, if we're going out of order. The vicar. Unlike you, I have no qualms about doubting a man of the cloth. Anyway, the Reverend Mitchell seems a bit too good to be true. Or too true to be good, or something."

"What are you talking about?" Jonty looked up from the empty glass he'd been contemplating.

"I'm taking after you, I suspect. Spouting a lot of nonsense. Please God, I don't do *that* as well when I'm giving my lecture." Orlando groaned. "Do you think another beer would help our brains?"

"Make it a half, or else I'll be nodding off." Jonty held out his glass. "And if there's any more of those rolls, kidnap them."

Orlando returned from topping up their troughs and nosebags to find his partner nodding over the table. "Are you having a crafty sleep?"

Jonty's eyes flew open. "No just a crafty think."

"Hmm," Orlando snorted, putting the beer and rolls on the table. Maybe witnesses could lie to him, but he could see through Jonty. "And what conclusions did you come to, if any?"

"That our next suspect, Rosalind Priestland, is a loose cannon, and I'd hate to be within her firing range."

Orlando was impressed. That sounded good, especially for what he suspected was spur of the moment.

Pulling the new glass closer, Jonty seemed to warm to his theme. "And she enjoys acting. We know that now. She's playing the part of the grieving widow while she tries to get her hands on her mother-in-law's jewels."

"But we have no proof, Dr. Stewart. Not one bit of it." Orlando looked bleakly into his beer. "Not of murder, nor of intent to profit by Peter's death. We might as well admit defeat. Have you ever known a case to have so little to offer us?"

"We must be missing something awfully obvious. It's such a shame young Billy doesn't seem to hold the key."

"He's too busy mistaking buzzards for red kites and wondering how many dead soldiers had their faces covered." Orlando shuddered, sudden memories bubbling up of places and times he'd rather forget.

"Were these *honey* buzzards, perchance?" Jonty grinned. "No, you don't need to answer. I can tell. Poor Billy. He said the flu hit his family badly. If they always covered the faces of their dearly departed, then it was a sight he'd have seen more often than was good for him. No wonder he's obsessive about it."

"He said he'd only seen it happen once, so I'm not sure where that bee came into his bonnet." Orlando sighed. Even the beer wasn't helping his mood. "I just wish we could prove Mrs. Hamilton was poorly sighted and somehow missed someone entering the house and smothering her master."

Jonty groaned. "Or Rosalind Priestland slipping from her side long enough to commit murder."

Chapter 14

Orlando's back hurt. His throat hurt. His feet hurt. He had a suspicion that it would be easier to list the parts of him that *didn't* hurt, although that would probably just amount to his eyebrows. Bad timing, to have arranged for guests to come to Forsythia Cottage so hard on the heels of his inaugural lecture, but what with investigating both plagiarism and inheritances, their diaries had become a little overloaded.

The lecture had been hard work, as all his aches and pains attested, but it was done and by all accounts, it had been a rip-roaring success. The rounds of back slapping and hand shaking he'd had to undergo afterward had added to his aches, but he'd felt too elated, and relieved, to worry about that.

"Well done, you." Lavinia, all smiles, had eschewed back slapping in favour of a hearty kiss.

"Was the lecture acceptable?" Still the nagging doubts. At least Lavinia would tell the truth.

"It was magnificent. I didn't really understand every single word of it, so I'll have to go home and consult the notes I've taken in order to clarify one or two points . . . Do behave, pest." The last part was aimed at Jonty, who'd appeared at her side and started making faces at her explanation. "That lecture was on the whole far better than I'd expected from a talk about numbers. Far better, even, than those roses you gave me."

Orlando wasn't sure he believed that, but he'd smiled, going along with whatever subterfuge was going on. And by the time everyone, including Jonty, had told him they'd enjoyed his talk, he'd begun to believe it.

The state of his body wasn't helped by dinner at the University Arms, after which he had barely twelve hours to lick himself into shape before he had to preside over *another* meal.

Jonty didn't seem bothered. Even as the years passed, that little toad still appeared to have the capacity to feast every day of the week, if need be. It was quite sickening at times. However, it was always a pleasure to have the Sheridans at their table, and Matthew Ainslie had proved to be a good friend on the occasions they'd needed one. Orlando would just have to bite the bullet and play the part of host with graciousness and a smile or two.

Whether it was due to a good dose of Epsom salts, willpower, or sheer schoolboy-like excitement, once the time came round for the much-vaunted and highly anticipated dinner, Orlando felt really quite enthusiastic despite his lingering aches. He leapt out of his chair at the sight of a carriage outside and insisted he be allowed to open the door to the first of their guests.

Dr. and Mrs. Sheridan were waiting on the step, beautifully turned out in black dinner suit and elegant purple dress. They were both in their sixties, but their sprightliness of gait and mind belied the fact. Seen behatted (to cover the greying locks) and from behind, linked arm in arm and strolling along the Backs, they might have been taken for a married couple just into their thirties, or even a very well-dressed butler out on his afternoon off with some equally respectable housekeeper.

And if, when she turned, Ariadne Sheridan's face didn't quite live up to her figure, just like Marian in *The Woman in White*—one of Orlando's favourite books—her intelligence and resourcefulness shone through and enhanced her looks. When animated, and discussing planarian worms, she was almost beautiful.

"How wonderful, to have the door opened by a real live professor!" Ariadne's smile lit up the October evening.

"I shall never tire of the title." Orlando stepped back to let them in.

"Neither will St. Bride's." Robert Sheridan's appearance reminded Orlando of Jonty's late, lamented father. He must have been stunning in his youth and remained handsome now; even Mrs. Ward's granddaughter gave him an appraising look as she took his hat and coat. The distant but approaching squeak of a bicycle wheel that needed oiling announced the imminent arrival of another guest.

"Dr. Panesar." Orlando nodded. "It has to be."

"I'd concur. Only one bike in the city makes that particular noise." Dr. Sheridan cocked his head to one side. "And about twenty yards away, I'd estimate."

"Robert!" Ariadne tapped her husband's arm. "He's only pretending he can calculate the distance from the noise. We passed Dr. P. on the road so it's easy enough to guess. See?" she said, as the man in question pulled up by the gate.

"It's going to be quite a party." Jonty appeared at the door to usher everyone in. Coats were taken, sherries were handed out, and small talk was made until the sound of a motor cab drawing up outside and deep masculine voices emerging from it stung Jonty into action again.

"It's like Piccadilly Circus in here!" he said, managing to get out of the room first to let in their next guests. All that could be heard from the sitting room was a lot of loud insults, back slapping, and a deep, pleasant American voice asking where the professor was and if he would be allowed to kiss the hem of his academic gown.

"Mrs. Sheridan!" Matthew Ainslie came through the door and greeted her with a huge smile and a kiss, just stopping himself short of actually kissing her cheek and settling for her hand instead.

"Oh, now what's all this? You should call me Ariadne. All of you, please." She stood up on tiptoes to kiss Matthew's cheek, looked as if she'd do the same for Jonty, and then evidently remembered she should be behaving herself. Dr. Sheridan shook hands with the new arrivals, which was a great relief to Orlando, who wasn't sure he wanted an outbreak of continental-style slobbering.

"Might I present my business partner, Rex Prefontaine?" Matthew presided over the introduction with a particular look of pride in his eye. If Ariadne had worked out just why there seemed to be such affection in a commercial relationship, she was too well-bred to suggest it in her glance.

Once the orgy of hand shaking and back slapping and general small talk had stopped, Jonty proposed a toast to the college, even if it wasn't strictly form to do it at this point in the evening. Rex followed up with a toast to Orlando's newly acquired status. Then, thank goodness, Mrs. Ward announced that dinner was about to be served, or they might all have been toasted out—and half-cut—before the evening had barely begun.

Talk over the meal inevitably started with college matters, but then, in deference to Matthew and Rex, swiftly turned to more general things. And, in an unprecedented move, one no doubt fired by all the preprandial sherry, Jonty proposed that they use Christian names; the world was changing and maybe it was time for them to all change with it. In an even more unprecedented move, Orlando seconded the proposal.

Rex turned to Maurice Panesar, a bright look of curiosity on his face. "Now, would it be improper of me to ask if you're the chap who wants to build a time machine? Jonty keeps telling me you're brilliant."

Maurice smoothed his luxurious black beard with evident pleasure at the compliment, then bowed to his hosts. "Knowing Dr. Stewart—sorry, knowing Jonty—he followed that up with the words 'but eccentric.' No!" He raised his hand to stifle any argument. "You don't need to either deny it or apologise. I'm proud of the fact that I'm unconventional. And yes, I *would* like to build a time machine, although that's just one of the things I have in mind. Calculating machines and Orlando's computable numbers interest me, as do means of communication. I have this vision of a device that would allow people to communicate instantaneously all over the world."

"But we have that," Rex said, bewildered. "It's called a telephone."

"And don't forget the telegraph," Jonty chipped in.

"Ah, but that can be so slow, especially when the telegram boy dawdles on his bicycle or the operator takes too long to put a trunk call through. When I say instant, I mean it." Maurice's eyes were now alight with enthusiasm.

"That sounds even more far-fetched than a time machine." Rex raised an eyebrow at Matthew, who shook his head.

"Gentlemen!" Ariadne looked around the company, shaking her head. "I remember the idea of man taking to the air being thought of as far-fetched, yet now it seems almost commonplace."

"Hear, hear." Orlando had been keeping his powder dry but now he had to leap to his friends' defence. "We've barely begun to explore the capabilities of technology."

The conversation flowed down the river of scientific and engineering advances for better and worse, until the dinner plates were cleared and Jonty could turn the talk to things he always valued a lot more than matters technical.

"I wonder what there is for pudding?"

Mrs. Ward and her granddaughter had laid on a feast: good reliable beef Wellington with heaps of vegetables. Not likely to leave room for any sort of sizeable pudding, although a man had to show stoicism and valour in these circumstances, the latter if something suety and substantial turned up and the former if it was replaced by fruit salad.

"Don't you know?" Rex seemed shocked at such a poorly ordered household.

"Usually not. I want an element of surprise. Papa never used to specify the sweet part of the nosebag and what was good enough for him is good enough for me. Maybe it'll be jam roly-poly." The opening of the door made Jonty look up expectantly, like a little boy at Christmas.

"That smells like toffee pudding." Matthew beamed, equally childlike in delighted anticipation.

"I think you're right." Jonty eyed the plates with evident relish as they appeared on the table, the great steaming jug of custard reverenced as if it contained holy water. "If there isn't toffee pudding in heaven, I'm not sure I want to go."

"We should eat this with due respect, as befitting," Matthew pronounced, like a priest making a blessing. Everyone obeyed, not insulting the noble dessert with talk of machinery. They returned to everyday subjects over coffee in the sitting room.

"Now, considering the brain power we have gathered here," Jonty said, waving his coffee spoon like a magician's wand, "it's a shame we're unlikely to be able to solve some of the frustrating bits of our current case."

Matthew grinned. "Not like you two not to be able to sort it out on your own."

"I'm not sure we've had a case before where every time we get to the bottom of one piece, another bit appears." Jonty wrinkled his nose, looking less like a fellow in Tudor literature than a puzzled little boy.

"Like Hercules's hydra?" Rex, like a sailor who's heard the drum beating him to quarters, seemed ready for the fray.

"Perhaps. I actually had Ariadne's planarian worms in mind." Jonty smiled, nodding at his guest. "Perhaps I'd better elucidate. Planaria are most remarkable things. If you bisect their tails, each part will grow an entirely new one. Clever little blighters, eh?"

"Absolutely," Ariadne confirmed. "The same with their other ends, so you can create little monsters with a whole handful of heads. I have some remarkable photographs at the lodge if anyone would like to come along tomorrow and view them?" She looked hopefully at Matthew and Rex, but only Maurice cheerfully piped up and booked himself a private viewing.

"Exactly that." Jonty brought the conversation back to mysteries as opposed to slithery things. "Every little incision produces a new direction to take. We have a woman accused by her brother-in-law of murdering her husband—or maybe her brother-in-law was actually the one who murdered him, despite the finger pointing. Or possibly it was the nephew, although he called us in. And that's just the start."

"And some sort of complication in the form of who was born first," Orlando added, muddying the waters further. "I'd better explain. Logically." Orlando clearly aimed the last word at Jonty. He took his guests through the whole story as he and Jonty had learned it, so that the layers of the case unfolded as he spoke. "We have no concrete evidence from back then. Collingwood's hounds confirm that nobody found any signs on the body to suggest poisoning or violent suffocation or the like. We may not even have a murder. What we *do* have is more suspects and leads than we know what to do with, but we don't have enough time to chase them all. We need to make some assumptions. We have to focus on Rosalind alone and her possible guilt. That's our brief from the client, after all."

Ariadne narrowed her eyes. "And if you can't establish this one way or the other by the time the inheritance falls due . . .?"

"Then she gets the money, while we have all the time in the world to pursue the case," Jonty cut in. "And we'll carry on down every avenue, dead end or short cut, until we discover the truth and ensure justice is done, if it needs to be."

"That's all I wanted to hear." Ariadne nodded, as though giving her benediction. "No shoddy thinking."

"Heaven forbid," Orlando said, maybe a touch too quickly.

"Now," Rex said, "if mathematical logic and Shakespearean inspired intuition can't move us forward, what a shame science can't come to our aid. We could do with one of Maurice's time machines to take us back and see what went on in the conservatory."

"And what happened to that baby. I'd hate to think he was just thrown out with the rubbish." Jonty grimaced. "I wouldn't suggest we would actually witness any of the actual . . . you know . . . confinement, just be stationed outside and count the little blighters, keeping a record of them on a slate."

Ariadne smiled, indulgently. "I never thought for a moment you would. Maurice's machine would hover gracefully by the door while I—if you would permit me the pleasure of accompanying you—could enquire of the midwife."

"How extraordinary, my dear. You speak of this as if it's real." Dr. Sheridan shook his head. "Making minute plans for the execution of the scheme."

"And why not? It may never happen in reality but it could take place in here." Ariadne tapped her forehead. "Which is almost as good."

"We could all employ our imaginations until the cows come home, but we'd be no further forward. I never thought I'd say I simply wanted some good, solid facts, but that's exactly what we're lacking," Jonty said, staring into his coffee cup. "Or a nice solid witness for the prosecution."

"But you have a witness. You've told us about him, twice." Maurice raised his hand, perhaps to stop anyone sneaking in and stealing his thunder. "That grocer's boy."

"He was there, and he saw what we presume is either Simon or the Reverend Bresnan lurking around, but he and his boss were gone by the time Peter died." Orlando tapped the notebook he'd been referring to when describing the case. "I verified that when we were last at Downlea."

"It's a shame one of those ladybirds couldn't have lived to tell the tale and shake Rosalind Priestland's alibi." Jonty grimaced again.

"I thought you had no truck with alibis?" Matthew winked at Rex before he faced Jonty again. "You always say you'd never trust someone who's got one."

"I suspect I have an alibi for the murder. Do you think I did it?" Rex grinned.

"Rosalind might not have an alibi."

Everyone turned to Maurice.

"Sorry?" Orlando broke the stunned silence. "She says she was with the housekeeper and the housekeeper agrees. Jonty, do you think Mrs. Hamilton was lying about them being together?"

"No, I don't. That's the odd thing. I don't trust Rosalind herself, or either of the two vicars in the case, but Mrs. H.?" He shrugged. "If she says they were together until they found the body, then I'm inclined to believe her."

"But are we sure that Peter Priestland was dead when they found him? Think of some of our fellow members of St. Bride's and the way they snooze in the Senior Common Room. Anyone would think they'd passed on, or been fossilised, they're so dead to the world." Maurice jabbed his finger at nobody in particular. "The housekeeper might have thought her master dead, especially if her mistress told her so. Rosalind Priestland is a good actress, we've established that."

Dr. Sheridan shook his head. "But Peter Priestland was recovering from his illness. We know he was wheezy. He may have looked dead, but wouldn't Mrs. Hamilton have heard his breathing?"

"Not if she only stood at the door of the room, and her mistress made a lot of noise," Maurice countered, belligerently.

"And not if she's a touch deaf," Jonty said, slowly, as if considering some new revelation. "Thinking back to when I was first at Thorpe House, she accused Billy of mumbling to us, but he spoke clear as a bell. And I don't think she heard me crunching over the gravel towards them."

Maurice smiled. "She sees but doesn't hear. She is sent to use the phone and may take her time over the call if her hearing isn't all that. Time enough for Rosalind to act."

Silence fell back on the room as everyone came to terms with what had been said.

"And so we come full circle." Jonty laid down his coffee cup with a frown. "We all think Rosalind did it. And we can't prove a thing."

Chapter 15

The guests had gone. Two tired fellows of St. Bride's sat in bed, books and—in Jonty's case—spectacles discarded, discussing, for the umpteenth time, the case they'd seemed to be losing their way in for so long.

"Right. Rosalind Priestland decides to kill her husband because he's showing signs of living forever and she fancies that nice young vicar who might not wait around if another nice rich widow comes along. How can we prove it?"

"That's three times tonight you've said something like that. Our guests couldn't answer, *I* can't answer, and the pear tree certainly couldn't answer." Orlando poked Jonty's arm.

"I didn't realise you were watching me out there."

"You can see a lot with the benefit of moonlight. Did you enjoy your cigar?"

"Yes. And thank you for letting me indulge."

"My pleasure." It wasn't. Orlando hated the smell of cigar smoke on his lover's breath, but it was a sacrifice that had to be made at times. Jonty in a particularly good mood might lead to Jonty in a particularly amorous mood. He'd never admitted that *he'd* taken to having the odd cigarette at the end of the war. One day that would all come out, along with confessions of how low he'd felt at the time, but not yet.

It seemed as if Jonty's sojourn in the garden had worked its magic when he snuggled in closer and said, "There's one more thing, apart from solving this bloody problem, that would make this evening perfect."

"At least that's not a hard riddle to solve, not where you're concerned," Orlando murmured, slipping his arm round Jonty's shoulder and rubbing his cheek. "But is gluttony not a deadly sin? And would we not be condemned for our indulgence if we kept coupling?"

"You're unusually poetic tonight. Where did those lines come from? It must be the pudding inspiring you." Jonty smiled, bringing Orlando's fingers to his mouth for a kiss. "And is heaven not the place where you get what you most desired and it is as good as when you only desired it?"

"Then heaven must be this bed," Orlando replied, eager to move from words to actions, not least because Jonty might ask more about the origin of his flowery phrases and he'd have to admit he'd been scribbling them down when he was supposed to be working on his lecture.

"And do we wish to have our heaven light, dark, or dappled?" Jonty slipped out of bed, ready to deal with lamps, curtains, or whatever was necessary.

"Dappled with moonlight, please." Orlando could hardly speak for anticipation. Once the room was illuminated only by a silver stream of light from the window, a silver stream that made Jonty look like one of those statues of athletes in the Louvre, the expectation turned from cerebral to physical. Jonty's attractive silk pyjamas needed to come off, however, so Orlando could catch a glimpse of even more attractive skin. "Come here. I need to get you ready."

Jonty came back to the bed, loosening his buttons en route to sliding in close. "I can tell *you're* ready. I have solid verification of the fact." He chuckled as he gently took the evidence in hand. "Quite the most magnificent exhibit to come before the court tonight." Jonty leaned over, kissing Orlando's shoulder. "And one that seems to require immediate attention if it's not to be spoiled." He gave it some appropriate attention, while Orlando lay back and tried to keep himself under control. "Members of the jury, I bring before you . . ."

"Will you ever hush?" Orlando, not without regret, moved his lover's hand away from where it was causing havoc. "There's only so much a man can take! If you want me to mount you, then you'd better stay within safe limits!"

"What?" Jonty, eyes wide, laughed at Orlando's brazenness.

"Mount you. As the bull comes to the cow or the stallion to the—"

"Spare me the agricultural analogies. I understood what you meant. I was just surprised at you being so daring in your choice of words." Jonty edged up the bed, turning onto his back and pulling Orlando with him. "If you ask so nicely, of course I will."

"No asking nicely about it. Once the bull is in the mood, he mounts you and you stay mounted." No matter how brazen his words, Orlando couldn't help but be his usual tender self. They rocked as one until the crisis had passed for them both, lying together afterwards without speaking.

"A bravura performance there, Orlando." Jonty stroked Orlando's head. "Please don't ever say, 'I have walked too long the paths of lust with you, Jonty, and drunk too deeply of the well of your delight. Let me rest.'"

"You honestly think I'd say that? Stuff and nonsense. I'm no sonnet writer. Have you been composing again?" Still, they weren't getting any younger. When would they turn from the delights of the flesh? In ten years' time? When death did them both part? He didn't voice the thoughts, because Jonty was blethering again and it seemed, as usual, that he'd been reading his lover's mind.

"I have. A double sonnet, question and answer. 'We'll tread more paths and drink more deeply yet.'" His stroking fingers wandered to Orlando's shoulders. "'If music truly be the food of love, I'll play you like a harp until we've both had excess of it.'"

"That makes no sense. You've twisted *Twelfth Night* beyond reason." Still, *excess* made him think. Weren't they supposed to be slowing down? And how much sex counted as enough? Was that quantity liquid, ebbing and flowing with abstinence and deprivation? When did satiation end and excess begin?

"Stop it." Jonty tapped his lover's forehead. "And before you say, 'Stop what?' I'll say it for you. *Thinking*."

"I was only thinking about whether we indulge ourselves too often." Orlando was pleased that the moonlight was unlikely to reveal the flush he could feel rushing up his cheeks.

"Not enough, I'd say." Jonty sighed and nestled into Orlando's embrace. "Remember that night here, on leave from Room 40?"

"I'll never forget." He could see it now, the scene etched forever not just in his memory but in his senses. Fresh scones with clotted cream, devoured until nothing was left but crumbs on a plate and smears on a knife. A pot of coffee drained and a bottle of wine opened. Simple pleasures, shared. "Soft tack and a softer bed."

"More poetry. Becoming a professor becomes you, if you'll excuse the pun." Jonty sighed again. "More of the same, as often as you can produce it, please."

"The poetry or the . . ." Words failed the fledgling poet. "Um, lovemaking?"

"Both. Give me excess of them."

"Excess makes me feel guilty."

"Guilt about rogering, or guilt because we survived and millions didn't?" Jonty gently caressed Orlando's chest. "Apply your brain to important things like Rosalind Priestland and how we'll ever prove our case."

"Maybe I should just apply my brains to murdering you, then we'd all get some peace." Orlando grabbed the counterpane, and pressed the silky material against Jonty's face.

"Get that off!" Jonty pushed the cover away. "That's not one of your surefire-yet-won't-leave-a-sign murder methods."

"Oh hell." Orlando turned and twisted the counterpane in his hands.

"Oh hell what?" Jonty stilled his lover's fingers.

"We've been complete and utter idiots." Orlando thumped the pillow again. "I knew we were losing our touch and this is the proof. We've concentrated on all the things we've enjoyed playing about with in the past, like riddles, puzzles, inheritances, family trees. We've been so intent on finding out who did it that we've never for a moment wondered how they could have done it and not leave a mark."

Jonty groaned. "I will not believe in the untraceable poison that leaves no sign."

"I'm not expecting you to. Smothering." Orlando shut his eyes again, as though replaying the scene. "If Peter was so weak with the flu that the doctor wasn't surprised he'd died, then he might not even have fought back. I can imagine her, crooning to him and reassuring him while . . ."

"I hate to be the bearer of bad news, but even smothering can leave a mark. I've got a book about it somewhere." Jonty leaped out of bed, then threw the covers from Orlando. "Come along, I'm not going to suffer the cold alone."

Orlando may have muttered an oath as he grabbed his dressing gown, but he wasn't going to miss this for the world.

The book was found and, as Jonty had suggested, dashed their slim hopes. Smothering, unless it was administered very carefully, wasn't as easy to get away with as they'd hoped. Some of the signs could be argued away as old age or the after-effects of flu, but not all.

Jonty smoothed the pages of the book, clearly thinking something through. "Hold on. We've missed something here. Billy's obsession with covering faces. Have we been too quick to dismiss that?"

"We might. Go on. I'm all ears."

"We've not really considered everything Billy said. Because we know he's definitely confused about the red kites and possibly confused about the man in the bushes, we've assumed the business with covering faces is the same. But could it be true? Could it be linked somehow to his having seen Rosalind covering Peter's face in the act of murder? Even if he's supposed to have left the house while the man was still alive."

"It could. It could indeed."

"Don't get too excited just yet. I have a feeling that method might leave too many traces. Fibres and the like."

"So you don't think she did it." Orlando eyed the wretched book as though he wanted to sentence it to two years' hard labour.

"Au contraire, I'm convinced she did. Illogically, intuitively, not-based-on-a-scrap-of-evidence-ly. I just don't ruddy well know how, because they've obscured the trail with scatterings of untruths." Jonty slammed the book shut. "I think lying runs in that family. Her, Bresnan, old man Priestland."

Orlando nodded, putting his arm round Jonty's shoulders. "I'm not even sure your man Mitchell's story of the theft is true. I bet she told him just to get his sympathy."

"Perhaps we should fight lies with lies, then." Jonty suddenly pulled free of his lover's embrace, then paced to the window and back, rubbing his hands together. "That's it. That's *it*. Maurice said we had a witness for the day of the crime. Billy. Maybe we can pretend he saw more than he did."

"I must be exceedingly obtuse because I don't follow you . . ."

Jonty stopped pacing and ruffled Orlando's hair. "That sounds like the old Orlando. I can remember when we first made love. You alleged you couldn't think straight for days."

"Ha-ha. Always my fault, never yours for being unclear." Orlando poked Jonty's ribs. "Explain."

"We ask Billy, purely in the interests of serving his country as he'll like that, to help us confront Rosalind. Perhaps we can panic her into confessing. He'll have to say he saw her smother her husband with the cloth she put on his face. It's not logical, maybe it's not even moral, but I'm not sure what else we can do." Touched by faint moonlight, Jonty resembled a statue again, but this time less athlete than philosopher.

"It's hardly a brilliant plan, but it's the sort of harebrained scheme that shouldn't work but just might. If she's been unnerved enough by all the interest from us and Collingwood's men." Orlando began to visualise the scene. "Mind you, it feels like the sort of thing that only happens in some creaky old play about lost inheritances and murderous vicars."

"And isn't that exactly what we've got here?"

"Maybe. But I'm still not convinced. It smacks too much of theatricality, if not of sheer desperation." Orlando ruffled his lover's hair. "You've always had a dramatic streak, and I don't want to appeal to it. And we have to do this by the book. How do you propose we organise the police side of things?"

"We invite our old friend Chief Inspector Wilson to come to Downlea and witness the proceedings. He'll see that fair play's adhered to, and can engineer an arrest if need be." Jonty seemed to have his entire strategy coming together.

"Wilson's retired, you chump. I know you weren't here when he had his big 'do' to announce the fact, but you can't have forgotten the conversation over dinner not a month ago." Orlando avoided referring to those lost wartime days.

"Of course I know he's retired, more's the pity for the safety of the good citizens of Cambridge. I thought we could invite him in a purely honorary capacity. Neither Rosalind nor Mitchell will know whether he's still serving, and if we persuade him to bring a hefty constable or sergeant with him, *he* can have the pleasure of making the arrest."

Orlando picked up the book again and thumped it in frustration. "Would they be party to lying? Not even in the cause of convicting a murderess?"

"I bet they would. Wilson's a pragmatist."

"True." That first rosy glow of dawn through the window might herald the first rosy glimmer of hope.

"I know it's a long shot." Jonty rubbed Orlando's hand thoughtfully. "But if Billy doesn't have to lie too much, he could play his part in the game."

"Murder's not exactly a game of croquet." Orlando squeezed his lover's fingers. "But you're right. We have to corner her into making an admission. If that fails, and she really is guilty, then she's won. At least for the moment."

"You've got that look in your eye. You'll never let this rest, will you?"

"Never. Even if we do it by cheating or sheer damned luck, we'll hunt down the truth."

Jonty grinned. "That's the spirit. Only don't let either Mrs. Sheridan or young Georgie hear you."

Chapter 16

"Are you sure this is going to work?" Jonty fiddled with his driving gloves while Orlando looked out of the window and avoided catching his eye. They couldn't actually see Thorpe House from the road, although Orlando was aware of some sort of brooding presence on the other side of the wall.

"Sure? I'm not sure it won't end up with *us* being arrested, let alone anyone else." Orlando kept his gaze fixed down the road. "But we have little choice."

"I wish Billy was here."

"Be patient. Sergeant McLaren will have him here soon enough. He wants to make sure we don't play any tricks."

McLaren was the antithesis of the redoubtable Sergeant Cohen, who'd formed half of the noted constabulary double act of Wilson and Cohen back at the times of the St. Bride's murders. While they'd left official police business behind, they still made a formidable pair when they met Jonty and Orlando over the dinner table at the Blue Boar. McLaren was Cohen's opposite in appearance, lithe and whippet-like, definitely built more for speed than endurance. Cohen had been stout, sturdy, and impossible to best in a fight. Orlando hoped McLaren would be able to handle himself if things came to fisticuffs.

"Play any tricks? Any more than we already have planned?" Jonty sighed. "I'm glad Papa isn't here to see us."

"Getting cold feet?"

"Just a touch. Are you?"

"Just a touch, even though it was *your* idea."

"I know. And when it all falls down about our ears, I'll be carrying the can."

Orlando pushed the car door open. "Here they come." He waited as the policeman and the bicycle-wielding grocer's lad came up the road. "Sergeant! All's well?"

"Yes, sir. This young man knows what's expected of him." McLaren didn't look as if he believed that expectation would turn into any useful reality.

"Good," Orlando said, starting the walk up to the house and hoping everyone would follow. Like going into no-man's-land. "We all know our parts?"

"I'd be a sight happier if there was less emphasis on the theatricals, Professor. It's only because Mr. Wilson recommended we agree to this that I'm here." McLaren clearly meant it. He'd not been happy with their scheme from the start, but Wilson—even a retired Wilson—wasn't someone to be argued with. And he had the chief constable's ear.

"We'll play everything by the book." Jonty looked solemn; one of the things his scar had added to his appearance was a gravitas not previously present. "And if it doesn't work..." He shrugged. "I suppose she'll sue us for defamation or something."

"We need to get through the front door first." Orlando swallowed hard; he hadn't realised just how imposing Thorpe House would look close up. Even though they were expected, they couldn't be certain of the reception they'd get.

"If Rosalind Priestland thinks we're here because of her mother-in-law's jewels, then we'll be welcomed." Jonty flicked some nonexistent specks from his jacket. "It's when she realises that we've got in under false pretences that we have to start worrying."

If Mrs. Hamilton was surprised at a policeman (and not the local bobby, to boot) with the grocer's boy in tow knocking at the door rather than the tradesmen's entrance, she was too well-bred to show it. Jonty saved his explanation for when they'd been ushered into the drawing room. Mitchell, looking every inch the spinsters' dream, was already present. To give moral support, Jonty assumed. Or maybe to confess to the crime himself, if they'd got it horribly wrong? He forced away any thoughts of them making fools of themselves.

"Dr. Stewart, Professor Coppersmith." Rosalind rose to meet her guests. "I'm so pleased to see you. I assume we can at last clarify the matter of what happened to Alice Priestland? I'm just sorry we couldn't have cleared this all up last year."

I bet you are, Jonty thought uncharitably. *Then you could have inherited Peter's part of* that *legacy as well.* "That's what we want to do," he said aloud. "We can confirm that we've located her jewellery and corroborate that she ran away and began a second life."

"So the letters were right?" Mitchell steepled his hands to his chin. "I wish the twins could have known. It would have eased things between them. Confession of error and forgiveness are at the root of a fulfilled life."

"I'm forgetting my manners. Please take a seat." Rosalind cut through the theological chat, indicating chairs for Jonty and Orlando. She seemed to think twice about McLaren and Billy, but in the end offered them seats too. "I assume you're all aware that my brother-in-law and his nephew were here the day Peter died?"

"We are indeed." Orlando's was the voice of authority; slow, measured, and displaying no hint of his misgivings.

"I suppose that's why young Billy's here. You saw them, didn't you?" Rosalind took a handkerchief from her pocket and twisted it in her lap.

"I saw somebody." Billy looked confused. "Don't know who it was."

"It was one of the family." Rosalind looked at Mitchell. "It sounds unchristian, but I can't help worrying about that. You don't think it possible they came in through the conservatory door when we were busy and . . . and did anything to my Peter? So they'd get a bigger share of the inheritance?"

"I suppose it's possible, although I find it most unlikely." Mitchell turned to Jonty. "Is that why you've come? To tell us some ridiculous tale about Peter being killed by his nephew?"

Jonty swallowed hard, ignoring the "ridiculous" bit. Was there any chance they'd got this arsey-farsey? That Rosalind's apparent acting was genuine and the real killer had taken them all for a ride? They'd soon find out.

"We're here to discuss the possibility that Peter was murdered, but not by his nephew. We have a witness to the deed." Screw-his-courage-to-the-sticking-place time. "Why did you kill him, Mrs. Priestland?"

If Jonty expected a stream of protest from Mitchell and a stream of invective from Rosalind, he was disappointed on both counts. Rosalind's voice was icily calm. Had she been preparing herself for this eventuality or had Simon—and they—read this all dreadfully wrong?

"I think you've been misled. Peter was already dead when I found him. When *we* found him. Mrs. Hamilton was with me and she'd been with me all afternoon up until then. How could I have had the chance, even if I'd had the inclination?" Rosalind still looked and sounded the picture of innocence, aided by a slight catch in her voice. "I loved him so much." She glanced at Mitchell, but he seemed to deliberately avoid her eye.

"Of course she was with you. That was the beauty of it, wasn't it? I believe your housekeeper's hearing isn't what it was?"

The sudden horrified look on Rosalind's face, quickly hidden, gave the lie to her response. "Her hearing is excellent, thank you."

"Hmm." Jonty cracked on, hoping his papa wasn't sitting up in heaven with a glass of malt whisky in his angelic hand, shaking his head at the speculative stuff his youngest son was spouting. "You saw your husband in a deep sleep, and saw your chance. A unique chance, perhaps not to be repeated. To pretend he was already dead, send Mrs. Hamilton off to get help and, while she was away, smother him. Peter was still weak after the flu, so it would have been easy. Billy, tell us what you saw," he said, sounding friendly enough but with officer-like authority.

Billy took a deep breath, as close to standing at attention as he could manage in a chair, and addressed a spot somewhere to the left of Jonty's head. "We'd been killing ladybirds, me and Mr. Houseman, that morning. I'd come back to see if I could get a glimpse of the red kites over the woods. Everyone tells me there's no such birds round here and I shouldn't hang around making a nuisance of myself, so I kept out of view. I didn't want Mrs. Priestland or Mrs. Hamilton coming and telling me off." He cast a quick glance at Rosalind, then pressed on. "I was round by the back of the house. Where they keep all those flowers."

"The conservatory," Jonty said softly.

"I suppose so. It's a sort of glass house." Billy smiled. "I saw Mr. Priestland in there, and thought that big thick blanket must have been uncomfortable up over his face. Mrs. Priestland must have thought the same, because she moved it aside. Then she covered his face with a little handkerchief. I guessed he was already dead, so she was doing what was required."

This wasn't quite what they'd asked McLaren to ask Billy to say. He was supposed to be talking about seeing Rosalind bending over the body, pressing a cloth over his nose and mouth. Nothing about a blanket. Jonty just hoped the lad's extemporising wouldn't spoil things.

"Why was it required, Billy?" Mitchell's voice had an attractive tone, the sort that invited confidences or confessions.

"I don't know. I'd never seen a dead body before. They didn't do it with my gran, but nobody's told me why. When I asked, they said to be quiet." Billy looked puzzled. "I don't know why Mrs. Priestland placed the blanket in the big tub, either."

"What big tub?" Jonty felt like his head was going to explode.

"The one with the strange plants in. Mr. Houseman says they keep it full of water so the plants don't get dry. Mrs. Priestland put the blanket in there after she put the handkerchief on his face."

"May we have Mrs. Hamilton in, please?" Orlando asked.

"You may have whom you like." Rosalind's voice was suddenly hard. "Reverend, would you be so kind?"

"Don't you worry yourself, sir." McLaren's voice was surprisingly authoritative. "I'll fetch her." The silence after he departed grew increasingly uncomfortable, but fortunately McLaren was gone only a short time. Mrs. Hamilton must have been lurking not too far away. "You have my seat, ma'am. We're discussing the day your master died."

Mrs. Hamilton cast a quick glance at her mistress, although whether that was to check it was all right to sit down or to communicate her support, Jonty couldn't tell. The faintest buzz of an idea began in his head, like a small wasp in one of his mental pigeonholes.

"Mrs. Hamilton," he said, rather quietly, and without looking at her, "can we clarify something?"

"I'm sorry, could you repeat that?"

Jonty, with a triumphantly knowing glance at the rest of the company, repeated the question, much louder this time, then continued. "On the day Peter Priestland died, where was his blanket when you came back from phoning the doctor?"

"In that ridiculous trough where he liked to stand his favourite plants. Such a mess. Mrs. Priestland said it had fallen in there by accident, in the panic." Mrs. Hamilton cast a quick glance at Mrs. Priestland, as if checking her answer was acceptable.

"Are you sure of that?" McLaren had evidently been making notes throughout, although nobody had seemed to have noticed. Now all eyes were drawn to his notebook and pencil. "Mrs. Priestland told you it had just fallen in?"

"Yes. She said it had dropped into the water as she'd tried to rouse him. It needed an age of drying out." The housekeeper spoke slowly and with what seemed absolute candour, her eyes constantly flicking between the policeman and her mistress.

Jonty took a deep breath. "Had that blanket been covering Mr. Priestland when you first found him, apparently dead?"

"Yes. He felt the cold terribly, poor man, so we'd made sure we tucked him up nicely. Not near his face, of course. Didn't want to suffocate him." Mrs. Hamilton's head turned sharply at the hint of a gasp from her mistress.

"Were you gone long? Making the call?" Jonty now had total charge of the interview.

The housekeeper looked confused at the change of tack. "I was a bit longer than I might have expected to be. The telephone in the hallway didn't seem to be working, so I had to go below stairs to the one we have there. There was a problem on the line, then the doctor was an age coming to his phone, then it seemed difficult to make him understand what the problem was."

"Time enough." Jonty nodded. "And when you returned his face wasn't covered with a handkerchief, either?"

"No." Mrs. Hamilton looked across at her mistress again.

"Time enough for what?" Mitchell unexpectedly cut in.

"To wet the blanket and use it to smother Peter Priestland. McLaren, I've got a book at home that tells me, if I remember aright, that if you smother someone with something wet and woollen it leaves very little in the way of marks. Would that be possible here?" Jonty shot a sideways glance at Rosalind, who looked distinctly unhappy.

"I couldn't say, sir, me not being a forensic expert like Bernard Spilsbury." McLaren frowned. "Although I've come across something similar before with a toddler."

Mrs. Hamilton suddenly spoke. "But you wouldn't have done anything like that, would you, madam? You'd have been too scared I'd have come back and caught you in the act."

"Of course." Rosalind shook her head, as if to say, *See how illogical people are.*

Jonty pressed on. "But what if your mistress happened to know there was something wrong with the phone line? She'd have been able to count on your being delayed."

"It was an error on Billy's part, surely?" Mrs. Hamilton turned to the grocer's boy. "You must have been mistaken about what you saw."

"I was not." Billy looked every bit as certain as he sounded. "The blanket was on the old man's face. She took it off and put it in the water. Then she covered his face with a cloth."

"This is ridiculous. Why would I do that?" Rosalind threw up her hands.

"To wipe away any drips of water? Or any other signs?" Orlando leaned forwards. "Or to check if he was still breathing? The almost imperceptible rise and fall of the cloth . . ."

"That's ridiculous. Why do you take the word of a silly boy who can't even tell a buzzard from a billiard ball?" Rosalind snorted.

"I'm not a silly boy. You'd not have called me that if I'd been old enough to go to France. I'm prepared to stand up in court and say what I saw."

"As am I." Mitchell spoke quietly, with eyes closed. "We should have the truth, Mrs. Priestland. Only that can set all of us free."

"You're right. We *should* have nothing but the truth." Mrs. Hamilton got up, went over, and stood by the door, where a shawl lay folded on a little table. She picked it up, twisting it in her hands. "Gentlemen, you've so nearly got this right. Peter Priestland *was* murdered, but not by Mrs. Priestland. After we'd finished looking for ladybirds, my mistress had to go and wash her hands. I could hear my master breathing in a hoarse, rattling way. I ran to him, but he was so very distressed, I couldn't but put him out of his misery. He'd been so ill . . ." She made the shawl into a flat pad, then handed it to Orlando, who was nearest to her. "Feel that material. How close the weave is."

She stepped back while he rubbed the shawl between his fingers, then held it to his face, every eye in the room watching him.

"What?" McLaren exclaimed, bewildered. "Would someone tell me exactly what's going on here?"

"I think we're being played like fishes but I'm not sure who the angler is." Mitchell got to his feet too. "Mrs. Priestland, can you . . ."

"Stop her! She's used that shawl to distract us!" Jonty was up like a flash but not fast enough to prevent the housekeeper from slipping out of the door. Just like the occasion he first met Billy, Jonty had the feeling he'd had his attention diverted while the magician produced his—her—piece of prestidigitation. The sound of a key in the lock stopped them in their tracks. "Break this down, Sergeant."

"No." Mitchell indicated another exit. "Through the dining room and into the hall. She can't have got far."

She hadn't. As Jonty, Orlando, McLaren, and Billy—who looked like he was having a day out at the fair, his smile was so wide—came into the hall, they spotted Mrs. Hamilton legging it up the stairs like a champion hurdler.

"Stop, in the name of the law!"

Jonty couldn't help grinning at McLaren's shout; the whole experience felt like being in something by Gilbert and Sullivan.

"She won't stop. Mitchell, where can she be going?" Orlando asked, barely stopping to hear the vicar's reply.

"There's a door to the roof, right up in the attic." The answer followed them up as they reached the top of the second flight.

"Don't bother," the housekeeper shouted down, almost at the top and not breaking stride. "It'll be easier all round if my guilt dies with me and I report straight to my Maker."

"Don't let her do it." Orlando's face was deathly pale. He'd seen suicide before, more than once. It still haunted him at times, especially since the war, which had stirred up all sorts of memories they'd thought long dealt with. "Dear God, don't let it happen, Jonty."

"I'm not sure I can catch her." Jonty was only a step or two ahead of his friend, although Billy was gaining on their quarry.

"Careful what you're doing there, Mrs. H. You'll make a terrible mess, and it's poor souls like us what'll have to do the clearing up." Billy's words must have hit home, as the housekeeper, pale and drawn, stopped halfway through the door.

"Stay there, Billy. Stay there until it's all done and then go straight home. I don't want you seeing this."

Mitchell suddenly held out his arm to stop any of them getting closer to their prey. They'd never reach her before she could close the door and lock it against them. "I'm not sure God will forgive you, my dear. Not if you're assuming responsibility for something you didn't do. Especially if that might let the guilty party go free."

Mrs. Hamilton still hesitated, face riddled with doubt.

"Hell." Orlando thumped the wall with his fist. "Who's keeping an eye on Rosalind?"

Jonty almost fell backwards down the stairs, so quickly did he turn round. Had this all been a diversionary tactic? One quick glance at the housekeeper's guilty expression settled matters.

"Leave her to jump if she will. Please God, the harm hasn't been done." They hared back down the stairs, the dramatic denouement of this murder play having descended into farce.

They reached the front door to see Rosalind Priestland halfway down the drive, carpetbag in hand. She'd been prepared for this, probably given warning by all the questions asked around the village. If she had a car coming for her—and she was just the sort of woman to have left nothing to chance—then she'd be away before they could reach her. Jonty cursed his having left his automobile out on the road.

"Stop!" McLaren shouted at the top of his not inconsiderable voice, but Rosalind wasn't having any of it.

The squeak of a bicycle caught Jonty's ear as he raced along. Billy had leapt on his trusty steed and was proceeding down the drive at a terrific clip. "Stop her!"

The bicycle flashed by, unswerving. It should have been comic, a grocer's lad chasing a respectable woman along her own drive, the stuff of Jerome K. Jerome or Weedon Grossmith, except that the woman's being a likely murderess took all the humour away.

It was soon done, Billy overtaking her, discarding the bicycle, and grabbing Rosalind with arms that were stronger than Jonty would have given him credit for. The lady, true colours maybe emerging at last, resorted to using her teeth to effect an escape, but all in vain. As the rest of them caught up with the scuffling pair, a motorcar screeched to a halt outside the gate, reversed, then headed off in the other direction. Whomever Rosalind had arranged to be her knight on a white charger had evidently taken his horse and run at the sight of trouble.

"Get off me!" Rosalind was willing to fight, even when surrounded.

"That'll do, Billy." McLaren took his rightful place as upholder of the law.

Jonty felt they should get some questions in before she was handed over totally to officialdom. They still hadn't had an admission of guilt or anything that could be used in a court of law.

"Yes, that'll do." Rosalind beat at Billy with her fists.

"No, Rosalind. That will do from *you*." Mitchell was barely out of breath, even though he'd been running. "There's nowhere to run where you can get away from guilt."

"You can't prove anything, any of you. There's just the word of an idiot boy." Rosalind looked contemptuously at Billy, while Jonty wondered whether he could get away with punching a woman.

"There's my word," Mitchell spoke softly.

Rosalind blanched, but there was still fight in her. "You wouldn't stand up in court and say anything."

"You underestimate me, my dear."

"You despicable swine." Rosalind reached out as if to scratch his face, but McLaren restrained her. "I told you what happened under the sanctity of confession. You can't testify to that in court."

"No I can't. But you didn't just refer to it in confession, did you?"

"My God . . ." Rosalind turned deathly pale.

"I remember standing at your bedroom door, and you spoke of it again." Mitchell appeared to be the calmest among them. "You must have thought me a helpless pawn in your game, that I'd ignore such a thing and not turn on my heel."

"Why not?" Rosalind, shaken as she was, still had fight in her. "Most men are idiots. Your dog collar doesn't protect you from the folly of your sex. Clearly."

"Alas, it doesn't. I liked you, Rosalind, and I still do, oddly enough. I could have loved you. But I couldn't wed you when I knew what you'd done."

"So pure, so clean." Slow burning anger flared in Rosalind's eyes. "I don't remember 'wedding' being mentioned. Bedding, yes."

Orlando looked as if he were about to interject, but Jonty's hand on his arm restrained him. Things were getting particularly interesting, so why not let them run their course?

She turned to Jonty, eyes flaming with anger. "You're all the same, only want a woman for the pleasure she can give. Our wonderful vicar—he'd have slept with a grieving widow, in wedlock or out. As soon as he knew my secret, he grew cold."

"The secret about the theft?" Jonty said, fingers crossed that a miracle was about to happen.

Rosalind rolled her eyes. "You're as big an idiot as he is. About my smothering Peter. I suppose *he'll* be able to testify about what I said to him in my house." She jabbed a finger at the vicar. "So you might as well know. I did it."

Mitchell sighed. "Thank you, my dear."

"What do you have to thank me for?"

"For a confession that *can* be used in court, as the ones to me couldn't, not even if they took place outside the church."

Rosalind gasped, but the vicar carried calmly on. "But I believe you have just admitted to murder. In front of these gentlemen and under God's blue sky."

Before the last few questions could be asked, Rosalind Priestland and Mrs. Hamilton had been taken away by McLaren and the reinforcements he'd summoned. Jonty and Orlando made their way slowly up the drive towards the car, with Mitchell at their side and Billy (plus his trusty bike) in tow. Hardly a word passed between them until they'd reached the road and physically as well as metaphorically shaken the dirt of Thorpe House from their shoes.

Jonty finally bit the conversational bullet. "Reverend, I had no idea how clever you'd prove."

"Not clever. Devious." Mitchell looked along the road, towards where the church stood. "I'd suspected her for a long time, and then I was constrained by what I'd heard as confessor. Not admissible evidence. In any circumstances." He sighed. "All I could do was drop hints and hope you'd be able enough to find the truth."

"I think it was less our ability than a mixture of luck and brass neck that succeeded," Jonty said, shaking his head. "Is that why you told me about Rosalind having committed theft, confessed, and been forgiven? And that there was more you could say, and couldn't? Was the misinformation you gave me for the same purpose?" It seemed obvious now.

"The order of birth? Yes. I just wanted to make you uncertain, get you to dig deeper. And I'm delighted you took my hint and took Billy seriously. He's the most honest of all of us, I suspect." The vicar held out his hand to shake theirs. "I have to go. I have other duties to perform."

They made their good-byes, Orlando waiting until he was out of earshot before saying, "What is it about clergymen and their inability to speak in anything but riddles?"

"We'll mull that over later. That's a three-sherry problem." Jonty turned to the grocer's boy. "Billy, you were magnificent. I wish I'd had more men like you out in France. Would you be insulted if I gave you a reward?" He produced a five-pound note from his wallet. There were no police present to have spotted that he might just be bribing witnesses after the fact or something equally bad.

Billy's eyes popped out like organ stops. "I've not got any change, sir. We could take it to the shop and . . ."

"No change required. It's all for you. To buy something for your mother." A sop for all their consciences and for not listening when they should have. If they'd taken Billy as a credible witness from the start, they'd have saved a wealth of trouble. Not judging by first impressions . . . they should have learned that in France too.

"I was glad someone listened to me at last, sir. I asked my mother about covering faces at the time, but she said I was being morbid. But you believed me, didn't you? You knew I'd seen something amiss that day. You knew and you came back to get me to do my duty." Billy's eyes shone.

Jonty smiled. "I told Professor Coppersmith here that we'd been blind, missing something obvious. You'll do a grand job in court if it comes to it. Only," Jonty lowered his voice, "maybe you might want to conveniently forget any conversations you had with Sergeant McLaren before you came here? We got that bit wrong. The truth will be enough."

Billy produced a reasonable impression of a salute. "I'll do just that, sir."

Ariadne Sheridan welcomed her guests with a small sherry and a big smile. "How wonderful to see you again so soon. Twice this week. I *am* blessed." She settled them into comfy chairs in the bay window, making the most of the autumnal sunshine.

"It'll be wonderful if you really *have* got a solution to the Owens mess to offer us." Jonty knew he shouldn't doubt his hostess's powers, but even Mrs. Sheridan couldn't work miracles. Could she?

Orlando had been calm, but now his hands trembled. The plagiarism case was to see a resolution in barely three hours and his optimism from the night before had ebbed. "Dr. Stewart has told me about the book. Isn't that just another arrow to his bow so he can blackmail the king about his unfortunate elder brother as well as threaten us?"

"I don't think Owens will dare carry out his threats. Lemuel's godfather would make sure he was incarcerated in the Tower if he so much as hinted at it." Ariadne beamed at Jonty. "You gave me the clue. 'Treason!' you shouted, and I nearly fell out of my chair."

"I apologise unreservedly. I suspect I was rather wound up."

"No need to be sorry. It was just the job."

"Your brother's godfather?" Orlando looked puzzled, but at least the trembling had stopped.

"Why, yes, didn't you know? The father of the Keeper of the King's Dignity was a great friend of our family, and he still takes a particular interest in my doings, even though Lemuel's now gone."

"Keeper of the King's what?" Jonty asked, draining most of his glass in his bewilderment.

"Dignity. It's an ancient role, not unrelated to the Keeper of the King's Conscience, back in the days of my beloved Richard of York." The titles seemed like they'd been pulled from a hat, but Ariadne was evidently deadly earnest. "That was the Lord Chancellor, but this isn't."

"Well, you've lost me now, but carry on. I'll just nod and pretend I follow," Jonty said with candour.

"I happened to ring him. The father, that is. He's a spritely old bird, the first man in his family to have a telephone, and he said he'd get his son on the case." Ariadne was clearly trying to look insouciant but it fooled nobody.

"*Happened* to ring him. I'll believe you, thousands wouldn't." Jonty winked, delighted to see his hostess blush. "Now, you'll have to excuse me, Mrs. Sheridan, if my mental powers aren't up to the task. Please explain all this slowly. You've got some clout with this Keeper chappie's father and he's going to persuade his son to do what, exactly? Apart from slap Owens in the stocks and let the ravens from the Tower deposit little presents all over him?"

"He's going to give him an ultimatum. Return the book to St. Bride's or be charged with treason."

"Treason? On what grounds?" Orlando looked as if *his* head was about to explode.

"He wasn't exactly sure. Some variation on 'If a man do violate the king's companion, or the king's eldest daughter unmarried, or the wife of the king's eldest son and heir.' Something to do with His Majesty's relatives and preserving their dignity at all times."

"Oh, I see." Jonty nodded. "Prince Albert Victor being the relative in question who mustn't have his reputation sullied any further. Would the law apply?"

"Oh, I don't think he'd even have to use it, just bamboozle Owens with enough legal verbiage. Even if he had the wit to go back and check the original Norman French, it's apparently ambiguous enough to cover almost anything. A sort of catch-all to protect the royal family." Ariadne went and fetched the sherry decanter while her guests thought about what she'd said. This was at least a one-and-a-half sherry problem.

"Could it work?" Orlando hissed from the corner of his mouth.

"I think it's potentially brilliant. Look at how twitchy everyone was about treason during the war; I'm not sure it's settled down yet. Ah, thank you." Jonty held out his glass for a top up. "I see the treachery bit, but I'm still confused. If Lemuel's godfather, or our guardian angel, whichever he turns out to be, scares Owens into returning the book, how will that help us?"

"The threat—sorry, persuasion to be applied—won't just be about paper and ink. Because of the nature of the scandal that might ensue should the whole story come to light, Owens will be warned not to make any accusations or insinuations of a similar nature affecting St. Bride's, as they might be used as evidence of him trying to execute his treason one step removed."

"And you're sure he'll fall for it?" Orlando looked hopeful, but the catch in his voice confirmed the doubts that always seemed to plague him.

"He'd better. The college next door was founded by old King Henry in what must have been one of his weaker moments and the royal family keeps a degree of control. They can give, and they can take away, including the post of master, should they so decide."

"Blimey. We asked for a piece of heavy artillery and you've unleashed a whole barrage. If I had my hat on, I'd take it off to you." Jonty settled for getting up, taking Ariadne's face between his hands, and kissing her heartily as near the lips as propriety, Orlando, and the possible appearance of Dr. Sheridan at any moment would allow.

"Well." Ariadne blushed like a schoolgirl. "Indeed. Now you go off and sort out that plagiarist, and I'll get on the phone again to my friend in a high place."

"Thank you." Orlando bowed. "I can't say how grateful I am." He bowed again. Then Jonty, smiling and winking at their hostess, dragged him from the room in case he spent the next half an hour bowing and scraping.

They made their way to the porters' lodge, Orlando silent and deep in thought until they reached the main gate when he suddenly said, "Splendid!"

"I should say so. Whatever it is you mean?"

"I mean that I can do my duty and have this plagiarist denounced, without fear." Orlando took a deep breath and nodded. "Terrible thing, plagiarism. To take someone else's work and claim it as your own. Don't you agree, Dr. Stewart? Dr. Stewart?"

"Sorry, I've just been thinking. No—" He put his hand up. "No smart remarks, this is important. What you said just now, how you phrased it. It's given me an extraordinary idea."

If Orlando's ears had been visible, rather than obscured by both hat and curls, they'd have been pricked up like a racehorse's. "Idea? About what?"

"About the final piece of this puzzle. Or maybe the first part, if we go right back to Bresnan coming to see us."

"I shan't pretend to follow. Just tell me what it's going to involve me in."

"Nothing more than a couple of phone calls and a luncheon engagement. And, in between, a pint of beer. You pay for the lot if I'm right."

"You're on."

Chapter 17

It felt like an eternity since Jonty and Orlando had stood in the porters' lodge, discussing wasps and the post and looking forward—with the benefit of hindsight, they could pretend they'd actually been looking forward—to Orlando being installed as professor. Since then, they'd had to contend with something much more vexatious than insects: human beings, with their lies and secrets, greed, and sheer stupidity.

But another case had been successfully solved, and Jonty could take pleasure in little sideways glances at his friend to see the smug satisfaction that he couldn't quite keep off his face. Orlando looked like that on only four occasions: when he'd solved some really abstruse piece of algebra; when he'd got one over on Jonty; when they'd rogered each other stupid; and, as now, when they'd brought a case to its successful conclusion and were lining up the last little piece of the problem before they wrote the metaphorical QED on the bottom.

"Penny for your thoughts?" Jonty whispered, as they pretended to peruse their mail.

"I was just counting my blessings. Owens sorted, tick. Plagiarist smoked out like the wasps in the porters' lodge, tick. Lecture given, tick."

"Lecture given with great success, tick," said Jonty, grinning like a mad thing. "I was so proud of you."

"Thank you. It meant a great deal to have you there." Orlando got out his handkerchief and blew his nose. "Rosalind Priestland brought to book, tick. Just this one little bit to get into place."

"It looks like your guest is just alighting from his cab, gentlemen." Summerbee, the porter, kept his eyes fixed on the view from the window. "And another chap with him. Maybe his father?"

"Have you developed psychic powers, Summerbee? Or are you practicing your Sherlock Holmes-type skills?" Jonty winked at Orlando, who probably wouldn't be best pleased at this intrusion into their business and would need to be kept sweet.

"Neither, sir. I've always had a good memory for a face and remember him from before. Clerical gentleman, I believe."

"That's right. But his father's gone to his long home, so you'll have to speculate about his companion for a while longer. And before you think you'll solve the matter by looking at the college visitor's book, you'll have no such luxury." Orlando, despite Jonty's misgivings, seemed in an excellent mood. "We're taking them out for lunch."

He grabbed Jonty's arm and hauled him away, leaving Summerbee to speculate all he wanted. "Not that Bresnan deserves lunch," he whispered as they paused in the entrance, "misleading us in so many ways."

"Grin and bear it. Ah!" Jonty strode forward as the little wooden wicket within the larger door opened. "Mr. Bresnan! Mr. B . . . Gurney?"

"Call me Bartholomew like everyone else does, please."

"I wasn't sure it *was* you, without the beard," Jonty said, shaking his head. An orgy of hand shaking followed, sprinkled with pleasantries and getting in the way of everyone else who was trying to get in or out of St. Bride's.

"We'd better go before the porters come out and beat us with brooms." Jonty led the way down to the Blue Boar where a private room, a laid table, and a bottle already being chilled awaited them. The bottle was half-empty and the first course done before they turned to matters investigational.

"Coppersmith's not happy with you, Mr. Bresnan," Jonty said, tapping the table. "Too many riddles and too much subterfuge."

"Ah." Bresnan took off his spectacles and cleaned them. "I think I should explain."

"Yes, you should," said Orlando a touch testily. Luckily, the waiter arriving to get the plates and Jonty deciding they should have another glass all around steered them through the treacherous waters.

"Might I interrupt you even before you start?" Jonty looked around the table. "Do you really want us to call you Bartholomew, or would you prefer Andrew?"

"Bartholomew's the name I was baptised with." Yes, there was a distinct resemblance, both to the pictures Jonty and Orlando had seen of the uncles and to Bresnan himself. No wonder Summerbee had hazarded a guess at a relationship.

"Your mother—adoptive mother—named you after an apostle as well, I suppose? To complete the association?" Orlando asked.

"Ah, no." Bartholomew smiled. "It was her grandfather's name. But it seemed apt. Especially when she heard it on my father's lips. Apparently he kept saying what a fine lad I'd turned out to be and how proud of me she must have been. Ironic, considering how he'd regarded me as being too weak to risk being left in charge of his estate."

"What a rash conclusion to have jumped to." Jonty shook his head. "Do you know why he felt that way?"

"Apparently it looked as if I had some sort of mental impairment. My father used to get fixed ideas about right and wrong and wouldn't be told otherwise. He thought I was the runt of the litter. He'd also convinced himself that I'd prove to be too much of a strain on his wife."

Jonty nodded, ruefully; everything they'd heard about old Andrew suggested he wasn't the nicest creature in the universe. "Did your real mother know you'd survived?"

"No. She wasn't around to see me grow, so she didn't suspect anything. She had an inkling he'd had me got rid of, though." Bartholomew addressed his nephew, as if such things should be kept in the family, at least on the surface. "My adoptive mother said it was one of the reasons she left him, Ian. Maybe she should have been braver and confronted him with it, although I'm not sure anyone would have wanted to do that. I was told that it all got too much and she had a bit of a breakdown."

Jonty looked briefly at Orlando. "A bit of a breakdown" was something they could both understand.

"When did you find out?" Orlando spoke quietly. He could appreciate the implications of a sudden discovery that your heritage wasn't what you'd been led to believe.

"When my father died and my mother decided to tell my brothers the truth."

"You never resented being taken away? Not having the life the others had?" Jonty had to ask the question, even though it risked causing pain to the person at the table he valued most.

"I was given life." Bartholomew smiled. "I was discarded, and she breathed life into me. Literally, as I understand it."

"And you weren't jealous of the rest of the family?" Orlando's voice was quieter still.

"Why should I have been? I may not have had their money, but I had something more precious from my parents. Love." No more needed to be said on that account. "We'd kept in touch with all the news about the family." Bartholomew laughed. "I used to have a chat with Simon quite often over a pint at the pub. He never cottoned on."

"He never had the slightest inkling? To my eyes, there seems a strong familial similarity, now that the beard's gone," Jonty said, replenishing their glasses. "Or am I seeing what I want to see?"

"That's the funny thing. Simon used to say I reminded him of his grandfather. Once he'd had a bit to drink and started wondering if I was descended from a by-blow somewhere. I steered him away from the subject. He wasn't to know." Bartholomew rubbed his chin. "That's why I grew the beard. I'd also picked up a lot of my habits from my adoptive mother, so I suppose those little quirks masked any familiar features of my face."

"Would you mind another potentially unpleasant question?" Jonty was going to ask it, whatever the answer. "I was told the letters your adoptive mother sent to your brothers were spiteful. Why did she feel so bitter? For your sake?"

Bartholomew shook his head. "I saw those letters. Maybe I'm the only person still alive to have seen them. There was not a word of spite, unless you call telling the truth spiteful."

More lies, then? Jonty wondered whether the truth—the whole truth—about this case would ever be known. The arrival of the next course gave everyone time to reflect on that, if they wanted to.

"How did you find out your uncle was alive?" Orlando asked Bresnan.

"It was just a piece of good fortune. I'd come down to see Simon and went to pay my respects at my grandfather's grave. Bartholomew was there. I'd met him before in passing, but I'd never even suspected."

"I was feeling a bit low. There'd been a couple of lads from the village—good, kind lads, never hurt a fly—who'd been killed out in France, and we'd not long buried their effects, not having the bodies to do the honours to." Bartholomew stopped to regather his composure. "It didn't seem right. Made me realise I could do what they hadn't, go to my grave with my body and name intact, if only I told someone the truth. My nephew seemed the right man."

"You discussed the will?" Orlando, a hound on the trail, was going to have every last bit of this out. "Alice Priestland's will, I mean?"

"We did," Bresnan cut in. "And the fact that Bartholomew here would be entitled to inherit his share, should we run it to ground."

"And if you could prove his consanguinity." Jonty wasn't sure that was the right word, although he was glad he'd managed to pronounce it after two glasses of wine.

"We don't need to. The fact that Alice's will was farsighted enough to mention issue, even though at the time her children were mere toddlers, means that I alone inherit, and I'll give my uncle his share." Bresnan laid down his knife and fork; for once he seemed entirely serious, all tricks and riddles played out. "I'll be content with what Simon left me. What I inherited from my grandmother will all go to Great Ormond Street. The good my uncle intended has worked out all round."

Bartholomew nodded. "I've two sons of my own, gentlemen, and they've given me three grandchildren. They'll be surprised at what their granddad leaves them."

"You won't leave them their real surname?" Orlando seemed as if he could hardly get the words out.

"No. I can't do that. But as it's not old Andrew's money, it's not tainted with his cruelty and spite, so they can have that with my pleasure." Bartholomew scooped up the last morsel of food from his plate. "Excellent. You'll let us treat you, of course?"

"We wouldn't dream of it." Jonty slapped the table. "You're our guests. You can repay us by answering one final riddle. Mr. Bresnan, why did you go back to Thorpe House on the day Peter died?"

"I think I can guess." Orlando's eyes had their *immediately postbreakthrough* look. "You'd had a shock. Intimations of Peter's mortality, and your own, made you decide it was time to tell the twins the truth. Before there was no time left."

"Yes. We contacted Simon before he left Downlea. He waited for us, so we could go together. The remains of the family . . ." Bresnan seemed near to tears. "We couldn't get near the house. Simon refused to enter it while Rosalind was there, but she hung around all morning. And then . . ."

"And then it was too late." Bartholomew patted his nephew's shoulder. "We were never a family blessed with luck. Or timing."

Jonty and Orlando had waved good-bye to their guests and were weaving a path back to the St. Bride's SCR where a short let-the-nosh-digest doze would be in order, when a deep feminine voice called to them.

"Mrs. Sheridan!" Jonty swung round to see their friend rushing across the Old Court grass, something that was never done unless in an emergency or at times of great celebration. "You look elated."

"I am. Have you not heard?" She stopped, catching her breath.

"Clearly not," Orlando said, looking from Jonty to Ariadne, then back again.

"It's Owens. He's had a double dose of comeuppance. St. Bride's is abuzz with it, which is appropriate given the circumstances." Ariadne grinned widely, as if her face might crack with delight.

"Tell us right now or I'll take off all my clothes and run round here until you do so. No, belay that." Jonty raised his hand at the look of horror on Orlando's face and delight on Ariadne's. "I'll change my threat. I'll tell Owens you have a secret passion for him."

"You can tell him what you like. I suspect he's past caring. Remember the wasps?" Ariadne asked, bouncing on her toes

"The play by Aristophanes?" Jonty wished he hadn't dined quite as well, because he couldn't quite follow this conversation as he wished.

"The ones in the pigeonholes?" Orlando asked, nodding.

"The very same. The process of smoking them out appears to have relocated them. They seem to have taken up residence at the college next door. In Owens's lodge."

"Glory be." Jonty felt like running across the grass too, just as if he'd scored a magnificent breakaway try.

"It's better than that. He tried to get rid of them himself. The little creatures, being highly intelligent, turned on him. Twenty-three separate stings, or so I've heard. Even if that's an exaggeration, it's wonderful." She clapped her hands like a delighted little girl. "I shall never kill a wasp again."

"Just in case it was one of the stingers? I think I'll join you." Jonty slipped his arm round her waist, then kissed her cheek, encouraging Orlando to do the same. This was a red letter day.

"Oh, you boys!" Ariadne blushed. "Let me get off to spread the good news. They need to hear this at Apostles'."

"You should cycle round Cambridge with a banner flying behind you, proclaiming it to all and sundry." Orlando bowed theatrically, and they let her get away.

"Isn't it wonderful? I should feel guilty, wishing harm on those who harm us, but I'll make my confession meekly kneeling on my knees next time I'm in chapel." Jonty took Orlando's arm and they walked on. "By the way, something's puzzling me. How did you guess our luncheon guest's reason for visiting Downlea? Did I miss some important clue?"

"You didn't. I just put myself in their position. It's what I would have done."

Jonty stopped, just at the bottom of the SCR steps. "How extraordinary. Fourteen years ago, you would never have been able to do that, not with such insight."

"I wouldn't have been able to do that at all. Full stop." Orlando smiled. "Different person. Different view of the world." He tapped his chest. "You saved my life. Just like Mrs. Gurney saved Bartholomew."

"Come along. People will hear." Jonty took his friend's arm and hurried them along. Such things should be said in the privacy of a college study or a double bed. "Professors aren't allowed to be big daft puddings in public. Only at home."

Dear Reader,

Thank you for reading Charlie Cochrane's *Lessons for Survivors*!

We know your time is precious and you have many, many entertainment options, so it means a lot that you've chosen to spend your time reading. We really hope you enjoyed it.

We'd be honored if you'd consider posting a review—good or bad—on sites like **Amazon, Barnes & Noble, Kobo, Goodreads, Twitter, Facebook, Tumblr,** and your blog or website. We'd also be honored if you told your friends and family about this book. Word of mouth is a book's lifeblood!

For more information on upcoming releases, author interviews, blog tours, contests, giveaways, and more, please sign up for our weekly, spam-free newsletter and visit us around the web:

Newsletter: tinyurl.com/RiptideSignup
Twitter: twitter.com/RiptideBooks
Facebook: facebook.com/RiptidePublishing
Goodreads: tinyurl.com/RiptideOnGoodreads
Tumblr: riptidepublishing.tumblr.com

Thank you so much for Reading the Rainbow!

RiptidePublishing.com

ALSO BY Charlie Cochrane

The Best Corpse for the Job
Second Helpings

Cambridge Fellows Series

Lessons in Love

Lessons in Desire

Lessons in Discovery

Lessons in Power

Lessons in Temptation

Lessons in Seduction

Lessons in Trust

All Lessons Learned

Lessons for Suspicious Minds (coming soon)

Paired Novellas
Home Fires Burning

Standalone Short Stories
Awfully Glad
Promises Made Under Fire
Tumble Turn
The Angel in the Window
Dreams of a Hero
Wolves of the West
Music in the Midst of Desolation
All That Jazz
The Shade on a Fine Day
Sand

Anthologies
Lashings of Sauce
Tea and Crumpet
British Flash
Encore Encore
I Do Two
Past Shadows
I Do
Queer Wolf

ABOUT THE Author

As Charlie Cochrane couldn't be trusted to do any of her jobs of choice—like managing a rugby team—she writes. Her favourite genre is gay fiction, predominantly historical romances/mysteries.

Charlie's Cambridge Fellows Series, set in Edwardian England, was instrumental in her being named Author of the Year 2009 by the review site Speak Its Name. She's a member of the Romantic Novelists' Association, Mystery People, and International Thriller Writers Inc., with titles published by Carina, Samhain, Bold Strokes Books, MLR, and Riptide.

Social media links:
Facebook: facebook.com/charlie.cochrane.18
Twitter: twitter.com/charliecochrane
Goodreads: goodreads.com/Charlie_Cochrane
Blog: charliecochrane.livejournal.com
Website: charliecochrane.co.uk

CPSIA information can be obtained at www.ICGtesting.com
Printed in the USA
LVOW10s1606200315

431394LV00005B/541/P